Riled Up

Anie Michaels

Riled Up
© *Copyright Anie Michaels 2017*

Edited by Hot Tree Editing.
Cover design © Pink Ink Designs

Chapter One

Riley

Camden and I had a pretty exciting relationship. Kiss Cams, basketball games, bachelor auctions, Skee-Ball, Batmobiles, halftime proposals—there was hardly ever a dull moment. So was I surprised when he sent me a text message with only an address and a note that said *Be there at seven*? No, I was not. But I was curious. And no matter how many sexy, pouty selfies I sent him, he wouldn't respond. Jerk.

My GPS took me through the heart of Portland and eventually spit me out in the Laurelhurst neighborhood. Right after college, I used to take the bus to that part of town to walk through the parks and look at the gorgeous houses. Laurelhurst was an older neighborhood, so all the houses were thoughtfully built, none of that cookie-cutter bullshit. They all looked intentionally different, and they were all beautiful.

The navigation alerted me that my destination was approaching, and I couldn't have kept my jaw off my lap if I'd tried. I pulled into the driveway of a gorgeous two-story, gray colonial with a red door. Cam's Batmobile was also in the driveway, but an unfamiliar SUV was parked in front of it.

I had barely stepped out of my car when the front door opened and Cam waltzed out, perfect sexy smile on his face. I couldn't help but smile back—until a leggy blonde followed him out.

"Riley," he said as he approached. "This is Julia. She's a real estate agent."

"It is so nice to meet you. Camden here has been telling me all about you for the last twenty minutes." She held her hand out to me and I gave it a polite shake.

"Nice to meet you too, Julia. Unfortunately, I've never heard of you, so you have me at a disadvantage." I shot Cam a glare and narrowed my eyes at him.

"She's here to show us this house," Camden said, putting his arm around me and tucking me into his side.

"What do you mean?"

"This is a 1942 colonial. Three bedrooms, two baths, a finished basement, fenced yard, updated kitchen, and tons of charm. It just went on the market this afternoon, so we're the first to see it. This is an extremely competitive market, so this house will likely be sold by tomorrow night, if not sooner. Let's go inside." She turned and walked toward the house, but as Cam went to follow her, I grabbed his arm and turned him to face me.

"What's going on, Camden?" Obviously, real estate Barbie wasn't going to clue me in, and technically, as my fiancé, it was Camden's duty to tell me these kinds of things. Especially if I had an inkling he was trying to pull a fast one on me. My eyes wandered over to the incredible house, and in the back of my mind I knew it would look just as incredible inside. But this was *not* what we'd been talking about. "I thought we were going to rent a house. You know, until after the wedding."

"And we can still do that," he said as he tucked a loose strand of hair behind my ear. "There's no harm in looking. This is a great house, babe." He cupped my cheek and I couldn't help but lean into it a bit.

"It looks really expensive," I whispered.

"Well, Portland is one of the most expensive cities to live in. Housing rates are only rising, so the longer we wait, the more we'll pay."

"But Cam, we don't need all this." I waved my hand toward the perfect house for emphasis. "We can live farther out from the city, get a smaller place, something more affordable."

His eyes darted back and forth between mine as he held my face in his hands, and I just knew he was trying to read my mind. More than likely he was doing a pretty damn good job too. I could never keep my thoughts well hidden, especially from him.

"We can afford this," he replied softly.

"No, *you* can afford this. We agreed to a 70/30 split. I cannot afford 30 percent of this house. I can, maybe, afford the little patch of grass between the sidewalk and the road."

His sexy lips flattened into a straight line. "Just look at it with me." He bent down so our eyes were level and stared me down.

I rolled my eyes. "Fine." At my submission, he placed a fast kiss on my lips, then took my hand and pulled me toward the porch. "I've always wanted a house with a red door," I said offhandedly.

He pushed the door open and then held it for me, forcing me to brush past him as I entered. "I know," he whispered in my ear as I scooted by.

I turned back and shook my head at him. "You play dirty, Camden Rogers."

"No, I remembered a key piece of information and then might have used it in my decision-making, knowing it could possibly help sway you. There's nothing dirty about that. It's completely fair." He shut the door and took my hand, lacing his fingers through mine. I held back a groan as Lawyer Camden made an appearance. I'm not sure what I was thinking, agreeing to marry a lawyer, but there were times—like the one I was living through in that moment—where I questioned my own decision-making skills.

"You're lucky you're so good in bed."

"*You're* lucky I'm so good in bed" was his quick retort. I'd walked right into that one.

"Are you ready for the tour?" Real estate Barbie was back.

"Do you mind if we just wander through on our own?" Camden asked, his voice gentle and sweet. Manipulative, even.

She looked surprised by his question, but then her professional mask slid right back into place. "Sure, that's fine. I'll just wait here and check some emails."

He led me through the house and I couldn't deny that it was beautiful. Big, open, and perfect. But also way too much space for us at the moment. Camden made sure to point out every beautiful thing we came across: exposed beams, travertine tile, a shower big enough for a dinner party, gorgeous hardwood floors, granite countertops, a walk-in closet even bigger than the shower, and a basement big enough to put almost anything down there.

I, however, was quiet through the whole tour. I was thinking plenty of things, but I had no words.

We walked back down the stairs and he led me out the perfect French doors to the backyard, where the patio boasted an outdoor kitchen complete with a built-in grill and hot tub.

"Well?" he said as he turned toward me and took my other hand in his, holding both between us. "What do you think?"

"I think it's amazing." My tone was less than enthused.

"But…?"

"But this is a house you buy *after* a starter house. Hell, this might be the house you buy after the house you buy after the starter house."

He chuckled and then moved our hands behind me, resting them on the small of my back and pulling me closer, forcing me to look up at him. "That didn't make any sense, babe."

I let out a sigh and leaned my forehead against his chest, loving the way he immediately pressed a kiss to my hair. He was giving me time to formulate my thoughts. After a few moments—and maybe I took a few extra moments because I liked the way he was holding me—I looked back up and met his gaze.

"This house is so much more than I ever imagined living in, Cam. It's a dream house. And it's scary."

"What's scary about it?" Genuine concern laced his tone.

I shrugged one shoulder and looked away. "It's a big financial commitment."

"Yeah," he said as he bent his knees and captured my gaze. "Most houses are."

"Camden, this is, like, four houses' worth of commitment. I wasn't expecting this. It's too much."

"Okay, maybe you just don't have the vision I do."

"Ha!" I barked. "I have more vision in my pinky finger than you have in your whole body, including your big head."

"Well, then let me tell you what I see when I look at this house. I see dinner parties and basketball games. I see a medium-sized dog running around the backyard and going on walks to the parks. I see friends and family on this porch on summer days. I see you riding me in that hot tub," he added, nodding over his shoulder.

"Camden," I yelled at him with my quietest threatening whisper, only to watch him smile at my outrage.

"I see you, round with my baby, walking through the house, getting ready to bring home a son or daughter. I see that dog chasing our baby around the backyard. I see Easter egg hunts and birthday parties. I see a life, Riley. Our life."

I tried to ignore the sting of tears behind my eyes, but his face became all blurry when I tried to blink it away. I pulled my hands from his, slid them around his waist, and pressed my cheek against his chest, letting him take my weight. Just as I knew they would, his arms circled my shoulders, holding me close. "I know you're afraid of getting in too deep, but you have to trust that I'm going to keep us afloat. Besides, it's just money." He said the last part in a way only someone who'd never been without money could.

"What about waiting to buy a house until after the wedding? A wedding and a house is a lot to take on all at the same time."

"Did you hear what Julia said? This house will sell by tomorrow evening. If we want it, we have to make an offer now. In a year this house will cost a lot more."

Stepping back, putting some distance between us, I looked out at the stupidly perfect landscaping. "Okay, well, that's not a good reason to just buy a house on impulse. Plus, people don't just buy the first house they look at. What if we look around a little and we find an even better, possibly cheaper, house? This is *crazy*, Camden."

"Let me make the down payment. I'll put enough down so you can manage 30% of our mortgage payment." His voice had moved from light and playful to almost pleading. Camden wanted this house—that much was clear. And thinking back to the last six months I'd spent with him, he'd never really asked me for anything. In fact, he'd done most of the giving and the compromising, always going above and beyond to make sure I was comfortable. Hell, at one point he'd confronted his own stepfather, threatening to cut off communication for me. "Let me give you a home, Riley."

His words cut deep, right down to my very core. My shoulders sagged with the weight of his words and I took the few steps to him, placing my hands on his chest.

"I don't need this house. My home is wherever you are." He opened his mouth to argue but I put my index finger right over his lush lips, silencing him before he got the words out. "But if buying this house will make you happy, then I'll let you."

Chapter Two
Riley

"Riley, I need you in my office."

The voice startled me, making me jump in my chair, so I was glad it was over the PA system on my phone. The last thing I needed was for Rose, my boss, to see me make an ass of myself. I was pretty good at doing that all on my own—I didn't need her help.

"I'll be right there," I managed with just a little bit of breathiness. I grabbed my iPad and headed out into the open-concept office, giving a finger wave to Rachel and Jasper as I passed them. "Lunch today?" I asked, turning and walking backward as I waited for their reply.

"Sounds good," Rachel replied with a smile.

"Sushi day!" Jasper exclaimed, pumping one fist straight up into the air. I hated sushi, but Jasper complained that we never let him pick our lunch spots, so Rachel and I relented and let him pick a sushi place every other week. Luckily, the restaurants he chose usually had something on the menu I could force down. Nothing raw and nothing with tentacles.

I gave them a thumbs-up and then continued to Rose's office. I could see she was alone through the glass walls, so I gently knocked and then opened the door.

Rose and I had an interesting relationship. Interesting because I could never figure out if she liked me or not. I thought, with a certain amount of certainty, that she appreciated my work and thought I was a good employee, but I could never pinpoint whether she wanted to hug me or throat punch me. She didn't give off the violent vibe, but she always seemed restrained. Almost as though she were afraid if she let her guard down or opened up about anything, there would be no way to contain herself afterward. I thought perhaps it was feast or famine when it came to Rose, and I'd only ever experienced her when she was in famine mode. She gave us bare bones all the time; you got what you needed from her, but nothing more.

It wasn't a problem, per se, but it was something I'd thought about more than once.

"Riley, take a seat." She motioned with her hand to the chair across from her desk and I smiled tentatively as I sat. I'd had meetings with Rose multiple times a week since my last promotion six months before, but most of them had been scheduled. To be called into an impromptu meeting put me on edge.

I hadn't even fully situated myself in my seat before she started talking.

"A good friend of mine is getting married this year and has asked me to personally handle the wedding coordination."

"Sounds exciting."

"Indeed, it is. I would like you to come with me."

"I'm sorry, you what?"

Rose gave a little laugh, which I'd never heard her do before, but then repeated what I'd heard her say already, but just couldn't process. "I would like you to come with me. To Arizona, where my friend lives and is getting married."

"Why me?" I asked before I could stop myself. I wasn't fishing for compliments, this was the 'what in the world could you want me for' version. I quickly tried to rephrase my confusion. "What I mean to say is that I'm just a little surprised by all this. It seems sudden and kind of out of left field. Not that I'm not grateful that you would think of me, I'm just… damn, I'm not sure what to think."

"Riley, relax. This is my best friend, and even though I'm very proud of my business and how far it's come and how much it's grown, I want to bring my A-game to handle this event. It means a lot to me that she gets the best people I have. That's you and me," she said with a little hint of compassion in her tone. "I've been watching everyone closely for the last year or so, and even though there're a lot of talented, hard-working people out there, I need the best people on this job. You're one of those people."

My mouth gaped open at her praise. "Thank you. I appreciate that." I tried not to stutter.

"We would leave middle of next week and be in Arizona for a few days. This commitment would also require trips to Arizona for the next few months while we plan the event. You won't have to go to all the meetings, but I'd like your help as much as possible. Of course, all travel and expenses will be covered." She paused, possibly waiting for me to say something in response, but I couldn't. My mind was reeling. "We'll need to make travel arrangements, and the sooner the better, so I'd like to know if you're interested in the opportunity by tomorrow morning."

"Tomorrow?"

"I'm afraid so."

"All right, I'll let you know by then."

A cool smile replaced the irritation on her face. "Good. Feel free to ask me any questions you might come up with between now and then."

"I will, and thank you for the opportunity." I stood and left her office, closing the door behind me, then walked to my office like a zombie because my brain was out of order. I collapsed into my chair, mouth agape, and mind completely blown. I knew I'd been doing well at work; the promotion had boosted my confidence and productivity. I was speaking up more, delivering better ideas, and backing all that up with stellar events, but never in my wildest daydreams could I have imagined Rose was going to ask me to help her put on an event for her best friend.

In fucking Arizona!

Arizona was my own personal hell.

I'd lived there for four years in high school, and once I left I never had any desire to go back. In fact, I hadn't. It had been years since I left Arizona to go to college, and I always made my mother come to Oregon to visit me.

Arizona was the setting for four of the most tumultuous years of my life. High school was traumatic on some level for everyone, but I'd spent it living in the servants' quarters of a mansion being treated like a second-class citizen. And that wasn't only at home—the hell encompassed my school life as well. Since I technically lived in the district of the most affluent neighborhood, I went to a very upscale high school. That was helpful when it came to opportunities as far as school-funded programs and sports—everything was the best of the best. But it was very obvious to all the other students that I was not one of them, and they voiced their displeasure daily.

I picked up my office phone and dialed Rose's extension. She picked up almost immediately.

"Rose speaking, how can I help you?"

"Hi, It's Riley. I was just wondering where in Arizona this was all taking place."

"Paradise Valley."

My heart lurched to a complete standstill at her words, but I had to force myself to respond.

A mousy "Okay" was all I could muster.

"Any other questions?" she asked, not unkindly.

"No," I managed to squeak out.

"All right. But let me know if any more pop up."

"Okay, thanks," I said before ending the call.

Paradise Valley. Of course.

For the next few hours I locked myself in my office and did my best to appear as though I was working. I clicked my mouse, typed on my keyboard, and at one point I did answer a phone call, but it was easily handled with only the quarter of my brain that was operating. When it was finally time for lunch, I couldn't figure out if I was looking forward to lunch with Rachel and Jasper or dreading it.

Jasper popped into my office at the exact moment my phone pinged with a text.

"You ready?" he asked.

"Yeah," I replied, swiping across the screen of my phone and reading a text from Hadley. Grabbing my purse from the bottom drawer of my desk, I headed toward Jasper and noticed Rachel waiting by the elevators.

"How's your day so far?" he asked, passing a hat back and forth between his hands.

"Stressful."

"Yeah? At least you're not knee-deep in bridezillas."

I couldn't hold back the laugh at the image he evoked with his words. Jasper, a giant, beating away giant lizards in wedding dresses and veils.

"Hey, I did my time." Rachel smiled as we approached and the elevator doors opened a second later. We all entered and Rachel hit the button for the bottom floor. "Do you guys mind if Hadley joins us? She's nearby and asked if I had plans for lunch."

"Of course not," Rachel said.

"The more the merrier," Jasper added.

"Thanks, guys. Same sushi place as always?"

"You know it." I could almost hear the excitement in Jasper's tone. He loved sushi. Luckily, so did Hadley. I shot her a text letting her know where to meet us and then put my phone back in my purse just as the doors slid open.

As soon as we stepped foot outside, Jasper placed the hat he'd been carrying on his head and it made me do a double take.

"Jasper," I crooned. "That hat is definitely my favorite accessory of yours. Is it new?"

"You like? I just got it. I'm trying it out."

"Oh yes, definitely a keeper," Rachel added. "What kind of hat is it?"

"It's called a flat cap," he said with a haughty tone and slight British accent, which made me laugh.

"Oh really?" I mirrored his inflection. "How proper." Laughs aside, I gave him props. He looked all kinds of dapper with the new hat and trademark suspenders. It was late spring in Portland and the sun was out. It hadn't rained in a few days, so everyone was chipper and walking around town without umbrellas or coats—a Pacific

Northwest dream. It almost made me forget about the meeting I'd had just hours before.

We made it to the sushi place Jasper preferred and found a table. Just as we'd opened our menus, Hadley walked in.

"Hey, bitch," Jasper said, a little too loudly for my liking, but Hadley gave him her warmest smile.

"Hey, yourself." She walked right to me and bent at the waist to wrap me in a hug. It hadn't been too long since I'd seen her, but our get-togethers were definitely spaced farther apart now that I was with Camden. Not that she'd ever mentioned anything of the sort. "Hey, friend," she said as she squeezed me.

I wasn't prepared to have a breakdown in public, but Hadley's words and her affection made something inside of me snap. She pulled away and immediately knew something was wrong—all three of them did. My chin was quivering with the strain of trying to keep the tears at bay and I was gnawing the hell out of my bottom lip. None of it worked though, because a rogue tear slipped down my cheek anyway.

"Oh my gosh, babe. What's wrong?" Hadley asked, taking the open seat next to me but keeping her hand on my arm, rubbing it up and down gently. Rachel swiped two napkins from the dispenser on the table and held them out, and I took them gratefully.

"I'm sorry. It's nothing. I'm crazy, obviously." And I felt a little crazy. I was laughing as we came in the door and now I couldn't stop the tears.

"Did something happen with Camden?" This came from Jasper and he sounded so concerned, his voice soft and worried. Double damn, the tears just continued.

"No, nothing like that." I wiped the tears from under my eyes and sniffled.

"Then what is it?" Rachel asked softly.

"There's just a lot going on."

"You're overwhelmed?" Hadley asked, her hand still moving soothingly up and down my arm. I nodded in response, using the napkins to dry my face.

"Is it the wedding planning? Because obviously, we can help with that," Rachel said.

"No, we haven't even really started planning anything."

"Do you want to talk about it?" Jasper asked softly.

I took in a deep breath and thought about his question. Did I want to talk about it? Yes and no. I knew if I told them about everything happening I would feel better, but I didn't want to tell them my list of complaints because I knew they wouldn't see them as such. The issues weighing heavily on me were problems some other people would kill to have. But I couldn't keep my thoughts to myself any longer, and my friends wanted to take some of the burden.

"Last night, Camden surprised me with a house."

"What?" Hadley exclaimed, her hand stilling against me.

"Yeah. It's a beautiful house and he really loves it."

"Wait, you bought a house yesterday?" Rachel asked, equally as shocked at Hadley.

I nodded as I blew my nose. Loudly. "And Rose just asked me to go to Arizona with her for a work thing."

"Arizona?" Hadley repeated, a knowing tone to her voice. I turned and gave a weak smile while I nodded. She

15

knew all about Arizona. "Well, no wonder you're freaking the fuck out."

"I know," I cried as I threw my hands up in the air. "I can't deal with all this at the same time. House, wedding, Arizona, *Camden*. That man," I said with a huff. "He just tells me to meet him at an address and then dazzles me with a beautiful house, telling me he wants our babies running around in the backyard."

"That asshole," Jasper said with no small amount of sarcasm. "I hate it when sexy-as-fuck fiancés threaten to buy me houses."

"Hey, he's not buying me a house. *We're* buying a house. I'm contributing."

"Good for you," Rachel added.

"You know what I mean," Jasper said, shrugging. "Camden wants nothing in the world but to make you happy. There's not one selfish bone in that man's body when it comes to you. Well, aside from just wanting you all to himself, but who could blame him?"

"He's right, you know," Hadley said, her hand finally falling away. "If he brought you to a house and convinced you to buy it, it's because he thinks it'll make you happy."

"Well, to be honest, I had a big case of sticker shock." I leaned over the table and my friends followed suit. I dropped my voice to a whisper. "It's a two-story colonial. *In Laurelhurst*."

"No," Rachel gasped.

"Yes," I said, nodding empathically. "How am I supposed to say no to that?"

"Clearly, you're not." Jasper laughed.

"So, it's beautiful, then?" I didn't have to look at Hadley to know she had a smile on her face.

"It's gorgeous," I groaned.

"Wait, what in the world does Rose need you in Arizona for?" Rachel asked, clearly catching on to the other piece of information I'd dropped.

I shrugged one shoulder. "She said her best friend is getting married, and she's bringing me along to help handle the event."

"Rose's best friend? Where in Arizona? What's the theme? Budget?" Rachel asked, leaning forward with interest.

"I don't know, I didn't ask a ton of questions." I took a deep breath and then let it out slowly. "Okay, I'm sorry for the breakdown. I've just been holding in all this stress and it just found a strange time to make its presence known."

"It's okay," Rachel said, reaching out and patting my hand softly. "That's what we're here for."

"I'm here for sushi," Jasper added, making me laugh.

I had the best friends.

Chapter Three
Camden

It had been a while since we'd stayed at Riley's apartment. The fact of the matter was the Batmobile wasn't safe there on the street, and I hated having to take an Uber home in the mornings just to get my car. I enjoyed staying in bed with her as long as possible, and both our offices were closer to my condo, so eventually we just stopped debating about it and Riley brought over a few big bags filled with everything she'd need to stay at my house indefinitely.

I'd been planning on talking to her about just giving up her apartment, but now that we'd put an offer in on a house, it seemed pointless—we'd both be moving soon.

I'd just popped the top off a Guinness and started pouring it into a frosty mug when my phone vibrated against the granite of my countertops.

Your girl needs a little extra attention tonight. She's had a rough day.

Hadley and I had a pretty good relationship. She was a good friend to Riley and I could tell the girls cared about each other a lot, so by default, I liked her a lot too. But we hadn't often texted each other, so her message caught me off guard. I read it again, and then again, and it made all kinds of red flags go up in my mind.

I hadn't heard from Riley all day, which wasn't necessarily worrisome—I just figured she'd been busy. But after Hadley's text, I was anxious.

Anything in particular I should be concerned about?

I sent the text off and waited for a response, sipping my beer.

Just talk to her when she gets home. She'll tell you.

Okay. Thanks for the heads-up.

That's what I'm here for.

When Riley walked in the door an hour later, I had everything set up. The lights were off, but the entire front room was lit with candles. Her favorite Chinese takeout was waiting at the table, and I had a cold six-pack of Hef waiting in the fridge. I'd also found *Girls Just Want to Have Fun* on Netflix, all cued up and waiting for her to relax on the couch.

So, when the door opened and she walked in, I enjoyed the confused look on her face. I also enjoyed watching the confusion melt away and a softer expression take over: love.

"What are you up to?" she asked with a smile when she found me standing in the kitchen leaning against the island.

"Waiting for you." I watched as the smile grew wider, knowing if there had been more light I would've been able to see the blush take over her cheeks. It was so easy to affect her.

"Is that Chinese I smell?" She dropped her purse on the island and came to me, pressing her hands against my chest and then resting her weight against me, our bodies aligning as she melted into me.

"You're my favorite bloodhound," I joked.

"Hey," she cried, slapping me playfully.

"You could smell Chinese food from a block away."

She shrugged and looked up at me. "It's my superpower."

"How was your day?" Immediately at my words, the laughter in her eyes disappeared and worry took over. I squeezed her closer. "What's wrong?"

"We need to talk."

"Well those certainly aren't good words."

"No, it's fine. *We're* fine." She tried to reassure me, but still, my pulse spiked. Something was up. "Let's get some food, and then I'll tell you everything."

"So, let me get this straight. Rose is taking you to Arizona, you'll be working in the town you used to live in—where your mom lives still—and this worries you, correct?"

"Yeah…." Her voice lacked the enthusiasm any young professional should exude when their boss gives them such great news and feedback.

"Babe, that's amazing. Why aren't you more excited?"

"Excited? Camden, we just made an offer on a house. Now doesn't seem as though it's the best time to be hopping between Portland and Paradise Valley."

Her shoulders dropped and that sexy bottom lip of hers jutted out. I knew she was about two-point-five seconds away from losing it. I pushed my chair back and crooked a finger at her. At my gesture, she practically bounced out of her seat and came to me. My hands met her waist when she was close enough to touch and I guided her down on my lap. She wound her arms around my neck and laid her cheek on my shoulder. I hadn't known Riley for years, but I knew her better than anyone, and in that moment she needed me to offer her reassurance. Somewhere along the line, in her past, she'd managed to convince herself she was subpar, that she wasn't deserving of the very best.

I pressed my lips to her forehead and rubbed my hand up and down her back.

"No crying, okay? I can't handle it when you cry. It makes me want to smash things." She laughed a little and I knew I was on the right track. "This is incredible news, Riley. You should be so proud of yourself. Rose is obviously impressed with your work."

She leaned her head back and pressed her lips against mine. Nothing compared to a kiss from Riley, so I took advantage of her mouth and took the kiss a little deeper. She didn't complain. In fact, she seemed to enjoy it, if the moaning and groping was any indication. When we finally broke apart, she whispered, "How'd you get so good at all this relationship stuff?"

"I'm not good at relationships, Riley. I'm good at being with you. With you is the only place I need to be." She nodded, but there was still worry in her eyes. "What else is bothering you?" I asked, tucking a stray piece of hair behind her ear.

She took a deep breath, seeming to try and calm herself, but then she spoke. "I never wanted to go back to Arizona. I hate it there. And not only does she want me to go back to Arizona, but also back to the same city I lived in when I went to high school."

Ah, that was where the insecurity was coming from. Riley had explained to me how high school had impacted the way she viewed the world—it had even affected our relationship in the beginning—but Riley wasn't the kind of woman to let something stand in her way.

"So don't go," I said bluntly. "Tell Rose no."

I watched as she took in my words and I knew she was mulling them over in her mind, thinking about all her options. Finally, she shook her head.

"Rose picked me for a reason, ya know? I feel like I owe it to myself, and her, to at least go there and see if it's a good fit. Right? Don't you think?"

"I do," I replied with a grin. "Arizona is just a place, and the people there are just people. They don't have to have any control over you."

She inhaled deeply, then exhaled, and nodded. "That's what I'm hoping for."

"How long will you be gone?"

"A few days."

I gripped her hips with my hands and picked her up, then rearranged her so she was straddling my lap. "Sounds like we're going to have to figure out some sort of Skype situation."

She giggled again, but that time the laughter reached all the way up to her eyes and her head fell back as her whole body shook with it. "You think you're going to get lucky with some Skype sex?"

"Oh, I know it." My hands slid up the backs of her thighs until the globes of her ass were in my palms. I lifted her as I stood and walked her back to the bedroom. She yelped at first, surprised by the movement, but by the time I was in the hall, her mouth was on my neck.

"The Chinese food," she rasped against my skin between kisses.

"It'll keep," I said right before I tossed her into the middle of my king-sized bed. "If you're going to be gone for a few days, I'm going to need to put in some serious work to make sure you don't forget about me while you're away." I peeled my shirt over my head and let it fall to the floor, then started on my pants.

"And how do you plan on doing that?" Her words were panted with sharp breaths, and I knew if I managed to get my hands on her right that second, I would find her already wet.

"Take off your clothes and I'll show you."

Chapter Four
Riley

One week and one practically tear-free goodbye to Camden at the airport later, I was standing next to Rose waiting to board our flight.

It had been hard to come to the decision to go with her because going back to Arizona felt wrong and uncomfortable. I wanted the chance to impress Rose even further, wanted to help her plan the wedding, but I wasn't sure if I could be useful there or if I would get caught up with the ghosts of my past. But Camden helped me realize that Rose wouldn't have offered the opportunity if she didn't want me there or want my help. So, I went.

Spring in Portland was nothing like Spring in Paradise Valley, Arizona. Shopping had been necessary, which gave me a perfect excuse for a girls' day with Hadley. I didn't need an excuse to spend time with her, of course, but it was good regardless. At the end of the day though, as I carried all my bags into Camden's condo, it only made me think about how adding trips to Arizona with Rose would inevitably make it even harder to spend time with Hadley. I made a mental note to work harder at fitting her into my life. I didn't want to be one of those friends who disappeared when life got hectic.

"Now boarding all first-class ticket holders for flight 329 with direct service to Phoenix, Arizona."

When Rose started to move toward the jetway I couldn't catch the words that came out of my mouth next.

"We're in first class? I've never flown first class before." It was stupid how unprofessional I sounded.

Rose kindly smiled at me. "With this carrier, there's no difference between first and business class. Enjoy, Riley. You haven't flown until you've done it in first class."

Rose was right. Before we even taxied away from the jetway I had a complimentary glass of champagne and a warm washcloth. I wasn't about to drink at nine in the morning on a business trip with my boss, but Rose had insisted and even clicked her own champagne glass against mine. Apparently, we were drinking to a successful trip with relaxing moments. I couldn't argue with her.

The flight attendants were giving all the in-flight safety instructions when I noticed Rose start to breathe a little deeper, her fingers gripping the armrests tightly. When I looked over at her, I was surprised to find her eyes clamped closed.

"Are you all right?" I whispered as I leaned closer to her. She was taking deep breaths in through her nose and pushing them out through her puckered mouth.

"I hate flying," she managed to quickly say between breaths.

The flight attendants finished their spiel and took their own seats, and before I knew it we began cruising down the runway, bumping along as we picked up speed. I hadn't flown very many times in my life, but I'd also never developed a fear of flying, so I couldn't relate to Rose's fear. But she was obviously petrified. As the wheels lifted off the pavement and the plane tilted up, she yelped quietly and, even though I wouldn't have thought it possible, gripped the armrests even tighter. She was trying to breathe but muttering something under her breath at the same time.

For the next five minutes as we climbed higher into the sky, she remained terrified. It wasn't until the plane leveled out and the flight attendants started walking about that she seemed to calm down. Her fingers unwrapped from the armrests and she waved at our flight attendant, asking him for another champagne. She used her warm towel to wipe her brow and then gave me a sheepish smile.

"Sorry. I probably should have warned you."

"No, it's fine. Lots of people have a fear of flying."

"It's actually just a fear of taking off and landing. I don't mind the time in between."

"Huh, I wonder why that is," I pondered aloud.

"It's because sixty percent of crashes occur during takeoff or landing."

"Oh," I said sullenly.

"And I hate to break it to you, but the odds of crashing double at landing."

"Well, that's... depressing."

"Sorry," she said, giving me a sad smile. "I try not to fly often, and when I do I usually medicate myself. But I didn't want to saddle you with a doped-up boss. Champagne will have to do," she said as she lifted her new glass to her lips. She took a hearty sip and then closed her eyes, resting her head back against the seat. She looked as though she was going to try to rest, so I pulled my Kindle from my purse, smiling at the idea of reading one of my romance books while I was on the clock, but then Rose's voice broke into my jubilation.

"Is your boyfriend going to have a guys-only poker night while you're away? Do something manly? Watch a sporting event in his underwear?" She turned her head toward me and peeped open one eye, then smiled. I

26

couldn't remember a time since I started working for Rose when she'd asked me a personal question.

"Camden? He's not really a sit-around-in-his-underwear kind of guy. But he might do something with his friend Justin." I shrugged. "We hadn't really discussed it."

"I forgot momentarily that you were dating the mayor's stepson. Of course he doesn't sit around in his underwear."

"I'm not dating him, actually. We're engaged." I got a little satisfaction out of the way her mouth fell open and her eyes went wide with surprise.

"He proposed?"

"Yep," I said, holding up my left hand where my beautiful engagement ring sparkled.

"Nice work. You closed that deal quickly."

I wanted to tell her that Camden wasn't a *deal* and I didn't *close* him, but I refrained. Instead I said, not unkindly, "When it's right, it's right."

"Yes, well, congratulations. I had no idea."

I admired Rose as a business woman, as someone who'd started and ran her own very successful business, but I couldn't help but think she'd be a little more approachable if she came out of her glass office every once in a while and interacted informally with her employees. But my opinion about Rose didn't matter one bit.

The rest of the flight was pretty typical. I let myself have one more glass of champagne and then spent the rest of the time reading. Rose fell asleep but awoke as soon as the captain announced we were making our descent, and then she was back to gripping armrests and breathing heavily. As soon as the wheels touched down and the plane slowed, she let out a large breath and gave me a smile.

"We lived," she said sleepily.

"Lucky us," I returned with a smile.

As first-class passengers, we were allowed to deplane first. After grabbing our bags, Rose led me through the airport where we eventually encountered a man holding up a piece of paper with Rose's name on it.

"Hello, I'm Rose Finch," she said, holding her hand out to the man dressed in a black suit with white shirt and skinny black tie.

He shook her hand and gave her a tight smile, almost painful, then motioned toward the sliding doors. "The car is right outside." He took our bags and then led the way to a shiny black town car. He opened the door for us and loaded our bags into the trunk before getting behind the wheel. "You're headed to Paradise Oasis, correct?" he asked before pulling away from the curb.

"Yes," Rose responded, all business.

Paradise Oasis? That was one of the most expensive resorts in the area. My senior prom had been held there. I hadn't attended, but still, I knew it was fancy. I didn't want to ask Rose if that was where we were staying, but I was undeniably curious.

I couldn't keep my eyes from the windows. Everything was familiar. I wouldn't ever consider Arizona my home, but it was strange to feel connected emotionally to a place you despised. I had hated it there, but for some reason the familiarity was comforting. I watched landmarks pass us by and memories came flooding back. We took the same exit off the freeway I'd taken a thousand times, passed the shopping center I'd spent many weekends wandering around in, even passed the road that led to my high school.

My eyes were glued to our surroundings as we approached the resort. The main building was classic Arizona stucco with red clay tiles. Tall palm trees lined the circular drive and high red cliffs stood behind the large resort. It was a breathtaking view.

Our driver opened the door for us and then placed our bags on the cart an employee of the resort had brought out.

"Welcome to Paradise Oasis," the man said as he pushed our cart into the building.

"Thank you," Rose replied with a friendly tone.

"Is this your first visit to our resort?"

"Not for me. I've stayed here a few times. What about you, Riley?"

I shook my head. "No, I've never been here."

"Well, you're in for a treat, then."

I stood in the foyer while Rose checked us in, gawking at the opulence. Everything was white and shiny, marble and granite with silver accents.

"Riley." Rose was waiting for me. I hurried to where she was standing with the man pushing our cart of luggage.

"This way, ladies," he said, leading us to a bank of elevators. He took us up to the fourth floor, which was the top, and walked us all the way down one end of the building. He stopped outside a door with a plaque that read "The Palm Suite," put a card in the reader, and pushed open the door. "Ms. Finch, this is your suite." He handed the card to her, then grabbed her bags and followed her inside, propping the door open with a little doorstop. I heard him talking to her but wasn't paying much attention, too involved in looking at the artwork lining the walls.

Beautiful paintings of the Arizona desert. My attention was drawn back to Rose, however, when she appeared in her doorway.

"We have a dinner meeting downstairs at seven. You're free until then. Tomorrow we start after breakfast. Sound good?"

I nodded. "Sounds great."

She smiled at me, turned to the man waiting to push my luggage and said, "Thank you for your assistance," then held out a twenty-dollar bill.

"Thank you very much, ma'am," he said while discreetly taking the money from her and slipping it into his pocket. "Enjoy your stay, and please do not hesitate to call the concierge desk if you should need anything."

I silently thanked Rose for tipping him in front of me because I wouldn't have even thought about it. I gave her a small wave as I followed the man down the hall to the next door with a plaque that read "The Valley Suite." He opened it for me, handed me the key, and then motioned for me to enter first.

The room was beautiful. The first thing I noticed was the view of gorgeous painted hills which I had never appreciated fully when I lived there. I walked through the living room and looked out the big picture window at the pool surrounded by more palm trees below.

"May I show you the amenities?" the bellhop asked.

"Sure."

He led me through the room, pointing out all the astounding features of the suite. He showed me how to use a tablet to open the blinds, turn on the television, and even order room service, plus how to control the temperature of the water in the shower and work the jetted tub. He finished the tour with the minibar and informed me that my stay was all-inclusive and not to worry about the cost as it was built into the price of the room.

I tried not to let my mouth gape open the whole time, but it was difficult. I had never stayed somewhere so fancy and it was a little overwhelming.

"Of course, if you have problems with the room or need anything at all, do not hesitate to let us know. We have staff on hand all hours to cater to our guests."

"Thank you so much, uh, what was your name?"

He laughed and said, "My name is Jason."

"Thank you, Jason. You've been very helpful." I pulled a twenty out of my wallet and held it out to him. He took it with the practiced discretion I'd witnessed with Rose.

"It is my pleasure, ma'am. Enjoy your stay." He gave me a polite nod and then left, closing the door behind him.

As soon as I was alone, I went back to the bedroom and collapsed on the bed, trying to wrap my mind around how nice the suite was. I'd never been in such a nice hotel. Camden's condo was nice, but not *that* nice. As I lay on the bed, I felt myself getting drowsy, but napping wasn't on the agenda. This was the closest I'd come to any sort of vacation in years, so I was going to get the most out of it.

I dragged my luggage into the bedroom and opened my suitcase, looking for my bathing suit. I knew there was a lounge chair sitting by the pool calling my name.

Thirty minutes later, I was sitting poolside, my Kindle on my lap, a drink in one hand and my phone in the other. I had my new sunglasses on, the ones I'd been wanting to buy for months but couldn't bring myself to do it. Portland has a good amount of sunny days, but when a ten-dollar pair did the same job as a hundred-dollar pair, it was hard to justify the cost. But I'd totally let myself splurge.

I held the drink up, placing the straw in my mouth just barely, pouted my lips just a little so they'd look plump, tilted my head to just the right angle, and snapped a photo. I took a sip of my fruity drink and then placed it back on the table next to me, inspecting the photo. I had gotten pretty good at taking selfies since I'd been with Camden, and that was a particularly good one. I quickly typed a flirty caption and hit Send.

Hope you're enjoying your day at work. Try not to miss my mouth too much.

It didn't even take two minutes before he was calling me.

"Hello, there," I said sweetly as a greeting.

"Well hello. I just received a picture from this number, but I didn't recognize the woman in it. This is my fiancée's number, but it seems a bikini-wearing, bronzed, happy sun bunny has stolen her phone and is sending me sexy photos."

"What can I say? I like Arizona better this time around."

"You're doing okay, then?" he asked, suddenly serious. I knew he was concerned about me going there alone, but to hear it so prevalent in his voice made my heart lurch a little.

"I am. I miss you though."

"I miss you too, babe. Thanks for the sexy selfie though. That'll come in handy later when I'm missing you even more."

32

"Oh God," I said with a groan, but secretly I loved the idea of him touching himself while looking at a photo of me. I loved it so much, I considered sending him a better one later, one more suited for what he was planning on using them for. "Hey," I said suddenly, a thought occurring to me. "You aren't going to have some bachelor night while I'm away, are you? Like, no strippers or prostitutes, right?"

"What? No. Why would you even ask that?" he replied, laughing through the entire response.

"Rose asked me if you were going to have a guys' night. She made it sound as if that was typical when girlfriends go away."

"Well, one, you're not my girlfriend. And two, I'm not typical."

"That's pretty much what I told her."

"Good," he said softly, and I could tell by the tone of his voice he was smiling. "Have you called your mom yet?"

My smile fell. "No. I've only been here an hour."

"All right. So, what else do you have planned today? Doesn't look like you're getting much work done."

"Dinner meeting, but that's it. Tomorrow is a busier day. Just thought I'd take the opportunity to soak in some vitamin D before I come back home."

"Hmmm, tan lines."

"Oh Lord."

"Well, as much as I'd love to talk to you all day, I've got to get back to work. Will you call me when you're done with your dinner?"

"Of course."

"Be good, babe. And enjoy yourself. You deserve a little rest and relaxation."

"Thanks, Cam. Love you."

"Love you too."

He hung up and I let out a breath. I did miss him, but I was a tiny bit glad in that moment that he hadn't come with me. But only because I knew he'd be hounding me to call my mother. I was planning on calling her, but not right away. Besides, if her job was the same as before, she would be busy during the day anyway. At least, that's what I told myself as I pulled my shades down over my eyes again, sipped my drink, and turned my Kindle on.

Chapter Five
Riley

At ten to seven, my phone chimed with a text.
Ready? I'm on my way to your room.

I couldn't remember a time when Rose had sent me a text message, so it surprised me to see one from her. It also surprised me how informal it was. Sure enough, a minute later there was a knock on my door. I stepped out, giving Rose a smile.

"You look as though you enjoyed the pool this afternoon," Rose mentioned. "A little sun looks good on you."

"Thanks. I did enjoy the pool. And the sun. Luckily I didn't get burned."

"You lived here before, right? So you're used to the sun."

"Well, I mean, one never really forgets the Arizona heat, but this is nothing. Try hanging out here in August," I replied with a laugh. We continued idle conversation until we walked into the restaurant where Rose gave the maître d' her name.

"Right this way, Ms. Finch," the tall man in a very dapper black suit said, just before leading us to a table toward the back of the restaurant. I was following them, taking in the scenery and lavish décor of the upscale restaurant, but put a smile on my face as we approached the table.

"Here you are, ma'am," he said, stepping to the side and motioning to the table.

"Rose, oh my gosh! It's been so long!" I watched as a blonde woman stood from the table and wrapped her arms around my boss. They hugged and swayed, both laughing. I let them have their reunion, waiting quietly until they parted.

Rose stepped to the side and held a hand out toward me. "This is my associate, Riley Smith. Riley, this is Lily Jameson, my very best friend from college."

"It's so nice to meet you," I said with a smile, reaching out and shaking her hand. She returned my smile, but hers was so warm and inviting, I instantly felt at ease around her. "Congratulations on the wedding," I added as we all took our seats.

"Yes, where is Adam?" Rose asked Lily.

"He got sent on a last-minute trip overseas for work," she said on a sigh, placing her linen napkin on her lap. "He sends his love, obviously." She gave Rose another warm smile. "How was the flight here?" Lily's eyes shot to me. "Did you have to wheel her off the plane?"

"Oh please, I'm not that bad," Rose insisted.

"I have pictures from spring break in Cancun our junior year that would absolutely prove you wrong." My eyes widened at the thought of Rose in Cancun. The image of Rose as a carefree college student was hard to conjure. Lily laughed and turned her attention to me. "She'd been dreading the flight the entire week we'd been there and ended up drinking herself into a stupor on the plane. They literally had to call ahead for a wheelchair to even get her down the jetway."

"Shall we start exchanging Cancun stories, Lily? Really?" Rose asked with a laugh.

"Okay, perhaps not. Besides, I think Penelope has the best stories—or the worst stories, depending on how you look at it. We should save the tales of college drunkenness for when she's around."

"Good plan. Will we be seeing her tomorrow?"

"Yes, definitely. She'd be here now but she had a date."

"Penelope, Lily, and I were all roommates in college," Rose said to me, filling me in. "Penelope and I are bridesmaids."

"Co-maids of honor," Lily corrected.

"I see," I said with a smile.

"I brought Riley because she's my best coordinator, but it hadn't occurred to me that bringing her meant I would be subjecting her to embarrassing stories."

"Well, let's face it. You're not Rose, her boss, right now. You're just Rose, my best friend. I'm glad you'll be helping to plan the wedding, but I don't want hard-ass, boss Rose. I want my best friend who happens to be spectacular at her job."

"Hey, I can totally appreciate that you have a life outside of work. And I promise I can definitely keep your confidence," I explained, giving Rose a smile. To be honest, it would be fun to see a different side of her, or to see her in a different light.

"Well, we might not have a choice after tomorrow," she sighed. "I love Penelope, but she can be a little over the top sometimes."

"She means well," Lily said softly.

There was the tiniest bit of tension falling over the table, so I did my best to clear the air. "Since I am obviously at a disadvantage here, can you fill me in on the plans you have for the event? Have you settled on anything yet, or are we on a blank slate?"

Lily clearly enjoyed talking about her wedding and the next two hours was filled with animated conversation about it. The drinks were flowing and the food was amazing.

"So, I think I want a blush dress and then I want the whole theme to be, like, rose gold. Very soft and feminine, but opulent."

"That sounds gorgeous," I said sincerely. It did sound breathtaking.

"And we can have the whole reception in a big tent with white draping, and use lighting to get the right effect. With gold embellishments and light pinks and reds, plus a few pops of sparkle, I think it'll be perfect."

"Dang, Lily, are you sure you don't want a job in event planning?" Rose teased.

Lily waved a hand at her friend. "I'm not a professional event planner. I'm a professional Pinterest abuser. Can I get paid to look at Pinterest?"

We all laughed as I was sure we could all relate.

"So, Riley, I know Rose is single because she's in a committed relationship with her job, but how about you? Seeing anyone special?"

A smile formed on my face thinking of Cam, but before I could answer, Rose spoke up for me. "Riley is recently engaged to a very handsome man, who happens to be the mayor's son."

"Oh really?" Lily said with enthusiasm.

"Show her the ring," Rose said while nudging me with her elbow.

I shyly held up my left hand and both women inspected the ring carefully.

"It's beautiful, Riley," Lily said softly. She was obviously a hardcore romantic. "So, tell me how you met your fiancé."

"Yes," Rose exclaimed. "I still haven't heard the story."

"Oh well, that's actually a pretty funny story." I took a sip of my cosmopolitan and then dove right into the best day of my whole life. "I'd just gotten a promotion, so I was celebrating by taking my best friend to a basketball game. Well, the couple sitting next to me broke up right before halftime, like, right next to me. And it was really awkward because I could hear everything. So, anyway, his girlfriend—well, ex-girlfriend—left in a huff and we're just sitting there next to each other. I felt bad for him because the woman seemed like a complete crazy handful, so I just kind of told him he'd dodged a bullet and was better off. We started talking a little, and then we noticed our faces were up on the Jumbotron for the Kiss Cam. You know, where they make people kiss in front of the whole arena?"

"No," Lily gasped, smiling.

Rose's hand was covering her mouth in surprise.

"So, I kissed him." My words came out all breathy and I knew I had a dreamy expression on my face. I always got all love drunk when I thought about that kiss.

"Must have been some kiss," Lily said with a laugh.

"The best kiss I'd ever had. Ever."

"Wow," Rose said wistfully.

"Yeah, after that he pursued me relentlessly." I laughed at the memory. "We've been together ever since."

"She had a ring on her finger within five months," Rose shared.

"Really?" Lily asked, looking to me for confirmation.

"Best kiss I *ever* had, ladies," I replied pointedly, raising my eyebrows. "That translates to all other pertinent areas of concern."

"Oh my," Rose said, fanning herself. She'd had at least three drinks and her boss walls were dropping.

"Oh yes," I said just before taking a sip of my drink, which I found to be empty. Bummer.

"Another round?" Lily asked, her voice hopeful.

"I'm down," Rose said in a very un-Rose way.

I looked at my empty glass—my *third* empty glass—and then thought about Camden.

"I should probably head back upstairs."

"Oh really? Just one more?"

"No," I said, making it sound as though I really wanted to stay, which wasn't hard because a big part of me did. I liked Lily and I enjoyed watching Rose be normal. And the two of them together was very entertaining. "I think I probably got a little too much sun this afternoon, and that third cosmo is totally hitting me. Time for bed." I turned to Rose. "What time are we starting tomorrow?"

"A car will be here to pick us up at ten. We're going dress shopping and then looking at a few venues."

Lily squealed and bounced in her seat. "It's going to be so much fun."

"I can't wait," I said with a smile. And I meant it. I couldn't remember a time when I was looking forward to planning a wedding more. "Okay, I'll see you then." I opened my clutch to put some money on the table, but Rose's hand covered mine.

"This is all covered by the company, Riley."

"Are you sure?"

"Absolutely. See you in the morning."

"Okay," I said sheepishly, feeling a little guilty for drinking with company money. "See you ladies tomorrow."

They both waved and then I made my way upstairs.

Walking into an empty room was unsettling, especially since I knew I was going to be there for the whole night. Alone. I hadn't spent a night alone in months. Even though I'd had a few days to prepare for this trip, I hadn't been able to prepare for the feeling of having something missing. It hadn't occurred to me that spending a night away from Camden would seem so foreign.

I pushed back the lonely feeling, changed into my pajamas, and washed my face. Only when I was deeply ensconced in my big, fluffy, mostly empty bed did I call Camden.

"Hey," he answered, his voice sleepy and gruff. "I was about to give up on you."

"Sorry. I wasn't expecting our business dinner to turn into a girls' night."

"Oh really?"

"Yeah, it was fun though. Seeing Rose in a whole new light. She's not all work and business. She's just like any other twenty-something woman with girlfriends. Weird."

"So it went well, then?"

"I think so. How was your day?"

"Boring, but that's to be expected. What I wasn't expecting was to miss you this much after just a few hours."

His words absolutely melted me. He missed me too.

"I know what you mean. This big bed is too empty. Feels weird to not be with you." I rolled on my side and brought the fluffy comforter under my chin.

"It's stupid is what it is. No more work trips." He sounded like an insolent, crabby child. His tone only made me laugh.

"Unfortunately, work trips are in my future. But only a few. Besides, we lived for twenty-some years without each other. We can make it a few nights."

"The difference, Riley, is that before, I didn't know what I was missing. Now I'm completely aware that you're not next to me. I can't just roll over and pull you against me, can't lean over and smell you or feel your warmth on the sheets."

"Cam," I whispered, moved beyond words by his declaration.

"It's pretty fucking stupid, babe."

That made me laugh. "I know, and I agree. But we'll make it."

"Speak for yourself," he said gruffly.

I laughed a little more, enjoying the sounds of his voice, even if it was irritated and grumpy with my absence.

"Did you call your mother?"

Suddenly I wasn't smiling anymore.

"I have not."

"Babe," he said in a warning tone.

"What?"

"You've got to call your mother."

"I will. I'm planning on it."

"When?"

"I don't know, when I've got time."

"How would you feel if you found out your mother had made a trip to Portland but didn't call you or try to see you?"

It would hurt my feelings. A lot.

"I don't know. I'd probably figure she'd been really busy."

"I know you hold some resentment toward your mother, babe, but you can't not call her."

"I know," I said, exhaling a large sigh. "It's just hard. I know she's going to want to see me."

"It won't be that bad," he said, his voice softer.

I knew down to my bones he was right, that I had to call my mother, but he was wrong when he thought it wouldn't be that bad. It might have been illogical, but the horror of my high school years and my mother were inexplicably linked in my mind. Even though she saw me suffer, watched me experience a horrid four years at that school, surrounded by those people, she never once stepped in to help me. She'd isolated me from the life and friends I'd had before, then left me to figure everything out on my own.

"I'll call her tomorrow," I concede.

"I think you'll be angry with yourself if you don't."

He was right, but I didn't need to tell him that.

"We're going to look at wedding dresses tomorrow. The bride wants a blush dress."

"Riley, you know that means nothing to me."

I couldn't help but laugh. "It means pink."

"A pink dress? For her wedding?"

43

"You don't like the idea of a pink wedding dress?"

"I don't know." He sounded contemplative. "I guess I just always imagined my wife walking down the aisle to me in a white dress. There's something picturesque about a bride in white. Something classic. I don't know, maybe that's stupid."

A slow smile spread across my face. My fiancé was a romantic.

"So, I should cancel the yellow dress I ordered?"

"Ha-ha-ha," he deadpanned. "Wait, have you ordered a dress? I didn't even know you'd tried any on."

"No, I haven't. You'd know if I'd found a dress. Besides, I need to know when we're getting married to pick an appropriate one."

"The date affects the dress choice?"

"Well, yeah. If it's a summer wedding and we're outside it'll be different than if we get married in the winter."

"So, when do you want to get married? What kind of dress do you want to wear? Summer or winter?"

His question, although completely in line with the conversation we were having, caught me off guard. I didn't think when I called him that evening we'd be trying to pin down a date.

"I'm not sure. I'm also three cosmos deep right now, so selecting a wedding date might not be the best idea."

"True. Do me a favor?"

"What?" I respond cautiously.

"FaceTime me."

"Really?"

"Come on, I miss your face."

Why did he always have to be so sweet?

"Okay, but I already got ready for bed. I'm in my granny pajamas. There's nothing sexy happening over here."

"Babe, you're always sexy to me."

I rolled my eyes but gave in to his request.

"There's my girl," he said when we finally connected on FaceTime. Something about him calling me his girl always made my insides tremble. He said it with such warmth and tenderness, as though I was his most treasured possession.

"Hey," I said, smiling at him. He was lying in bed, propped up against his headboard. He wasn't wearing a shirt, the bastard. Suddenly I missed him so much more than I had a minute before. "I miss you."

"I know, babe. It'll only be a few more days, and then you'll come home and we'll stay in bed all weekend."

"That sounds divine."

"You look like you got a little sun today."

"Shit, did I burn?" I asked as I inspected my face in the little window on my phone screen.

"No, you just look like you were in the sun. Tan, I guess." I watched as a slow smirk crept across his luscious lips. "Are there new tan lines for me to inspect?"

"Tan lines?" I laughed.

"Fuck, Riley, I promise I wasn't planning on getting all turned on. I just wanted to see your face. But now you've got me thinking about tan lines across your ass. *Fuck*," he groaned. I watched on the screen as his arm moved, looking like he was reaching for his pants.

"Hey, hand check! Hands where I can see them, mister!"

He laughed but didn't comply.

"You know you like it when I touch myself."

This was true, generally speaking. There'd been numerous occasions when Camden would be paying special attention to me, whether it be fingering me or going down on me, and the very distinctive sound of his hand on his cock, swiftly moving up and down… well, that sound could send me over the edge. Him being so turned on that he couldn't take it anymore and just had to touch himself was pretty fucking sexy.

"I like it when I'm there with you and we can enjoy each other. This just feels cheap and dirty."

"Feeling dirty?" He said the words on a gasp, and by the way his arm was still moving I could tell he was touching himself. Damn. I tried not to get turned on, but it was useless. He was shirtless and I could see all his muscles moving in sync as he ran his hand up and down his shaft. Well, I assumed that's what he was doing. I couldn't see him from the belly button down.

"I think you're feeling dirty enough for both of us."

"Fuck," he groaned, his head dropping back to lean against the headboard. I watched for a few seconds, fascinated by the visual, but then his eyes met mine again. "I don't want to do this alone, babe."

I worried my bottom lip between my teeth. I wanted to give him what he needed, wanted to be the sexy fiancée who'd have FaceTime sex with him and fulfill this new fantasy, but I didn't have it in me in that moment. Maybe it was the alcohol, or perhaps it was the loneliness I felt in that big suite all by myself, but I didn't feel sexy. I was actually a little sad.

"I'm sorry," I whispered with a wince.

He sighed loudly and it was clear his hand dropped whatever it had been holding. He looked at me with concern in his eyes. "You okay? I mean, is everything all right?"

"Yeah, I'll be fine. I'm just tired and homesick." I shrugged. "I think I'm just going to go to sleep."

"Okay," he said, sounding worried. "I love you."

"Love you too, Cam. I'll talk to you tomorrow."

I disconnected the call and pulled the covers up to my face.

There were so many things in my life that were right—my job was going great, my romantic life was practically perfect, and I had the best friends anyone could ask for. So why did it feel as though everything was so close to falling apart?

Chapter Six
Riley

The next morning I was determined to have a better day. I'd made a list of things I needed to accomplish, ways I could help Rose throughout the day, and I even added things to the list that were pointless just so I could cross them off and feel accomplished.

Shower? Check.

Get dressed? Check.

After I'd eaten breakfast—check—the next thing on my list made me pause.

Call Mom.

Damn.

I had twenty minutes until I had to meet Rose downstairs, but I figured that was good because it would give me a reason to cut the conversation short if I needed to. I took a deep breath, pulled up my mother in my contacts, and hit Call. I said a silent prayer that she was already working and I'd get her voicemail, but apparently the phone gods were too busy to hear my pleas.

"Riley?" my mother asked as a greeting.

"Hey, Mom," I said with what, to me, sounded obviously like forced cheerfulness.

"What in the world—is everything all right?"

I cringed at her voice. Clearly I didn't call my mother enough if her first thoughts were that something was wrong.

"Yeah, no, everything's fine. I was just calling because I happen to be in Paradise Valley and thought maybe you'd want to get coffee or something."

There was silence on the other end of the line for a few moments. I was about to ask if she was still there, but she finally spoke.

"Wait, you're here? In Arizona?"

"Yeah, Mom. I came for a work thing."

"I can't believe it. What a wonderful surprise." She sounded so happy and excited it made me feel even worse about not calling her sooner. "Why don't you come over for dinner tonight?"

"Oh, well, um, I'm not sure what my boss has planned for this evening. I was thinking maybe we could get coffee tomorrow before I leave."

"Oh okay. I guess I could meet you for coffee." I could hear the disappointment in her voice. "What time do you leave?"

Mom guilt was her superpower. "No, Mom, on second thought, let's do dinner. I can come to you." Even though my mother's house was the very last place I wanted to be.

"Oh, Riley, I'm so excited. I'll make your favorite."

"Pork chops and mashed potatoes," we both said at the same time. Just the thought of my mother's cooking had me salivating. She could definitely cook.

"Sounds great. What time should I come over?"

"How about five? If that won't work, let me know. Do you need a ride?"

"No, it's okay. I'll just take an Uber."

"That sounds dangerous. Let me pick you up."

I laughed. "Mom, it's fine. Uber is safe."

"Oh, Riley, I'm so happy you're here. It's been too long."

"I know, Mom. It'll be good to see you." I paused, realizing it was true. "I need to go meet my boss now, but I'll see you at five."

"See you then," she said with obvious excitement before disconnecting.

I let out a sigh, glad the conversation was over but nervous about going back to the house I hated. I took just a moment to text Camden before going to meet Rose.

Going to my mom's house for dinner tonight. Happy?

Good girl.

I smiled at his response, then tossed my phone in my purse and made my way downstairs to meet Rose.

I'd been in approximately one hundred wedding dress shops since I started with Rose and her company. You wouldn't think there were that many dress shops in Portland, but factor in all the surrounding suburbs and one would be surprised how many establishments sold wedding dresses. This was definitely not my first rodeo.

The particular shop we were in that morning was fancier and more exclusive than most. You needed an appointment to get in, and champagne was handed out immediately upon arrival. You were also given a private viewing room with a personal shopper who handled every aspect of the bride's needs along with anyone she brought along.

It became clear to me as soon as we arrived that Rose was there in more of a bridesmaid capacity than wedding planner, but I figured that was why she brought me along. I declined the expensive champagne and took notes as the morning progressed.

"Welcome to Paradise Bridal," Amy, our bridal assistant, said with a bright smile after everyone was seated with their champagne flutes in hand. "Is your entire bridal party here?"

"Actually, not yet. Penelope is coming, but she's running a little late. But other than her, yes. Everyone is here." Lily was floating on a happy bride cloud. Nothing could wipe the smile from her face. Even if I hadn't been introduced to her mother a few minutes before, I still could have picked her out of the group; she was the one wiping a stray tear every few minutes. It was everything wedding dress shopping was supposed to be.

"Shall we wait?"

"No, I don't think she'll be too long. I'm too excited to wait."

"Great." Amy smiled. "I've looked over the information you put on your initial interest form and pulled a couple of dresses that aligned with your vision."

Interest form? This place is legit.

"If any of the dresses aren't what you're looking for, let me know and we'll skip over it. But keep in mind, sometimes dresses look different on our bodies than on the rack." She gave Lily a sweet smile and then motioned for her to follow her back to a dressing room. Everyone watched Lily disappear and excitement pulsed through the room. I had to hand it to this place, they seemed to have their shit together.

I pulled my phone from my purse and opened my Pinterest app, searching for inspiration for Lily's rose-gold theme. I had to give her credit, everything looked beautiful. Soft and elegant, two words that perfectly described Lily herself. A light pink dress would be gorgeous surrounded by soft golden hues.

"Penelope!" I heard Rose excitedly call out and looked up to see a woman embracing Rose. When they pulled apart, my breath halted and my eyes shot open wide.

Standing not twenty feet away was Penelope Price. If I ever had an archnemesis, it was Penelope. Not only were she and her band of merry bitches from high school responsible for most of my torment, but it was her family my mother worked for and on her property I lived during those four years. She took particular pleasure in making my life miserable.

I watched and Penelope and Rose hugged again, both of them smiling and laughing. Eventually, Rose motioned to an empty chair next to her and Penelope sat, just in time for Lily to come out in her first dress.

Everyone gasped. Lily in a stark white strapless bridal gown was a sight to behold. She was glowing, smiling so wide I could probably count all her teeth. Her mother was crying full-on, and everyone was blown away. She was incredibly beautiful. Breathtaking, even. Stunning.

And that's how the next two hours progressed. Lily tried on dress after dress and looked amazing in every single one. And that wasn't even an exaggeration—she, quite literally, looked fantastic in every single dress.

I'd taken a picture of her in all the dresses she'd tried on from the back of the room, knowing that if she couldn't make a decision that day, she'd be thankful to have visual reminders. Luckily, everyone in the room had been so preoccupied with the dresses and Lily's stupidly stunning ability to look good in all of them that Penelope had yet to realize I was even in the room.

After Lily had put on the last one, she was nowhere close to making a decision. She'd tried on a few blush dresses, but none of them had had the *it* factor. None of them had been *the* dress.

"I don't know what to do," she said after Amy had left us all alone for a few minutes to ponder the decision. "I tried on twenty dresses. I thought for sure I'd find one I'd want. What am I supposed to do now?"

"The third dress was beautiful," one of her aunts chimed in from the front row.

"I really wanted a blush dress though," Lily replied, more to herself than anyone else.

"Lily?" I said gently from my perch at the back of the room. Her eyes snapped up to meet my gaze. "I took a photo of you in every dress and you were stunning in all of them. But if you didn't get that feeling you were looking for, that undeniable rush of knowing you'd just put on your wedding dress, then I would keep looking." As soon as I spoke, everyone turned to look at me, including Penelope. I didn't glance in her direction, keeping my eyes on Lily, but I could feel her gaze on me.

"Riley's right," Rose added from the front row. "You don't have to choose a dress today."

"I just feel bad. I tried on all these dresses and that woman spent so much time with us, and the champagne."

"That's her job, Lily," I said gently, trying to ease her guilt. "She understands that not every bride is going to purchase a dress every time. I guarantee you that. There's no rule saying you must buy today. Trust me."

"Okay," Lily said, still sounding unsure. "Thank you, Riley." She gave me a small smile and then turned back to return to the dressing room.

I walked around the seating area and followed her back, acting on a hunch.

"Hey, Lily," I called softly, catching her before she disappeared back into the dressing room.

"Yeah?"

"Would you like me to tell Amy we'll need some time to think about it? I can totally handle that for you."

"Really?" she asked, eyebrows tipping up, a hopeful expression crossing her face.

"Of course, that's what I'm here for." I reached out and patted her arm softly. "If you're not sure about any of these dresses, we should walk away and think about it."

"Okay. Thank you so much for your help." She gave me another soft smile and then disappeared into the dressing room as I went to find Amy. I found her in the showroom hanging up some dresses that I assumed Lily had declined. She saw me coming and put on a very friendly smile.

"Amy, I don't know if we got the chance to formally meet. I'm Riley. I'm here with one of the bridesmaids and we're acting as event planners for the wedding."

"Oh hi," she said with a smile, shaking my outstretched hand.

"This is truly one of the nicest places I've ever been with a client. We're based in Portland, so we don't usually get to explore other areas and scope out their best shops. You've done a wonderful job with Lily too. Those dresses were amazing."

"Well thank you," she replied, clearly appreciating my flattery. It was sincere though; it really was the nicest shop I'd been in, and she had done a great job.

"Lily is expressing a little bit of regret because she's overwhelmed by all the beautiful choices. I think she needs some time to let the dresses marinate, you know? She wants to make the best decision and she feels a lot of pressure."

"Oh, no pressure," Amy cried, her hand coming to rest on my shoulder. "No, she can take all the time she needs. I'm just a phone call away when she decides. Do you mind if I just go back there and let her know she doesn't need to make a decision today?"

"Would you? I think she'd really appreciate that. You and me, we do this all the time, but she's a first-time bride and she's too sweet for her own good."

"You're so right. Thank you for letting me know."

I watched as Amy disappeared around a corner to find Lily. Then I saw Rose appear from the same corner.

"That was smooth, Riley. I get the feeling you can sweet-talk anyone into anything."

I shrugged. "It's just now occurring to me that I might be a master manipulator."

"There are worse problems to have." She took a beat and her eyes swept over me in an assessing way. "The plan is to go get some lunch with the mother of the bride and bridal party, and then we all go tour two venues."

"Sounds good. Although, if it's not too much trouble, I made dinner plans with my mother, so if we run too late I might have to take off. I hope that's all right."

"Of course it's all right, Riley. I'm glad you'll get to see your mother while we're here. Let's go see if Lily needs anything else."

I nodded and followed her back to where her friend was waiting. Right before we made it there, my phone buzzed in my hand. I looked down and saw it was Camden. I sent him to voicemail, figuring I'd call him back later, but when I looked back up, Rose was watching me.

"You can take a phone call, you know." She laughed. "I know I'm usually a hard ass back in Portland, but hell, Riley, I've been drinking champagne all morning. This isn't the normal workday."

She said everything with a smile, and my shoulders lost a little tension with her words.

"Are you sure?"

"Yeah. Call your man back. I'm sure Lily's still getting dressed anyway."

"Okay, I'll just wait outside."

She gave me another smile and then went to find Lily, so I made my way out of the store. They had a nice entryway with some benches in the shade and I took a seat as I called Camden back. He picked up on the first ring.

"Hey, I'm glad you called me back. I was leaving you a rather lengthy voicemail."

"Is everything okay?" Camden and I weren't really voicemail people. We either talked or texted—only creepers left voicemails.

"Yeah, I just had a lot to say and didn't want to type it all out."

He paused and I was quiet, waiting for all the words he supposedly had.

"Cam, you're making me nervous. What's going on?"

"Oh, sorry, I'm packing."

"Packing?"

"Yeah, my flight to Arizona leaves in two hours. I've got to hurry."

"You're coming to Arizona? Why?"

"Because even though you pretend to be all tough and unbreakable, I know you and I think you could use me around tonight when you have dinner with your mom."

"Are you serious?" I cried, my hand coming to rest over my heart which was thumping away in my chest.

"Yeah. My flight gets in at three thirty. I'm gonna rent a car, and take you to dinner at your mom's."

"Camden," I said, breathlessly, fighting back tears. "There are no words. I don't even…."

"I know, babe. It's okay."

"I wish you were here so I could hug you," I said, half crying and half laughing. He was so right too. I didn't realize how much I needed him until he made himself available. "How long are you staying?"

"All weekend. You're gonna have to tell Rose to fly home alone tomorrow, because we're relaxing at the resort."

"Really?" Camden and I had never been away together, and spending a weekend with him in the sun and by a pool sounded incredible. "How in the world did I get lucky enough to brainwash you into loving me?"

"It's your ass, babe. Grade A."

"Shut up," I said with more laughter, wiping tears from my cheeks. "So you're coming to the resort? Or picking me up? What's the plan?"

"I'll text you when I land and then you tell me where to go and when." He sounded excited, but then his next words were softer. I could picture him standing next to his bed, a duffel bag open in front of him and a pair of socks in his hands. "I know it's only been one night, Riley, but I can't wait to see you."

"Me too," I managed to say, even while my breath was stopped in my lungs, throat stinging with tears.

"I'll text you in a few hours. I love you."

"Love you too. Be safe, all right?"

"You got it."

He disconnected and I took a deep breath, trying to rein in my emotions. Most likely I never would have admitted it, but I did need Camden there with me. Sure, I could get through the dinner on my own, but having him there would make everything so much easier. Plus, he needed to meet my mom sooner or later. It was important to him, and to me too.

I heard the door open behind me and Rose emerged with Lily, Penelope, and the rest of the group. I pulled my shoulders back, trying to steel myself for my first encounter with Penelope since high school.

"You ready to go?" Rose asked me, smiling widely.

"Definitely. Lily, I've got photos of you in all the dresses if you'd like me to email them to you later."

"Oh my gosh, that would be great." She sounded grateful.

"Lily and Penelope are going to ride with us to lunch. Penelope, this is one of my best employees—"

"Riley Smith," Penelope finished for Rose. "I thought that was you in the back. Wow, what a surprise."

I had absolutely no time to process before she pulled me into a hug.

"You two know each other?" Rose questioned, curiously.

"Know each other? Riley lived with her mother and brother in our guest house all through high school. Her mother still works for my parents. She's like an honorary aunt to me." She said the words as if she hadn't been personally responsible for most of my unhappy memories there.

"What a small world," Lily said, her voice happy and light.

"How bizarre," Rose added. The black SUV pulled up to the curb and all four of us climbed in. Once seated and buckled, I pulled out my phone, swiping through Pinterest, trying to look busy in hopes the other three would ignore me.

No such luck.

"So, Riley, what have you been up to since high school?"

I looked up to see Penelope giving me a smile. "Not much," I said on a breath. "I moved back to Oregon for college, then moved to Portland afterward and have been working for Rose ever since."

"And how's your brother? Your mom talks about him all the time."

"Tripp is doing well. I don't see him much as he's super busy all the time."

"Gosh, how long has it been since you've been back? Nine years?"

"That sounds about right," I replied and turned back to my phone. The polite thing to do would be to ask her about her life, but I just couldn't. I was hanging on by a thin thread as it was.

"Were you guys close in high school?" Lily asked with all the innocence of a lamb.

"Not as close as you'd think," Penelope answered thoughtfully. "We kind of ran in different circles."

I pressed my lips together at her response. Then I prayed whatever restaurant we were going to for lunch had a full bar. Working or not, I was going to need a strong drink.

A half hour later and we were seated at a very trendy restaurant with an impressive brunch menu. Everyone had mimosas, even me. I might have asked the waitress to add extra champagne to mine. I took a sip, practically moaning at the effervescent tingling of the bubbles in the large dose of champagne. Clearly the bubbly-to-orange-juice ratio was in my favor.

My phone pinged in my purse and I read a text from Camden.

Just got to the airport. Going through security. I'll text you when I land and have a car. Love you and can't wait to see you.*

His words made an enormous smile spread across my face.

"Looks like Riley got a message from her man," Rose said, not unkindly, but catching me off guard.

My eyes snapped up to her, my smile faltering slightly. Was I that transparent?

"Oh, do tell," Penelope said, eyeing me. She wasn't the only one either. Everyone at the table was staring at me, waiting for a response.

"My fiancé surprised me and bought a plane ticket to Arizona. He's coming to spend the weekend here with me." I looked at Rose. "I was going to tell you. Looks like I'm staying here, so you'll be flying solo tomorrow. I hope that's all right."

She waved away my worry with a dismissive hand. "That's fine. I'll get a credit for your ticket. Besides, now I can get sloshed since I'll be alone."

"That's very sweet of him," Lily sighed dreamily.

"It is. How long have you been together?" Penelope asked.

"About six months."

"It's been a whirlwind romance," Rose said dramatically. "He's the mayor's son."

Wide eyes snapped back to me. Penelope had one eyebrow that was almost reaching the ceiling. "Really?" she asked, drawing the word out like it was a fantastically salacious idea. "How did you meet him?"

My insides iced over and I wanted to change the subject. A large part of me wanted to keep everything about Camden and me away from Penelope. He was too precious to subject our relationship to her whim. I wanted to protect the thing in my life that was most important. But I knew it would be rude not to answer, and so far, Penelope had been completely polite to me, so I had no reason—in the eyes of everyone else at the table, at least—to keep the information to myself.

"We sat next to each other at a basketball game. Nothing too exciting."

Rose, who might have been lingering on the edges of drunkenness, picked up her flute and, just before taking a sip, said, "Her fiancé is probably one of the sexiest men in Portland. He was considered one of the most eligible bachelors until Riley came along and snatched him up."

Now both of Penelope's eyebrows were sky-high. "Impressive."

I had to repress a shudder. I hated the way the outside world viewed my relationship with Camden. Sure, it wasn't as if he was under heavy speculation—he wasn't the son of the President, after all—but Portland was its own little world and once the news of our relationship broke, we'd been subjected to lots of scrutiny and observation. Some news outlets painted our relationship as a Cinderella story, as though he was a prince saving me from a lowly existence. Other magazines had insinuated I'd used my feminine wiles to lure him in and trap him—they were expecting a pregnancy announcement any day now.

The truth was Camden and I fell in love just like any other couple had. But I always ended up being the lesser half of the equation, as though I was lucky to have him, never the contrary.

No one aside from Hadley had ever told Camden that he was fortunate to have me. Well, all right, maybe his mother. But even though I knew Camden felt as though he'd gotten the better end of the deal, it was hard not to let the weight of everyone's view settle heavily on my shoulders.

"So, Lily, what kind of venues are we going to be viewing today?" It was my desperate attempt to change the subject. Lily welcomed the departure.

"Well, we're going to tour two resorts: The Pointe and Royal Palms."

I'd heard of both venues but never been to either. Just like the Paradise Oasis, they'd been places I knew I could never afford to step foot in.

"I think I'm leaning more toward The Pointe simply for the view from the ceremony space. You're literally standing on a cliff and the desert mountains are behind you. It's gorgeous."

"It sounds breathtaking." My brain was working, conjuring up an image, trying to picture how to work in a rose-gold theme in the setting she described.

"I'm just so excited!" she squealed, bouncing up and down in her seat. She was simply adorable and obviously ready to be married.

"It's going to be amazing," I promised.

Chapter Seven
Camden

A year before, had someone told me waking up alone in my bed would make me grumpy, I would have laughed. Laughed pretty hard, actually. But, sure enough, I woke up that morning reaching for Riley and jolted when I felt a cold and empty bed. It took me a few seconds to remember she was out of town for work, but as soon as my brain wrapped around the idea that I was alone, I was instantly irritated.

There's nothing in the world that can prepare you to feel as though you're incomplete without a certain person close to you. Riley was more than just my fiancée—she was a source of comfort, someone I wanted desperately to make laugh just so I could hear her giggle and watch her eyes crinkle in the corners. I wanted, more than anything, to make her need and want me as much as I craved and longed for her.

It took me about thirty minutes to say, "Fuck it," and book a flight to Arizona. I hadn't taken a vacation day in a while and I could accomplish just as much on a plane as I could sitting at my desk. To hear Riley get just as excited as I was about seeing her made me feel as though I'd made the right decision.

I also knew renting the sexy red Mustang was the right decision. The fact that it was a convertible was just icing on the sexy car cake.

The flight had been typical, and I'd managed to get enough work done that I'd relieved the small amount of guilt I felt for bailing on the office, but once I'd landed in

Arizona, I was officially in vacation mode. I had my shades on and the top down, and I would be lying if I said I didn't feel like a complete badass.

I'd texted Riley and she'd told me to head to the hotel. She'd given the concierge my name and allowed them to grant me access to her suite. I knew she'd be another hour or two, so I took a detour through the desert, testing out the capabilities of the 'Stang.

I pulled up to the resort and immediately knew it was going to be a good weekend. The hotel was obviously top of the line. I parked in front of the elaborate entrance and a valet approached, eyes trailing the Mustang from the hood to the bumper. I shut the door and then leaned over the back, grabbing my duffel bag from the back seat.

"Good afternoon," the valet said with a polite smile.

"Hey, man. Here ya go," I said, handing him the keys. He gave me a ticket and then his eyes went wide as he climbed into the driver seat. I knew it probably wasn't the nicest car he'd ever driven, especially not at this resort, but it wasn't anything to balk at either. No one could deny the beauty of a classic American car.

I had no problem getting a key to Riley's room. As soon as I slipped the key card in the door and pushed it open, I knew Riley was in there. I could smell the soft powdery scent of her and feel her presence deep inside me.

"Babe?" I called out, shutting the door behind me.

She didn't answer me with her voice, but I heard her footsteps from deep inside the suite, thumping along the floor until she appeared at the doorway to my left just before she made a running leap into my arms. I caught her, held on tight, and her legs wrapped around my waist.

"Fuck, I missed you," I said as I swept my hand down her dark brown hair, my other hand wrapped tightly around her waist, holding her to me.

"I missed you too," she mumbled into the skin of my neck, and God, she felt good. Her body pressed against mine, the warmth of her core hot against my stomach, her fingers threading through my hair. She pulled back, her hands framing my face, and pressed her lips against mine.

I was done for.

Always gone for her.

Her lips nipped at mine, her tongue teasing, but when she opened for me, I took advantage. She moaned as I swept my tongue through her mouth, and I needed to be inside of her, to have no barriers between us.

"Bedroom?" I rasped against her mouth.

"Door behind me," she answered in an equally urgent and raspy voice.

I stumbled my way through the suite but found the bedroom easily enough and wasted no time dragging Riley into the middle of it.

"How long do we have?" I asked just before I pulled my shirt over my head.

"Long enough," she replied breathlessly, propping herself up on her elbows to watch me undress. I stood up and unbuttoned my pants, quickly pushing them down my thighs along with my boxer briefs, my cock standing straight up, aching for her. I crawled back over her and pushed her shirt up her torso, exposing her stomach before kissing up the middle. She took over, pulling the shirt over her head, then reaching behind her back to unclasp her bra.

As soon as her breasts were free, my mouth pulled her nipple in, sucking and nipping.

"Oh God," she breathed as she writhed beneath me.

I could have stayed at her breasts forever—she had a fantastic rack—but I wanted more. Wanted to give her more. I moved lower and unbuttoned her slacks, loving how she wore sexy-as-fuck lingerie under her work clothes. I peeled the pants down her thighs and my eyes locked on the black lace covering her pussy. I could smell her arousal and absolutely could not stop myself from burying my face between her thighs and nuzzling her before I yanked her lacy underwear down her legs.

We were naked, both of us ready, and I couldn't drag my eyes from her.

I sat back on my ankles and gripped her behind her knees, dragging her into my lap. Her legs fell open over my thighs and I fucking loved that she was on display for me. I trailed a finger over her opening, and my cock grew impossibly harder finding her wet.

"You're so ready for me, babe."

"I've been ready for you all morning, thinking about seeing you. I need you, Cam."

"Fuck," I ground out harshly, sinking two fingers knuckle-deep inside her. I watched her eyes flutter closed, felt her hips arch up to meet my fingers, heard her groan as I rotated my fingers inside of her, stretching her, finding that spot that made her absolutely lose her mind. I stroked that spot over and over again, feeling her wetness flood around my fingers and watching her skin become flushed and splotchy. One of her hands grasped the sheets and I grunted as the other palmed her breast, kneading and pulling to the rhythm of my fingers.

"I can't take much more of this, Riley. I want to feel you come around my fingers, and then you're going to come around my cock."

"Yes," she whispered, lost in her own world of lust.

I started moving my fingers quicker, putting more pressure on that rough spot inside of her, and smiled as I watched her climb. She grew louder, uninhibited in the fancy hotel suite, rocking her hips against my fingers until I pressed my thumb against her clit and circled, sending her into orgasm.

Her mouth dropped open, back arched off the mattress, and she trembled uncontrollably. It was fucking magnificent to watch. Her pussy gripped my fingers, pulling them farther into her channel, and I couldn't wait to feel her work against my dick.

I pulled my fingers out while she was still reeling and thrust my cock inside, watching her react to the sudden intrusion.

"Camden, I can't—"

"You just did, Riley. Take it."

I pulled out and thrust in again, pulling her knees farther onto my lap, then dropped my hands next to her head and gave in to the instinct to claim her, to make her remember she was mine. I pounded into her, every thrust met with a strangled cry from her luscious mouth. I couldn't tell if she was still coming from the first orgasm or if she was building rapidly to another. It didn't matter. She could come all night long as far as I was concerned.

I slowed my thrusts, taking my time, leaving kisses all along her neck and shoulder.

"I didn't realize how much I'd miss you until you were gone," I panted, using my hips to push deep inside of her. "I need you."

"I'm right here," she said, her voice somewhere between a cry and a moan.

"You're everything." The words fell from my mouth. I meant them but hadn't realized I needed to say them until they'd already been said. Something inside me was desperate for her to know how much I needed her with me.

She used her hands to bring my mouth back to hers and wrapped her ankles around my waist, her heels digging into my ass, meeting me thrust for thrust.

"Get there, babe. I can't hold out much longer." I wanted to. Lord knew I wanted to spend eternity wrapped inside her heat, but sometimes Riley was so good for me, so perfect, I couldn't keep myself from coming. There was a primal logic there, some baser instinct; my body wanted to fill hers, to mark her, to mate. And it was happening whether I was ready or not. "Get yourself off, Riley. Touch yourself."

I leaned back enough to look down at where our bodies were connected, where I was slick and coated with her wetness and sliding in and out, where her body was swallowing my cock whole. Her delicate hand reached between us, finding her clit and gently circling it with two fingers.

"Yes," I growled. Did it get any sexier than watching Riley make herself come? No.

"I'm close," she whined, eyes shut again, head tilted back.

I dug in, rutting against her deeper, making sure she was taking every inch of me without fail, pushing into her harder.

"Oh fuck," she cried as she came.

Feeling her already-snug grip tighten around me sent me over the edge as well. I thrust once more, then stilled inside her, letting my release roll through me. I leaned down to kiss her and fell to the side, but she rolled with me so we stayed connected, kissing like teenagers. Her hands cradled my face and I slid mine around her slim waist, making sure there was absolutely no space between us.

Finally, when I'd kissed her enough to make up for the twenty-four hours we'd been apart, I released her lips, but still held her close.

"Hi," she said on a sigh.

Even though my eyes were closed, I knew she was smiling by the sound of her voice. She sounded sated and sleepy.

"Hi back," I said, peeping one eye open.

"That was a little unexpected."

At that, I opened both eyes and gave her a narrowed glare. "Really? You didn't think the moment I got my hands on you this would happen?"

She lifted one shoulder in a coy shrug. "Obviously I expected us to have sex while we're here. I just didn't expect it to be the instant you walked in the door. It's only been a day. Was it really that hard?" She tried to keep the smile from her face, but she was too proud of her own pun to stop her lips from turning up at the corners.

"You loved it," I said dismissively.

"I definitely did." She let out a large sigh. "We should probably get cleaned up and head out to my mom's house."

Before she could climb out of the bed and end the spell that came over me when I walked in the hotel room, I leaned over and kissed her gently one more time.

"I fucking missed you, Riley," I said, my forehead pressed against hers.

"I missed you too."

Forty-five minutes later, we were driving through town heading toward Riley's mom's house. I knew she was nervous because she had a vice grip on my hand. I let her squeeze it, though, because I knew it made her feel better, even if just a fraction.

"Go right at that light," she says. She didn't sound like she was directing me toward her old home. Her voice was heavy, full of worry and fear.

I wasn't exactly sure what she was afraid of, but if I had to guess it probably had to do with Riley being afraid I'd view her differently after meeting her mother and seeing where she spent part of her childhood. I think on some level she was embarrassed about where she came from.

I took the turn and observed the town giving way to a neighborhood. The houses were exactly what I would expect in Arizona—stucco, red clay tiles on the roof, rock gardens instead of grass. The houses were decently sized with ample room between them, but as we drove the houses and the lots they were on grew larger. With more size came more finery; instead of a standard two-car garage, there were three and four, then houses with circular driveways and detached garages.

Eventually, after a few more turns taking us deeper into the suburban area, the houses were no longer visible because they sat far off the road and were blocked by big gates you could only gain access to with a code.

"Turn into the next driveway on the left," she said softly.

I rubbed my thumb against her knuckles, trying to calm her as much as possible.

When we reached the gate, I pulled up to the box and rolled down my window.

"The code should be one-nine-eight-five. That's the year Mr. and Mrs. Price were married."

I punched the code into the dial pad and sure enough, the gate started to slowly open inward.

Palm trees lined the driveway which led, finally, to a house that could only be described as colossal. Excessive. It was simply massive. A huge fountain was the focal point around the circular drive, and a grand white marble staircase led up to two mahogany doors that must have been fifteen feet high. I thought back to when I took Riley to my parents' house for the first time and the way she had reacted looking at their rather large home. This mansion made my parents' quaint home pale in comparison.

"Holy crap," I said before I could think better of it.

"I know. It's ostentatious, isn't it?"

"It's something, all right. What in the world do these people do?"

"Mr. Price got in early on a bunch of nineties Internet stocks. I think he's one of the original owners of America Online. Might have a piece of Explorer as well.

Even though those companies are not exactly top of the line anymore, he made all the money he'd ever need decades ago. Now I think they live off interest and dividends."

"Lucky bastard," I mumble.

"Go all the way around the driveway. Right after the house, you'll see a little access road. That'll lead you down the south end of the property."

I followed her directions and took the Mustang off the nice smooth pavement and onto a gravel road. It wasn't terrible, but it definitely wasn't as nice as the main driveway.

The sun was setting and the bright sun was waning, casting an orangey-pink hue over everything. After a few moments on the access road, we came upon what I would have called a normal house. In fact, it looked much like the houses in the neighborhood we'd passed before we encountered the long gated driveways.

Riley's hand tightened in mine, and I realized why when my eyes landed on her mother standing on the porch. Pulling the Mustang up next to what I assumed was her mother's car, I put it in Park and then turned to Riley, cupping her cheek.

"I love you and this is going to go great. You'll see."

"I love you too, and I hope you're right."

I pressed a chaste kiss to her lips, then let her go. It looked as though her mother was one second away from pouncing down the steps of her porch if we didn't make it to her soon. Riley met me at the front of the Mustang and we walked together to her mother, who was practically bouncing in her shoes.

"Riley, my baby, I can't believe you're here," she said, wrapping Riley in her arms and swaying back and forth. I watched as Riley allowed her mother to hug her. Her body was stiff at first, only returning the embrace out of politeness or obligation, but after just a few moments I watched her body relax. She squeezed her mother tighter and pressed her face into the crook of her neck. I stood a few feet away, silent, simply observing and letting them have a moment together.

When her mother pulled away, it was only far enough to cup Riley's face and smile brightly at her. "How are you?"

"I'm good, Mom. Promise. I'm really good." I could tell Riley wasn't saying the words just to make her mother feel better—Riley believed them. A wave of warmth spread through me at the realization. I couldn't take credit for all the good things in Riley's life—she was responsible for most—but I knew our relationship made us both better, made us both happy, and hearing her say the words made me love her a little bit more.

Riley's mother's eyes moved to me and I gave her my best smile.

"Camden," she said happily. "I'm so glad to finally meet you." She walked toward me with open arms and I accepted her hug, glad to finally be meeting her as well.

"Sorry I crashed your dinner, Mrs. Smith."

"Nonsense, you're always welcome. I'm glad our first meeting won't be at the wedding. And call me Nora, please."

"Well, thanks for having me, Nora."

Riley walked to me and slipped her arm around my waist, and I eagerly brought her to my side.

"He surprised me too," Riley said, looking up at me. "But I'm glad he did."

"Me too," Nora said, her voice weepy. I noticed her eyes tearing up but didn't want to call attention to it, so I tried to change the subject.

"We'll have to get my parents out for a visit soon, or you can come out to Portland. We're all going to be family soon."

"Oh, that would be fun," she said, turning away and trying to wipe her tears without us noticing. "Come on inside. I've got dinner almost on the table."

I waited for both women to enter and followed.

Nora's house looked just like any other typical middle-class house in America. It was warm and homey, with pictures hung on the wall, overstuffed couches that looked extremely comfortable in the living room, and knickknacks placed delicately on shelves. With a little observation it occurred to me that Nora and my mother had something in common.

"You collect salt and pepper shakers?" I asked as I approached a cabinet with shelves full of them.

"I do," Nora replied, smiling. "I picked up a set at the Grand Canyon twenty years ago and it kind of took on a life of its own."

"I can see that."

"It sure made birthdays and Christmas easy for a while though," Riley added.

"I know exactly what you mean. A holiday never passes without a new set for my mother."

"I didn't see your mom's collection at her house." Riley gave me an inquisitive look.

"She keeps them at the beach house."

"Ah," she replied. We hadn't made it to the beach house yet.

"Please, sit," Nora said as we entered the kitchen. There was an attached nook with a round table, set for three. "What would you like to drink? I've got Guinness, but no Hef though, Riley. Sorry. Couldn't find any on such short notice. White wine?"

"Wine's fine."

"I'd love a Guinness," I said happily, smiling widely at Riley.

"Ugh, don't encourage him, Mom." She turned her eyes to me and I could tell she was trying to look annoyed. "I hope you brought your toothbrush. I hate Guinness breath."

"There are other things I can kiss besides your mouth," I whispered to her, fully aware her mother's head was buried in the refrigerator and more than likely couldn't hear me. I got exactly what I was looking for when Riley's mouth dropped open in shock.

"Camden," she whispered harshly, then narrowed her gaze at me.

I shrugged and then smiled at Nora as she set the beer down in front of me. Then, like Riley and I were royalty, her mother brought us enough food to feed an entire village.

"Mom," Riley laughed, "you did not have to cook all this food."

"It's in a mother's nature to feed her children, and I have a lot of time to make up for."

"Let her feed you," I said, piling food on my plate. "This all looks delicious. Why don't you cook like this, babe?"

"Oh, I'm sorry I don't cook enough. I'm just a little busy trying to build a career."

"You know I'm kidding," I said, elbowing her lightly.

"Besides, if I tried to cook anything more complicated than spaghetti, I'd burn the house down."

"Well then, let's get you some lessons before we move into the new one."

"You're moving?" Nora asked as she took the seat next to Riley.

"Oh… yeah," Riley replied, looking a little guilty. "We, uh, bought a house."

"You bought a house?" Nora replied. "Purchased a house? With a mortgage?"

"Yeah," I interjected when Riley seemed quiet. "It happened kind of quickly. I kind of sprung the house on her and then talked her into buying it. Just a few days ago."

"That's so nice," Nora said, her voice noticeably sadder than it had been just a moment before. "I'm so happy for you. I can't wait to see it. You'll have to send me pictures."

"I'm sorry I didn't mention it to you. Like Cam said, it happened really fast. We weren't even looking. Well, I wasn't looking. And work's been crazy. I was planning on telling you."

"That's really exciting. I'm glad you'll have a place you can call home."

An awkward silence fell over the table like a storm cloud. Nora was obviously upset that Riley hadn't shared the exciting news with her, and Riley seemed both irritated at her mother's reaction but also guilty for not telling Nora she'd purchased a house. And I had no fucking clue what to say to move us all past it. Luckily, Nora spoke again, saving us all from the silence.

"So, what brings you to Paradise Valley? What kind of job are you working on?"

"A wedding."

"I thought your promotion got you out of doing those? I know you didn't like that part of your job very much."

"No, I didn't. Weddings definitely aren't my favorite, but the bride is a friend of my boss's and she said she'd help. Oh my gosh, I can't believe I didn't tell you," Riley said, turning to me, suddenly amped up.

"What?"

"So Rose's friend, Lily, is getting married. Guess who one of her bridesmaids is?"

I had absolutely no idea who she could be talking about.

"Who?"

Riley looked back to her mother. "Penelope Price."

"What?" Nora said with a laugh. "Penny is in the wedding you're helping with? What a small world."

"Yeah," Riley replied with a scoff. "*Penny* is a bridesmaid."

"Who's Penny?"

"*Penelope* is the daughter of Mr. and Mrs. Price, the couple my mother works for."

Oh shit.

"Well, that must have been fun catching up with her," Nora said just before taking a bite.

"Nearly as fun as that one time I got stitches in my knee." Riley looked at me with a new expression in her eyes. She looked angry and hyper, like she might steamroll over anyone in her way. "Twelve stitches. Right knee. We were in gym class in ninth grade and Penelope tripped me while we were playing tennis."

"Oh, Riley, she did not trip you."

"She *did*, Mother. She tripped me and I ripped my knee open on the turf."

Nora rolled her eyes and Riley stabbed a piece of lettuce on her plate. I picked up my Guinness and took a very long, deep pull. Then I took another one.

"Why in the world would Penny trip you?"

"Um, because she *hated* me," Riley responded, her words dripping with anger and indignation.

"Stop it, Riley. I don't want to have this argument with you again. I just want to have a nice dinner."

I carefully slid my hand under the table and placed my palm on Riley's thigh. I had seen her angry before, but this was a whole different animal. I didn't know why she was so upset, but I didn't like it and I wanted to do anything I could to soothe her.

"Babe, take a breath," I said quietly, squeezing her leg gently. "It's okay."

"No, it's not okay. My mom spent all four years I lived here ignoring anything negative I had to say about the Prices. I don't know why I'm even surprised right now that she doesn't believe me—again," Riley spewed, caring not one bit that her mother was only three feet away and could hear everything she was saying. "This is why I never come back here. Somehow, Penelope Price was always the perfect princess and I was always, *always*, the one in the wrong."

"You could never forgive me for bringing you here, for taking you away from your home, and you never gave anyone here a fair shot, Riley. You took all your anger at me out against everyone else. They all tried to make you feel welcome, but you shut everyone down before they could get through your armor."

"So making me feel welcome is physically harming me? Or spreading rumors about me to the whole school?"

Nora's hands went to her forehead and even I could tell she was exasperated, but I didn't know what to do to calm either one of them.

"Do you know how humiliating it was to stand out on that street every morning, waiting for the school bus to pick me up, while all the other kids from my grade drove by in their new BMWs? Or their Range Rovers? I watched them all drive by and laugh at me as I waited for a bus with only five other kids on it who didn't have their own top-of-the-line vehicles. Every day, Mom."

"So now it's my fault because I couldn't afford to get you a car?"

"No, that's not what I'm saying." Riley took in a deep breath and then pushed it out, trying to calm herself down, which I was thankful for in the moment. I took her hand in my free one and brought it to my mouth, kissing her knuckles. There was no way for me to anticipate Riley getting into an argument with her mother. I knew there was tension there, but not to that degree. I'm not even sure Riley knew that was coming.

Her eyes met mine and even though she was angrier than I'd ever seen her, they softened a little with my touch. I might not have understood her anger, might not have agreed with her method of problem solving at the moment either, but I would hold her hand and support her while she figured out whatever she was working through.

"Not a week went by where something didn't happen, Mom. Whether it was big or small, something happened every week to make me feel inferior to them. But you always took their side. You always told me I was being immature or irrational." Riley's voice cracked and I watched as she shoved her emotions back, forcing herself not to cry, not to let that last wall down. "Just once it would have been nice for you to take *my side*, to believe what I was saying, or even acknowledge what I was feeling."

Silence fell over the table again, but it wasn't awkward that time—it was absolutely uncomfortable. Riley seemed to be waiting for her mother to say the words that might heal almost ten years of heartache, and Nora looked as though she was lost, as though she had no idea how to bridge the gap that suddenly exploded between them.

"I am always on your side, sweetie," Nora finally whispered, clearly overcome with emotion. She and Riley had matching tears tracking down their faces. "Always."

Riley nodded slightly, wiping tears from her face as she said, "I could have really used those words back then, Mom."

"And I probably should have said them to you, but I was busy being a single mom trying to give her kids a good life on her own, working a full-time job, trying to put food on the table and a roof over yours and your brother's head, clothes on your backs, and not completely lose my mind. I might not have been a perfect mother, Riley Marie, but I did the best I could. Now, I'm sorry if you feel like high school was a terrible time for you, but you might want to just stow that away in the 'you and everyone else' category of life and stop letting it affect you so much now." Nora placed her hand over Riley's free one and said, "You are such a strong and capable woman. I admire that about you. I don't know where you got it from, but I'm so happy and proud of how independent and self-sufficient you are. You're smart and beautiful and funny, and I love you more than you'll ever know."

I let out a breath of relief. I didn't know where Nora was going with the first part of that tirade, but she pulled out all the stops in the end. If I knew Riley, I knew being called independent and self-sufficient was the way into her heart. She didn't ever want to feel like she needed anyone, which was why I considered myself lucky that she needed me. I'd managed to break through that barrier she built around herself, and I sat there hoping she'd let her mom in too.

Finally, Riley broke.

"I'm sorry, Mom," she said on what would have been a sob if she hadn't been holding in so much. "I didn't want to fight with you."

"I know you didn't, sweetie," Nora replied, patting Riley's hand.

I leaned closer to Riley and kissed her temple. I felt awkward sitting there while they had this mother-daughter breakthrough, but nothing could have torn me away from Riley in that moment. She so rarely let me see her vulnerable. And it wasn't even that I wanted to see her hurting or broken, I just wanted the opportunity to show her that being vulnerable around me wasn't a weakness, that I wasn't going to run the other way when she showed me her imperfections. I wanted Riley, real and raw, and I wanted to see every facet of her, wanted to understand her to the very depth of her character, and watching her and her mother have a personal and long-time-coming conversation was weirdly gratifying.

"I still don't like Penelope," Riley grumbled as she wiped away a few more tears.

"I surely hope someone wouldn't hold something you did as a teenager against you for nearly ten years. Why don't you give Penelope the benefit of the doubt and try to forgive her? I know you've had your issues with her, but I think she's grown into a wonderful woman, truly."

"Well, hopefully I won't have to see her very often."

Nora let out a sigh and I imagined she was holding back some more words, but she kept them to herself.

"How often do you think you'll be in Arizona to help plan the wedding?"

Riley shrugged. "As often as Rose wants me here, I suppose. It's hard to tell. I don't think we're here in an official capacity. We're not treating it as a regular job, but Rose is definitely offering her help and mine. So, whenever she needs us, I guess we'll be here."

"Well, I'm selfishly looking forward to seeing more of you. I was worried I'd have to wait until *your* wedding to see you again. When is the wedding, anyway?"

"Yeah, Riley. When is the wedding?" I asked her with a smile. She rolled her eyes at me.

"I don't know," she sighed. "Now that we've got the house, planning a wedding seems like a lot of work. And a lot of money."

I hated that she was stressed out about anything wedding related, especially now that she was planning someone else's wedding again. The only thing I could think of to alleviate her stress was to put the wedding off, but that made a tight knot form in my belly. I wanted to be married to Riley, and postponing the wedding wasn't my favorite idea. But I also loved her more than anything, so I carefully broached the subject.

"We could always plan a date far enough in the future that you don't have to worry about it immediately." Even saying the words made me sick to my stomach. I wanted Riley tied to me in every way possible. I wanted my ring on her finger. My last name on her driver's license. I wanted her. Period. And as barbaric as it might have sounded, I wanted to own her and feel as though she belonged to me. It was totally Neanderthal of me, but it was an honest emotion.

"You want to put off the wedding?" she asked, turning to me with concern in her eyes. Shit.

"No, not at all. I want you to be happy and not stressed. I'm not worried about the wedding itself, I just want to be married. To you. Whenever that happens."

Her shoulders dropped at my words, but she didn't look any less worried.

"We don't have to think about it now," I said, running my hand up her back.

"Okay," she agreed.

"No, there's no hurry. Besides, a long engagement might not be such a bad idea, seeing as how you've only been together for a few months."

I could almost feel Riley holding her words back. I knew how she felt. That was the usual consensus, that Riley and I couldn't be ready for marriage after only a few months. Or that our marriage was bound to fail. We'd had a million discussions about it and we both agreed it was all bullshit.

I ran my hand up her back again but continued up into the hair at her nape, tugging it gently but firmly enough to have her look up at me. I leaned down and kissed her gently. Nothing obscene—her mother was right there, after all—but it was enough of a kiss to erase the tension in her body and let her know I wanted her, regardless of when.

When I pulled back, it was only far enough to look her in the eyes.

"Whenever we get married, nothing about it will matter except that you're there, and I'm there, and when it's over, you'll be mine forever." I whispered the words, not caring for anyone except Riley to hear me, but if Nora heard, maybe that was better.

"I love you," she answered softly.

I kissed her again, quickly, then pulled back and released her.

"This is delicious, Nora," I said, turning back to my meal. "You said this was Riley's favorite?"

"It was." She laughed. "I couldn't make enough pork chops and mashed potatoes when she was younger."

"Who doesn't like mashed potatoes?" Riley said, taking a bite.

"Crazy people," Nora responded with a smile.

Chapter Eight
Riley

"Thanks for dinner, Mom."

"No thanks necessary. I'll cook for you any time you're in town. Call me whenever, okay?" she said, then gave me the biggest hug ever.

I pulled her in close and took a breath, remembering the way she always smelled of cheap vanilla perfume. It wasn't a bad smell. In fact, I loved it. But the brand was one you could get at any drugstore for less than twenty dollars. Regardless, the smell evoked many memories of childhood and familiar feelings of warmth.

She pulled away and took the fragrance with her.

"Camden, it was so nice to finally meet you. I can see why Riley was so smitten with you from the beginning." I watched as Cam leaned down to hug her, and something about the visual tugged at me. I wanted my family to get along, and it meant a lot to me that my mother approved of Cam. "Let me know when you get home safely, okay?" she said as she pulled away, her voice squeaking with the tears forming in her eyes.

"Mom," I said, laughing a little. "It'll be okay. I'll probably be back soon."

"I know. Don't mind me. I'm just happy you were here."

"I love you."

"Love you too, baby. Tell your brother to call me too."

"Okay."

"Good night, Nora. Thank you for everything," Cam said, smiling.

She waved and we walked to the Mustang. I climbed in and buckled up, waving to my mother as we drove away. Something about saying goodbye and not knowing exactly when I'd see her again made more tears spring to my eyes, but I tried to push them back. I'd done enough crying already.

Camden had put the resort's address into the GPS, so he followed directions, silently making turn after turn, letting me be. He did, however, reach out and take my hand, offering me that support.

Finally, I let out a sigh and said, "Well, that was intense." Nervous laughter followed. "I'm sorry you had to watch us fight."

He gave my hand a reassuring squeeze. "Don't worry about it. I'm glad I was there. That's exactly why I got on a plane today. I wanted to be here if something came up. And something did." He took a second to look my way, then turned back to the road. "Do you think it helped?"

I blew out another breath. "I don't know. I guess time will tell. I don't want to feel this distance between my mother and me, so I hope finally telling her that I never felt like she had my back will help me move on."

"What about Penelope?"

"Ugh, what about her?"

"Well, I mean, your mom seemed pretty convinced she was a pretty decent woman."

"I don't know. She could save a bunch of orphans from a burning building and I'm not sure it would change my opinion of her. It's hard to separate the teenage girl who hurt me so badly from the put-together woman I encountered earlier today. She could very well be a fantastically wonderful person, but that doesn't change what happened."

"No," he said softly, drawing the word out in a way that I knew he had more to say.

"But...?" I goaded him.

"But maybe it's time for you to be in charge of how people make you feel. Don't give her any power. Besides, I bet she doesn't even realize she bothered you that much. Did you ever tell her? Did you ever say anything to her about it in high school?"

"No. Does anyone sit down with their tormentors in high school and have rational conversations?"

"No, but adults do. Maybe you should talk to her now. If talking to your mother made you feel better, perhaps talking to Penelope will help too."

"I thought your degree was in law, not psychology." I tried to hold back a smirk, but it didn't work so well.

"Maybe I'm just educated in all things Riley."

"Oh my God," I said through my laughter. "That's a terrible line."

"It was, wasn't it?" He started laughing too.

"How about enough deep, emotional conversations for one day? I just want to think about the next two days and how much time we're going to be spending by the pool."

"Hey, I propose equal time spent in the pool and in the bed."

"Hmm, Counselor, I think we might be able to reach an agreement that satisfies both parties."

"Oh, you know how I get turned on by courtroom talk. Say it for me," he said in his best sleazy voice, making me giggle.

I managed to calm myself, and dropped my voice to a sultry level. I turned to him, narrowing my eyes and pouting my lips. "Your Honor," I said with a breathy tone. "I object."

"You know how much that turns me on." His hand squeezed mine tighter and I couldn't control the laughter any longer.

When I managed to catch my breath, I looked over at him as I wiped my eyes, removing happy tears instead of sad. "How do you always manage to make me feel better?"

"Luck," he replied quickly, shooting me his most adorable smile. The one with the dimples.

"No, seriously, Cam. You always know exactly what to say, exactly when to be serious, when to make me laugh, *how* to make me laugh. I'm not sure what I'd do without you." Even I was surprised by the sudden sentimentality I was spewing, but he seemed unfazed. He simply lifted my hand to his mouth and kissed the back of it.

"It'll be my greatest accomplishment to spend the rest of my life anticipating your every need."

"That sounds incredible," I said just as I leaned over the console and pressed my lips to his neck, using my tongue and teeth to make sure he knew I wasn't giving him the obligatory sweet peck. I kissed up his throat, making my way behind his ear to the spot I knew could make him hard in seconds.

"Uh, babe. This is a really expensive rental car. I'd hate to wreck it." His voice was gravelly and I knew I was affecting him. Just to check though, I reached my free hand down between his legs, palming his erection and making him gasp. "Riley, seriously, this won't end well."

"It might," I said against his neck. "I can almost guarantee a happy ending."

"Is it weird that I'm turned on by that statement but also really want to groan at your lack of originality?"

I didn't bother answering him. Instead, I continued to kiss everywhere I could reach that wasn't covered in clothing and wouldn't obstruct his view. I wanted to be daring and adventurous, but I didn't want either of us to die for a handy in the car.

"Babe, seriously."

"Just let me touch you," I said, slowly unbuttoning his pants and then sliding my hand under the waistband of his boxer briefs. It always surprised me how Camden's cock was both hard and still felt soft, like velvet. It was a strange combination. He was straining against his pants so I pushed them down, along with his underwear, and set him free.

"Fuck," he growled, and I felt the car veer off to the side of the road. "I can't drive when you're doing that to me."

"Good. Lean your seat back a little." I felt him put the car in Park and then he moved—rather quickly, I noticed—to recline his seat. Since the car was so fancy, there wasn't a quick lever to pull, so we both sat there, trying not to laugh, as the motor that moved the electric seat whined. His cock was in my hand, and he was reclining at a snail's pace. Eventually, I couldn't keep a straight face any longer and I laughed out loud, leaning my head back. I let the laughter work itself out of my system and finally Camden's seat stopped moving.

When I looked back at him, I lost my breath.

"You're so beautiful when you laugh," he said, sincerity flowing through every word. He wasn't laughing anymore. He was looking at me with the same expression I'd seen before—the one where he looked like he loved me more than anything in the whole world.

His hand came up to my jaw, his thumb rubbing over my cheek gently, and then he moved it back to my nape, threading his fingers through my hair and pulling me down and kissing me. He groaned into my mouth at the contact and swept his tongue inside, as though he were desperate to taste me.

I started to slowly move my hand up and down his shaft, loving the feel of him.

Camden had, in my opinion, a perfect penis. He was everything a girl could wish for in the length and girth department. He was just big enough to be impressive, but not so big you'd need an Advil afterward. And I loved feeling him, whether it be between my legs or between my fingers. Just touching his dick when it was hard was a turn-on. And knowing it was *me* who made him hard? Oh yeah, it was the absolute best feeling in the world.

I pumped him a few more times, then ran my thumb over the head. The sticky drop of precum there caused my sex to jolt and I pressed my legs together to try and alleviate some of the pressure.

I continued to move my hand up and down his cock, all the while doing my best to kiss him senseless, when he suddenly pulled away.

"Fuck, Riley, climb over here and ride me."

"No," I whispered. "I just want to watch you come."

"Maybe I want the same thing," he said, then gasped as I gave his cock a squeeze.

"This is just for you," I argued, shutting him up as I pressed my mouth against his again.

I used all my best tricks. I sped up, slowed down, let him watch as I spit into my hand and wrapped it around him—that pulled a really sexy groan from him. Though not as sexy as when I used my fingers to tease the crown. That particular trick made his whole body shudder. When I got the idea that he was done fooling around and was ready for the main attraction, I turned serious.

"Tell me what you need," I rasped. I knew how to get him off, but I also knew he liked to be bossy sometimes.

"Squeeze me tighter," he groaned, then gasped when I did as he asked. "Harder, Riley. You're not going to break me."

I smiled at that, pulling back and watching his beautiful face as I gave him exactly what he needed. His eyes were closed, mouth open slightly, his breath panting out in short spurts. His hips started thrusting up into my hand and I looked down to where I pumped him. He was hot and hard, nearly purple he was so ready to come.

I leaned down and whispered in his ear, "Come on, Camden. I want you to come for me."

"Fuck," he growled. His eyes were still closed but his free hand came up to the nape of my neck and gripped my hair, tugging it just to the point of pain.

My breath caught as he spilled over my hand, the warm fluid covering both of us. I was watching as he continued to come, his hips thrusting upward, when he used his hand to angle my head back toward him and pull me in for a rough kiss.

"Jesus, that was crazy," he said, out of breath. "You're crazy."

I lifted one shoulder in a shrug. "You're the one who's always telling me to be more daring. You've practically trained me to take risks."

"Ah, the grasshopper becomes the master."

We both smiled and he pulled me in for a kiss. It was my favorite kind of kiss, where we were both smiling and laughing so our teeth touched, lips thin. Happy kisses made everything inside me light. All my problems disappeared when Cam was laughing with his lips pressed against mine.

"Babe?" he said quietly.

"Yeah?"

"Got any napkins in your purse?"

That only made me laugh harder.

I managed to find a small travel-sized package of tissues, and after we got him all cleaned up and put back together, he continued the drive to the resort.

After giving the Mustang to the valet, Camden and I were walking back to our room, his large, warm hand enveloping mine.

"Are you tired?" he asked as we approached the door.

Shrugging, I replied, "Not really."

"Wanna go sit in the hot tub?" He opened the door for me and I smiled as I passed by.

"That sounds like an excellent idea."

"Got that bikini?" His eyebrows waggled with his question. My eyes rolled.

Thirty minutes later I was in heaven. Absolute heaven. The water was hotter than I anticipated, but once the heat made its way into my muscles after the initial dip, I could feel the tension seeping out of me.

I was sitting with my head lolled back, resting on the concrete behind me. Camden was right next to me and my legs were draped over his lap, his hands resting on my thighs.

"I feel like a piece of wilted lettuce," Camden said, his voice soft and sleepy.

"Wilted lettuce?" I was almost too relaxed to laugh, but not quite.

"I don't know. Something weak and droopy. A noodle?"

"Feels amazing, huh?"

"Indeed. I'm just not sure how I'm going to make it back to the hotel room. Do you think if we tipped enough, the concierge would come and wheel us back on one of those luggage racks?"

I opened the eye that was closest to him and he looked just as relaxed as I felt. We did look like a pair of wet rags. His normally golden complexion was rosy, and I could see beads of sweat on his brow.

"Probably not." I closed my eye, content to simmer in the hot tub for a while longer.

"Everyone has a price," he mumbled.

"I don't think it's so much about his price as it is company policy not to give lazy guests rides on the luggage carts."

"So you don't think if I offered him a million dollars, he'd do it?" Camden's voice was now less tired and he was seriously debating the issue with me.

My eyes were closed, but I rolled them anyway.

"You don't have a million dollars."

"Shows how much you know," he said under his breath.

I snapped my head up and glared at him.

"Camden Joshua Rogers. You do *not* have a million dollars."

"That's beside the point."

"What point?" I asked, irritation lacing my words.

"The point that if I offered him a million dollars he would wheel us back in a luggage cart."

"You're ridiculous. Now I'm all agitated."

"Agitated? Because of a hypothetical question? *That's* ridiculous."

Instead of arguing more, I took in a deep breath through my nose, held it for a moment, then pushed it out through my mouth.

"Wait, are you really upset?"

"I'm not upset—I'm irritated. I'm sitting here relaxing and you're arguing with me over a dumb question."

Suddenly there were hands gripping my waist and I was being hauled over to Camden. His big hands brought me to him and planted me down on his lap, straddling his thighs.

"Don't be grumpy, babe. I was just kidding around."

"I know," I said with a sigh. "But seriously, you don't really have a million dollars, do you?"

His hands cupped my ass under the water, giving me a squeeze. "A million dollars isn't really that much money nowadays."

"Oh my God. Says the guy who has a million dollars."

He laughed and his hands moved over the tops of my thighs, his thumbs running along the seam between my legs and hips, making me shiver even in the hot water.

"It's not like there's a million dollars sitting in my bank account." His hands continued to run over my skin, pulling my core closer to him, eliminating the space between our bodies. "But…." He drew the word out as he caressed my skin. "If you take my condo, the Batmobile, my trust, my savings, *and* my checking account, it might all add up to a million dollars."

I let out a sigh and looped my arms around his neck. I shouldn't have been surprised by the amount of money he has, and I wasn't really. But knowing something in the back of my mind and hearing it confirmed were two different things. The most surprising part, however, was that hearing he was worth a million dollars didn't bother me. In fact, it kind of made me want to roll my eyes— again. He had money. And if I expected him to love me despite my lack of money, I had to love him despite his abundance of it.

That being so, I was done talking about it.

"What do you want to do tomorrow? Aside from lounge by the pool?"

"Whatever you want to do." His reply was soft, as were the hands running up my back. They stopped at the tie where my bikini top was fastened, and I narrowed my eyes at him.

"Keep moving, Rogers."

He smirked and gave the strings a tug.

"You pulled my cock out on the side of the road earlier this evening, I might remind you."

"Yeah, in a car on the side of the road. We're in a hot tub in the middle of a resort. Anyone could walk out here and see."

"You're worried about people seeing you without your top on?"

"Well, yeah," I replied, sardonically.

"Come to think of it, I have a problem with that as well." His eyes sparkled with mischief as he released the strings of my top. His fingers tickled their way down my side. When he reached my waist, he slipped inside my bikini bottoms at the same spot he was teasing just moment before, where my thighs met my hips.

"Camden, no." I tried to sound firm, but the words were shaky.

"I promise I'll make it feel good," he vowed. I didn't doubt him. Camden always made me feel good. Exquisite, even. I'd never felt with other men what I did when Camden touched me. He trailed his fingers over the seam of the fabric, just barely grazing the sensitive skin of my core. When I didn't move away or say no again, his fingers moved deeper, his thumbs brushing over the lips of my sex, making me gasp.

I closed my eyes, holding on to the widely undisputed fact that if I couldn't see anyone, no one could see me either.

I made a decision in that moment, albeit swayed by the way his fingers felt inside of me, to trust Camden to keep strangers from seeing my O face. The way we were situated in the hot tub, he had the better vantage point and could see anyone who might happen upon our indecent activities. So I kept my eyes closed and let Camden take me away.

His fingers slowly pushed into me, one at first but then two right after, and it was fucking fantastic. Perhaps it was the way I was situated on his lap, or the angle at which his fingers slid so deftly into me, or it could have been the fact that we were out in the fucking open and anyone could have come across us, but I was absolutely wired. I went from zero to sixty in a heartbeat.

"Oh," I cried out when his thumb brushed across my clit.

"That good, babe?"

I nodded, biting my lip to keep myself from crying out again.

His thumb continued its delicious torture, circling and pressing in tandem with his fingers curling against the sensitive spot inside of me.

Within a few minutes I was absolutely done, moments away from coming unhinged. I wrapped my arms tightly around his shoulders, burying my face in his neck, sinking my teeth into him to stifle my moans, all the while grinding my pussy down on his hand, trying to find that euphoric release.

"Yes, Riley. Fuck, yes. Get there." Camden's voice was harsh and choppy, and so fucking sexy. Before him I never would have thought hearing a man demand I come would be such a turn-on, but it *so* was. So sexy, in fact, that it pushed me over that proverbial edge and I came *hard,* riding my fiancé's hand in a public hot tub. And it was awesome.

"Holy shit," he breathed a minute later, when I'd finally regained my faculties and sat upright. "That was hot."

"Well," I said, my voice dreamy and sleepy, completely sated, "we are in a hot tub."

"Funny, Smith." He gripped my hips and pulled my core against his erection, which was impressively hard, and said, "We're going to sit here for a few minutes to let my dick calm down, and then we're going back to the suite. I'm going to make you come again with my mouth, and then I'm going to bend you over the counter in the bathroom with all the mirrors and watch as I take you from behind. From all angles."

I was instantly aroused again, which was, quite honestly, ridiculous. But that was Camden for you. He had the innate ability to be the sweet, caring partner one minute and then the rough and demanding lover the next. He was the best.

"Can I make one small request?" I asked, shamelessly rubbing my core up and down his erection just to watch him squirm.

"Hmmm," he said, his fingers digging into the flesh on my hips.

"Can I make you come with my mouth too?" I batted my eyelashes at him, feigning innocence.

The corner of his mouth tipped up into a sexy smirk.

"I think that can be arranged."

Chapter Nine
Riley

A few weeks passed, but they flew by in what seemed like a blink of an eye. All of a sudden—without warning, it seemed—warm weather was welcomed to Portland. Portlanders only enjoyed three months of sunny weather, so when it started, it came on abruptly. Suddenly boats filled the Willamette River and people were flocking to the beach at every opportunity.

The city streets were filled with people walking, rain boots replaced with sandals. Large coats replaced with tank tops. Smart pants replaced with sundresses. It was my favorite time of year.

Unfortunately, I was so busy I hardly noticed the change in weather.

Rose had me working a few big events, and even though I hadn't been to Arizona since the first trip, I was doing some work over the phone for Lily, making sure everything was set for her big day.

When I wasn't working, I was packing. My place, Camden's place—I was a packing fool. On the rare Saturday neither Camden nor I was working, we were at the home improvement store looking at paint samples and appliances.

I woke up one day and I was suddenly an adult.

It was both wonderful and scary.

Nothing was more adult, however, than sitting next to Camden in the office of our mortgage broker, signing our names on the contract that made us homeowners. My name was right there next to Camden's and we had purchased a house. Together.

It was both wonderful and scary.

When the kind woman who'd brought us through the hour-long process of signing the paperwork handed us each a key, I could've fainted. It was a surreal feeling.

"You two enjoy your new home," she said with a smile, our cue to leave. Funnily enough, I had no idea what to do next. We'd just bought a house. Were we supposed to just go back to the condo and pretend as though something huge hadn't just happened? But Camden rose, sure of himself, so I followed suit. He shook her hand and thanked her, and I did the same. Then he took my hand and led me from the building straight to the Batmobile. I slid into the passenger seat right after he'd opened the door for me, and I watched as he calmly walked around the front of the car and slid into his own seat.

He started the car, the nearly silent purr now familiar but still impressive. When he glanced over at me, I was sure I looked like a deer caught in headlights.

"We own a house, babe. You and me. It's *ours*." The emphasis he put on 'ours' made my heart melt a little. Sometimes I forgot how sentimental Camden could be. He was a lot of things: funny, smart, sexy, protective, sensitive. But he was also caring. The idea that he was just as excited to be linked in this legally binding way as I was... well, it was sweet.

I leaned over and kissed him, at a loss for words. I was still kind of in a stupor over the whole thing.

"Let's go see the house," he said, excitement filling his voice.

We'd only been able to get inside the house once since we made the offer and that was during the inspection. We'd taken a thousand pictures, or so it seemed, but I had to admit I was dying to go inside again and look around *our* house.

"Okay," I replied, my excitement matching his.

He held my hand the entire trip, and as we pulled into our new neighborhood, I couldn't help the smile or how it spread wider across my face. He must have felt it too because his hand squeezed mine. When we pulled onto our street, my heart rate spiked and I almost felt like I was going to burst with joy.

As we approached our beautiful home, I was completely shocked.

Standing outside the house holding a huge banner that read "Welcome Home" were Hadley, Rachel, Jasper, Camden's mom and stepdad, and Justin.

"Oh my gosh. What are they doing here?" I asked, looking at Camden.

"Surprise" was all he said in response.

"Did you plan this?"

He shrugged. "I thought it would be fun to have everyone over."

I leaned over the console and kissed his cheek.

He pulled the Batmobile into the driveway and our family and friends crowded around us, smiling and waving.

"Who wants a tour?" Camden practically shouted as he got out of the car.

I was met with hugs from everyone. Camden's mother, Meg, pulled me in for a long embrace, whispering in my ear, "We're so excited for you two."

"Thanks," I said after she pulled away.

Camden's stepfather hugged me too. We'd come a long way in the months since we first met. And any resentment I'd felt toward him in the beginning had faded completely. He loved Camden, and I knew anything he'd ever said about me had only come from a good place. And the fact that he'd apologized and had since treated me with nothing but kindness and graciousness went a long way to endear me to him. "It's a beautiful home, Riley," he said, patting my shoulder.

"Thank you. It's more than I ever wished for." And that counted toward my whole life in that moment. Everything I had, the job, the house, the man—it was all more than I ever dreamed of having.

"You both deserve it, and all the happiness I know you'll have inside of it."

"Thank you," I said again, tears stinging my eyes, unsure of what else to say.

"Stop making my girl cry," Camden said with a smile, pulling me to his side and leading me to the front door.

The door opened and we all flooded in. My chest filled with emotion watching the people I cared about most wandering around my new home. It didn't even matter that it was huge and expensive; what mattered was that it was ours and our friends and family were there, together, enjoying it.

"Hey, stranger," Hadley said, sidling up to me where I leaned against the kitchen counter. "Long time no see," she teased.

"Oh, Hadley, I'm sorry I've been absent lately. This has been a huge undertaking. Buying a house is crazy."

"I can imagine." Her words were kind, and I knew she wasn't really upset with me for not being around, but I could also tell that she missed me. "It's beautiful, Riley," she said, looking at me and smiling. "It's perfect, really. I hope you aren't planning on changing much."

"Not a ton. Just some paint colors and putting up window treatments. Really boring stuff," I said with a laugh when I realized she probably didn't care about drapes and paint samples. Hadley's eyes drifted to where Justin was standing in the empty living room. "I notice the two of you haven't really said much to each other since I've been here. What's the update with him?" I asked, nodding toward where Justin was talking with Camden and his stepfather.

"No updates," she said quickly, her eyes darting away from him.

"So he still hasn't admitted he wants you desperately?" I joked. I knew there was something between Hadley and Justin, and I also knew that even though she denied it, she felt something different for him than she did all the other guys she hooked up with.

"Whatever happened between us is in the past. I've moved on."

"Good," I said, bumping my shoulder against hers, even though I didn't believe her in the slightest.

"Babe," Camden called as he headed toward the French doors that led to the backyard. "Come on." He waved a hand at me, beckoning me to follow him.

"My presence is requested," I said to Hadley.

"Keep pretending like you wouldn't follow him anywhere," she said with a wink.

I smiled at her, then went to Camden.

He took me outside and my mouth dropped open in shock. The entire backyard was set up for a party. There was a huge table with chairs with a beautiful tablecloth, complete with place settings. There was a free-standing hammock, food on the counter by the grill, an open cooler filled with beer and soda—it looked like the most beautiful summer cookout.

"Who did all this?"

"Well, Justin brought over all the food, and my mom put together all the decorations and stuff."

I turned and looked at him. "I can't believe this is my life right now."

"It's our life, babe."

"Who wants a burger and who wants a dog?" Justin called out as he stepped outside. People all over called out their orders and I just leaned into Cam, wrapping my arms around his waist. The day couldn't get any better.

"There's no way my sister lives in a house this nice."

At the familiar voice, I spun away from Camden, only to have my eyes land on my baby brother.

"Tripp? What are you doing here?" I screamed, running toward him and wrapping him in my arms as soon as he was in reach.

His arms circled me and held tightly. Tripp only lived a few hours away, but he was busy all the time with school and work so I hardly ever saw him. After a very long but not-long-enough hug, I pulled away and looked up at him, trying to hold back the tears. He was my little brother by four years, but he was tall and broad and I hadn't been able to look down at him in a long time.

"Camden called and said you were having a housewarming party. I finished classes yesterday. Here I am." He smiled and held his arms out like he was an offering, so I hugged him again.

"Tripp," Hadley said, coming up beside us. "You grew up since I saw you last." She hugged him too, and like always, Tripp's eyes turned into big cartoon hearts. He'd been crushing on Hadley ever since I met her in college. It started innocent enough since he was just a boy back then, but he'd never outgrown his infatuation.

"Hey, Hadley," he squeaked, hugging her back.

"How long are you here for?" I asked him, wiping the happy tears from my face.

"Just the night. Have to be back at work tomorrow evening."

A huge frown pulled at my face.

"Sorry, sis. Someone's got to pay the bills."

"Don't let her guilt you too badly. Riley works harder than anyone I've ever met." That came from Jasper, who had just walked outside with Rachel.

"That's the truth," Rachel added, smiling widely at me.

"Tripp, this is Jasper and Rachel. They're my friends and coworkers."

"Nice to meet you," Tripp said, holding a hand out to Jasper. But when his eyes turned to Rachel, it was as though he lost his words for a moment. "Um, hi," he stammered. "I'm Tripp." He reached out to her slowly and I watched as sparks ignited between them. Rachel blushed as my brother shook her hand for much longer than socially acceptable, but she wasn't complaining.

"I'm Rachel."

I didn't know why it had never occurred to me to talk my brother up to Rachel. They were the same age and she was one of my most favorite people. I'm not sure I'd ever spoken about Tripp to them though, which was sad.

"Tripp is getting his MBA at University of Oregon," I tell them, even though he and Rachel hadn't taken their eyes off each other.

"That must be really interesting," Rachel said. She sounded nervous, and Rachel was never nervous. "I took a few business classes in college."

"Really?" he asked, smiling.

"Yeah."

"Can I get you something to drink?"

I'd never seen my brother try to pick a girl up before, and I found it very entertaining. He wasn't half bad, actually.

"Oh, I wouldn't want to take you away from Riley. I'm sure she wants to catch up with you."

He didn't even look my way before he replied with, "I'll see her plenty. I'm helping them move. Come on."

I watched, mouth gaping, as he smoothly pressed a hand to the small of her back and led her across the patio to where the giant red cooler sat with all the beverages inside.

"Did that just happen?" I asked anyone and everyone.

"Your brother better not screw Rachel over," Jasper said, a warning tone to his voice.

"Hey, Tripp is a decent guy."

"That may be so, but I stand by my statement." Jasper was also a good guy, and I couldn't fault him for wanting to protect Rachel; she was so smart and sweet. I didn't think Tripp would ever do anything to intentionally hurt anyone, though.

"Maybe they'll hit it off," I said with a shrug.

"Okay," Camden broke in, wrapping an arm around my shoulder. "He's getting her a beer, not an engagement ring. Chill out, guys. Let's not start planning their wedding."

"Yeah," Jasper said eagerly. "Let's plan yours instead."

"Did someone say wedding?" Camden's mother asked, coming up behind him.

"Have there been new developments?" Hadley asked.

And suddenly I was anxious. We were standing on the patio of my brand new house—which I couldn't afford on my own—asking about wedding plans. The job, the house, the fiancé, the wedding—I absolutely couldn't do it all, and my brain knew it.

"No wedding talk tonight, guys," Camden said firmly, and I watched as all three of their faces fell, Jasper's the most.

"There's no hurry, dear," Meg said, reaching out and squeezing my hand.

"Do you even know which season you want to be married in?" Hadley asked, clearly exasperated with me.

"Not in the winter," I said without thinking. But as soon as I said the words I realized they were very true. I didn't want to be cold on my wedding day. "I want it to be warm. Maybe on a beach."

"Hot damn, we've got details!" Jasper's voice was so full of excitement I thought he was going to burst.

"Quick, ask her some more questions, Hadley. Get her to answer while she's on a roll."

"No more questions," Camden practically growled. "Let's just enjoy the house."

"Can I get a tour?" Meg asked politely, and I knew she was trying to distract Camden and get him to cool down.

"Sure thing, Mom." He pressed a soft kiss to my temple, then led his mother inside the house. He stopped by Justin, who was manning the grill, on his way in, and I knew he was asking him to keep an eye on me.

Hadley placed a hand on my arm, urging me to look at her. "Can we talk for a minute about how manly Tripp is?"

"Ugh," I groaned. "Do we have to?" Sure, Tripp was handsome and swoony, but he was my brother and I wanted to think about him in feetie pajamas forever.

"I agree," Jasper said, leaning toward us like he had a secret. "Why have you been hiding him from us?"

I laughed. "I wasn't hiding him. He's a busy college student. Plus he works a full-time job. I hardly ever see him."

"Well," Jasper said with a lilt, "if the way he's devouring Rachel with his eyes is any indication, we'll be seeing a lot more of him."

"I need a drink," I sighed, then left Hadley and Jasper to gossip and headed toward the cooler. I smiled when I saw the Hef on ice. Of course, it was right next to the Guinness. I needed a pillow with the two beers cross-stitched on it. Maybe with a caption that said 'Opposites Attract.'

"Hey, nice house." Justin smiled at me and nodded toward the aforementioned house.

"Thanks," I replied, wearily.

"So, uh, how's Hadley doing?" He was trying so hard to seem uninterested I almost laughed.

"You could go talk to her yourself and find out," I offered kindly. I knew there was something going on between them, but I also knew Hadley was somewhat of a man-eater. It was entirely possible that she caught Justin in her trap and then set him free without realizing he had formed an attachment. It wouldn't have been the first time.

I watched as he looked over at her, his eyes zeroing in on her face, but then he turned back to the grill with a sad expression. "Nah, she looks busy. I was just trying to make conversation."

"What happened between you two?" I asked softly, taking another step toward him, trying to make him feel like our conversation was private even though we were standing in the middle of my backyard.

He shrugged. "We hung out a few times. Nothing serious."

"Is that why you're always looking at her with sad puppy dog eyes?" I joked, trying to get a genuine smile from him. Luckily for me, it worked.

"I do not," he said with his handsome smile across his face.

I'd gotten to know Justin a little over the past few months, and even though he seemed a little aloof sometimes, he was obviously a good guy. Still very much in his bachelor stage, but a good guy regardless. But it was strange how fascinated he was with Hadley and how little time of day she gave him. It wasn't unlike her, but something about her attitude toward him, her indifference, didn't ring true all the time. It felt forced and artificial.

However, I had my own damn problems to worry about without trying to figure out why they couldn't get their shit together.

"Hang in there," I said, patting him on the bicep. "She's not all bad. If it's meant to be, she'll come around."

"Thanks, Riley." His tone was solemn, but then he turned to me and I watched as a mischievous grin spread across his face. "Do you want a burger or a wiener?"

I gave him a playful wink. "Don't ask me questions you already know the answer to."

He laughed as I walked away, and I was glad I could give him just a little bit of a mood lift.

I walked into the house and took a moment to just look around. The floor was empty, everyone still outside except for Camden and his mom, who I assumed were upstairs by that point. There was light coming in the windows, and the sounds of people laughing outside. I imagined many weekends filled the same way, with friends and family here, enjoying this crazy house that I never dreamed I would ever own.

My future happiness has never been wrapped up in possessions, or even my address. I didn't need a house in a fancy neighborhood. But what I hadn't realized was that I *wanted* a home and a family. Could I be just as happy someplace else? Definitely. But for whatever reason, Camden wanted this to be our home. And even though it was sappy and mushy, I was home wherever Camden was. So if I had to live in the big beautiful house to be with him, then I'd suffer through it.

My phone buzzed in my pocket and I pulled it out to see I had a text from Rose.

Please advise any clients you may have meetings with this week that you'll be out of town Monday and Tuesday. We need to take another trip to Arizona. Just a quick dress evaluation and catering appointment. Flight leaves at nine Monday morning. Meet you at the airport at seven.

I sighed after reading the text. Another trip to Arizona was inevitable, but I'd been hoping to stay away a little longer.

Message received. I only had one meeting that was high priority, and I'm sure Rachel can handle it for me. See you on Monday.

At least I'd have the weekend to relax before being thrown back into the lion's den. The last trip had gone okay as long as I kept my distance from Penelope. That was my plan going forward as well. I let Rose do her thing, took notes, and offered suggestions when they were needed, but it was definitely a different role than I was used to. When I was planning an event for a client, I was in beast mode. I had dedicated folders full of information: quotes, bids, renderings. Sometimes I even had collages if I felt the client was particularly visual.

Luckily, Rose seemed to be playing down our involvement as planners, but I wanted to focus on the planning so I didn't focus on Penelope. Or, to be completely honest, so Penelope didn't focus on me.

I heard footsteps upstairs and went to find Camden.

"This would be a wonderful room for a nursery, Cam," I heard Meg say just before I pushed the door to the spare bedroom open.

"Yeah," he said softly, not sounding too committed to the agreement. "When the time is right, maybe. We've got plenty of time for kids though. I kind of just want to spend some time with Riley, have some time where it's just the two of us for a while. Maybe travel a little."

I smiled at his words, loving his vision for us in the foreseeable future. I did want kids with Camden, but I agreed with him—there was plenty of time for that.

"Hey," I said as I stepped into the room, trying not to startle them.

"Hey, babe," Camden replied, his face softening as I entered the room. "We were just talking about you."

"Good things, I hope."

He lifted his arm slightly, just enough for me to press into his side. "Always."

"I was just telling Camden how this room would make a wonderful nursery," Meg told me.

"Mom," he warned.

"You think?" I asked sincerely. "The other spare room is much closer to the master, so I figured we'd make that into the first nursery."

"First nursery?" Camden asked, clearly surprised by my response.

I gave him a wink.

"Oh, I didn't even consider that," Meg said as she walked out the door to inspect the other room.

Once we were alone, Camden looked down at me. "Are we really going to need more than one nursery?"

I shrugged one shoulder. "I have no idea. I'm not even sure the other room is closer."

"So you don't want a house full of babies?"

"That sounds horrid." I couldn't help the laughter that erupted from me, or the visual his sentence conjured up.

"You know what I mean," he said, smiling while rolling his eyes at me.

"I want kids. Someday. Not any time soon though. There's no rush." I gave him a gentle pat on the chest to try and ease his worries. I didn't want him or me to stress about that; we had enough on our plate at that moment. "Oh, before I forget, Rose just texted me and needs me in Arizona again Monday and Tuesday."

I watched as his eyebrows drew together.

"You're going out of town again? In, like, two days?"

"Yeah," I said softly, looking up at him. "I know it's bad timing, what with the house and all, but I have to go." He didn't respond right away, not with words anyway. But I could see in his eyes that he was working something out in his mind. Almost as though he were weighing whether or not to say something. I wanted to know what he was thinking, wanted him to just come out and say it, but not if he wasn't ready. "Will you be all right here by yourself?"

He turned toward me fully, taking my face in his hands and looking me right in the eye. "I'm never okay when you're not with me. But yeah, I'll be all right." He moved in and pressed his lips against my forehead, resting them there and breathing me in. "Maybe I'll stay at the condo."

"Why?" I was itching to be in the new house, to move all our stuff in, to make it our own. To see Camden walking around in his boxer briefs in *our home*.

"Doesn't seem right to sleep here without you."

And like so many times in the last eight months, Camden left me speechless and emotionally raw with just one sentence.

"I'll never understand how, in this entire huge world, somehow I managed to find you. And what's even more mind-blowing is that, out of every woman on this huge world, you want me."

At my words a smile spread across his face. "Do you remember our first kiss, babe? Who wouldn't come back for more after that?"

Oh, I remembered all right. So did the other twenty thousand people at the arena that night.

"It was pretty impressive. For a first kiss, anyway," I teased.

"All our kisses are impressive," he argued.

"That's true," I relented. And almost as if he was trying to prove his point, he bent at the knee and captured my mouth, pulling me closer with his arms snaked around my waist. I let him lead the kiss, let him show me how he was feeling through it. The kiss was hungry and a little urgent, as though he was trying to keep me close.

We both heard his mother's heels on the hardwood floors, the sound getting louder as she got closer the room we were in. He tugged gently on my bottom lip with his teeth, sending shivers to all the good places, then pulled away, scraping his teeth along my lip as he went.

"You're terrible," I rasped, hating the fact that he knew he'd gotten to me with that lip bite and there wasn't a single thing I could do about it with all our friends and family around.

"I think you meant to say 'impressive.'"

Chapter Ten

Camden

The sun was setting over our new backyard, flames roared out of our fire pit, everyone had a drink in their hand, and the night was perfectly warm. It was, by all accounts, pretty fucking perfect. Exactly as I'd imagined it when I'd explained my plan to Justin.

"Thanks for pulling all of this off," I said as I turned to face him. We were sitting on the patio, looking out over the yard where everyone else was. Riley, Hadley, Rachel, Jasper, and Tripp all sat around the fire pit chatting, laughing, and smiling. Justin and I hung back though, as I figured he was trying to keep his distance from Hadley.

"Hey, man, no problem. It's not every day your best friend buys a house."

"Let's hope not," I said, lifting my Guinness in a cheers and watching as he did the same. We both took healthy pulls from our beers, but then we were quiet again. When I'd called Justin the day before and laid out my whole plan, he'd been onboard from the first word. My condo didn't have an outdoor patio, so pretty much everything I saw around me was brand new. I'd ordered it online and Justin had gone today and picked it all up. We'd still had to enlist a little more help with all the food and beverages though.

"Did you have a hard time working with Hadley?" I asked, never quite sure if I was going to get the laid-back Justin or the Justin who was transparent about his feelings for her. It was a toss-up, really.

He sighed. "She basically said just enough words to get the job done."

So Justin was being a little transparent today.

"Have there been any developments in that department?"

"You mean the department where Hadley won't give me the time of day? No. No, there hasn't."

"And how do you feel about that? Usually you'd be moving on before you even got your pants all the way back on."

Justin's eyes met mine and I was surprised to see he looked a little bit angry.

"I can't really explain it, but man, she's driving me crazy by ignoring me. Do you think she's doing it on purpose?"

My eyes swept over to Riley and Hadley, the fire casting an orange hue around their faces, both of them laughing and talking. Hadley looked happy. Completely carefree.

"Of course she's doing it on purpose. Women talk. If she weren't upset with you, she wouldn't be avoiding you or ignoring you."

"See, and the stupid thing is I know that. I understand that on a basic level. But I still can't get her out of my mind. What's her deal?"

"I've got no idea. But Hadley is, for the most part, a great girl. So if she's really this adamant about not giving you a chance, well, you kind of have to let her go and give her the benefit of the doubt. Maybe it doesn't have anything to do with you. Maybe she's hung up on someone else and doesn't want to string you along."

"Did Riley say she's hung up on someone else?" he asked, his voice suddenly full of rage.

"No, man. Chill out. No wonder she won't talk to you—you're fucking psycho."

Justin let out a large breath and took another pull from his beer.

"I think you gotta move on. It's obviously not going to happen."

"We'll see," he mumbled under his breath. I wasn't sure if he knew I could hear him, but I didn't give him any indication that I had. Justin and Hadley needed to figure out their own issues. Either that or Justin really needed to get over Hadley.

Movement from the campfire drew my gaze that way and I saw Jasper rising from his chair, then hauling it behind him as he made his way toward Justin and me.

"I am legit the fifth wheel over there," he said as he dropped his chair next to Justin and took a seat.

"Tripp and Rachel seem to be getting to know each other pretty well," I said before taking another drink.

"They're real close to planning a double wedding with you and Riley," he replied, sarcasm clear in his tone. "Anyone want to take bets on whether Rachel is leaving by herself tonight?"

"Nope," I replied. I didn't know Tripp very well, but even I could see the two of them were minutes away from jumping each other.

"I think I'd rather take bets on how long until they make some excuse to leave." Justin's tone was much more upbeat, and I was glad Jasper had come to distract us from his woes with Hadley.

"Twenty minutes," Jasper said quickly.

"Ten," Justin countered.

"I'll be a radical and call thirty."

We all chuckled, but then a silence fell over us. It wasn't awkward—quite the opposite, in fact. I was watching Riley, loving the smile on her face and knowing it was because she was surrounded by her favorite people. Justin was watching Hadley—I didn't have to look over at him to know it. He was probably trying to figure out what he had to do to crack her open. Jasper was probably watching Rachel, deciding whether he needed to be protective over her. He was probably fighting the urge to drive her home himself. He, Rachel, and Riley were a close unit, and I knew he felt like a brother to the girls. He might wear suspenders and bow ties, but I knew without a doubt that he would protect my girl at any cost. And the same went for Rachel.

"Tripp's a good guy," I said coolly, trying to ease any tension Jasper might be feeling about Rachel and Tripp spending time together. Or a night.

"I'm sure he is," Jasper replied quietly. "But it's not Tripp I'm worried about. Rachel's innocent, ya know? I mean, she's no virgin, but she's not the kind of girl to just sleep with someone and not catch some feelings."

"I hear you," I said with a nod. And I did.

"Maybe Hadley could teach her a few things." Justin's words were cold and angry. I knew he didn't mean them, but it didn't mean I'd excuse him for saying them either.

"Dude," I snapped. "Let it go. If she doesn't want anything more from you, move on. But don't sit here and bad-mouth her."

Justin put his beer to his mouth and drained it.

"I'm out of here," he said grumpily.

"Dude, don't leave angry," I said, even as he stood and put his phone in his back pocket.

"Nah, man, you're right. I shouldn't be here if I'm going to be an asshole. I need some distance."

"Justin, after everything, she's just another girl." I held his gaze and watched as his shoulders slumped.

"I wish that were true." He gave us a nod and then disappeared into the house.

"Well, that was dramatic," Jasper said, nearly making me laugh.

"Yeah, that's not like him. He's usually pretty easygoing."

"Sounds like someone's salty."

That *did* make me laugh.

"I think he got more than he bargained for with Hadley. He thought they'd have a good night together, and then it turned into more. Maybe. I don't even really know what happened. Neither one is talking about it."

"Well, they're adults. They'll figure it out. Or they won't. But I'm not going to lose any sleep over it."

"I'll drink to that," I said, lifting my beer again and tapping it gently against Jasper's martini glass. "What are you drinking?"

"Dirty martini," he deadpanned.

"Of course you are," I responded with a chuckle. The quiet came back, but I took the opportunity to focus on Riley, to listen for the lilt of her laughter. If there was one thing I could count on with Hadley around, it was Riley laughing. "Can I ask you something?" I said to Jasper after a few quiet minutes.

"Sure, Cammy. You can ask me anything."

I shook my head and laughed at his nickname for me, then got on with my concern.

"How's Riley doing? You spend a lot of time with her at work—how does she seem to you?" I watched as his face moved from playful to contemplative.

"You know, the last few months she's been pretty determined to prove her worth to Rose. I think she wants to make sure Rose doesn't regret promoting her or giving her the opportunities she is, like the whole Arizona thing. And I think it's stressing her out."

"Yeah?" I said with a sigh, even though it's exactly what I suspected.

"Yeah." He sighed too, and it reminded me of how much Jasper had grown to care about Riley in the last few months. "She puts a lot of things on the back burner in her personal life to make sure she's doing well at work."

"Oh, you mean like a wedding?" I asked sardonically.

"Perhaps."

Truth be told, I didn't care when Riley and I got married. We could've gotten married five years from then, or the next week. I just didn't want to watch her keep putting it off because it was another thing weighing her down. I knew she loved me and she wanted to marry me; she just couldn't take anything else on. I wanted our marriage to be something she enjoyed and remembered fondly, not something she dreaded.

"But to be honest, Cammy, springing this house on her didn't help any."

"She could have said no," I said in defense.

He raised one perfectly coifed eyebrow at me. "Really? Come on, you know she would never say no to you if she knew a yes would make you happy."

"She also knows she doesn't have to pander to me."

"Okay, Mr. Lawyer." Jasper rolled his eyes dramatically. "She loves you, more than she's ever loved anything, and if I know Riley, she's worried, somewhere deep down in there, that you'll wake up one day and realize you want something different. So when you tell her you want this big extravagant house, something she'd never be able to give you on her own, what did you expect her to say? Did you expect her to argue? To say no? Of course not. You wanted the house, and she wants you to be happy. So she said yes."

"I want Riley to be happy," I said defensively, and loudly. Loud enough that the other conversations in the yard stopped and all eyes darted to me—including Riley's.

Jasper leaned over the arm of his lawn chair and whispered, "I know that, and so does she. But you asked how she was. She's overwhelmed, Camden. People keep dropping things in her lap instead of trying to unload her burden."

Before he even finished his statement, Riley was walking toward us, a worried expression on her face.

"Everything okay over here?" she asked, her eyes darting between Jasper and me.

"Everything's fine," I replied before Jasper had a chance, opening my arms and giving her the cue to sit on my lap. "We were just discussing work, and it seems Jasper and I both care very much about your happiness."

"What are you talking about?" she asked sweetly as she took a seat, her legs dangling off the side of my leg.

She wrapped an arm around my neck and looked at me like I'd just dropped another weight atop all the others she was already carrying around.

"Nothing, babe. I just don't want you overworked or overstressed."

Her hand came up to my cheek and her brow furrowed.

It still baffled me sometimes how strange the notion was to her that someone wanted to take care of her.

"I'm fine, Camden. There's nothing to worry about."

"The thing is, babe, you wouldn't tell me if there was something to worry about." She opened her mouth to argue but I continued. "And that's mostly because you push and push and give and give until there's nothing left." My hand twined its way into the hair at her nape, pulling her closer. "You give so much of yourself to others, and I'm afraid you don't have enough of yourself left over for you."

"Camden," she whispered, resting her forehead against my own.

"I'm worried about you." My voice sounded even smaller than hers, and I realized it was because I was afraid that what I was saying was truer than I could even comprehend. Riley would push herself past her own limits and no one would ever know because she was so good at hiding it—even from herself.

"We're gonna head out," I heard Hadley say softly from somewhere behind us.

Riley started to sit up fully and make her way off my lap, but Jasper intervened.

"No, Riley, it's fine. We'll show ourselves out."

"Thank you for coming," Riley said softly. "And Hadley, thank you for everything. It was amazing."

"Anything for you, best friend for life." She blew Riley a kiss and then made her way into the house with Jasper following behind.

"I'm going to take Rachel home," Tripp said as he and Rachel headed toward the house too. I noticed her hand was firmly clasped in his, and I tucked that away in the back of my mind as something to worry about later.

"Wait," Riley cried. "We hardly got to talk at all."

"Don't worry, I'll be back tomorrow."

"Where are you staying tonight?"

"Camden said I could crash at his place."

"Oh," she said on a sigh, relaxing a little.

"See you later, sis," Tripp said just before he placed a kiss on her cheek.

"Bye, Rachel. See you next week."

Rachel gave a shy wave, and it was obvious she felt weird about leaving with Riley's brother. But not weird enough to find a different way home. I gave Tripp access to my condo, but I suddenly wondered if he'd be staying there alone.

"Come on, let's go upstairs."

"What's upstairs?"

"You'll see," I said softly as I brushed a tendril of her dark brown hair behind her ear.

She stood and I followed, her hand in mine as I led her to the house. I took her up the stairs to the master bedroom where the air mattress I'd purchased was fully inflated and covered in fluffy blankets and a mountain of pillows. I couldn't get our actual bed there in time, but this would do.

"I wanted to spend the night with you in our new house," I said when her eyes fell upon the setup.

Her mouth parted slightly but no words came out. She looked at the makeshift bed, then back at me. Then back at the bed for a moment. Then back to me.

"I can't with you." Luckily, she said the words with a smile, then wrapped her arms around my waist and pressed her face into my chest. "Why are you constantly doing things like this? I can't keep up with you. I never know what to expect."

"Just expect to be happy," I said against her head, running my hand down her soft hair.

"How happy?" she asked, pulling back and looking at me with all kinds of seriousness across her face. "On a scale of one to ten, where should I expect my happy-ometer to be?"

"If you're not at a solid seven for eighty percent of the time, I'm not doing my job." I pulled her closer, peppering kisses from one side of her jaw to the other. I couldn't fucking handle it when she tried to be cute.

"And when should I expect to be in the eight-to-ten range?" Her words were breathy and she pressed her breasts into my chest as her hands slid up my shoulders and her arms wound around my neck.

"Whenever I'm inside you," I growled.

"Can we arrange for me to be at a nine-point-five in about ten minutes?"

"I think I can make that happen."

Chapter Eleven
Riley

"How come every time I come in this house, I find you sitting on your ass?"

Tripp's voice caught me off guard, making me jump. Luckily, I'd just unpacked the box with the throw pillows for the couch, so I tossed one at him.

Of course, he caught it.

"I'm obviously in a supervisory role," I said just before he tossed the pillow back at me. We both laughed when it smacked me directly in the face.

Camden and Justin went to return the moving truck we'd rented and were going to bring home pizza for lunch. We'd been moving all morning and afternoon, and even though there were a few things left here and there at the old places, we were pretty much done. And we were pretty much exhausted.

Tripp came over to the couch and plopped down next to me, letting out a large sigh.

"Moving all your shit is hard work."

"I know, right?"

"Did you pull any muscles carrying the pillows?" he asked sarcastically.

"No, but I broke a nail."

Suddenly, his big arm was wrapped around my neck and my face was shoved against his side, his other hand purposefully messing up my hair.

"Hey," I cried out. "Knock it off."

After thirty seconds of struggling against him, trying my hardest to break his hold and being completely unsuccessful, he finally let me go.

"When did you get to be such a bully?" I said with mock irritation as I tried to fix my hair.

He shrugged. "Just making up for all those years you were bigger than me and used it to your advantage."

"Remember how Mom used to always warn me that one day you'd be bigger than me and that the roles would reverse?" I let out a loud laugh. "Guess she was right."

"Funny how when you're young you think your mom knows nothing. Turns out Mom is pretty smart."

"Yeah," I sighed, pulling my hair through the rubber band and then leaning back against the couch, my arm touching Tripp's.

"Did you guys have a good visit when you were down there? I know things have been tense between you two for a while."

"I think so. It was definitely cathartic."

"How so?" he asked, looking over at me.

I pulled my knees up to my chest and wrapped my arms around them, nibbling on my bottom lip, trying to think of a clear and concise answer to his question.

"You don't have to tell me if you don't want to."

"No, it's fine, I'm just still trying to process everything." I took in a deep breath and decided to let my thoughts out, unrestrained. "I guess for a really long time I'd been a little selfish in blaming Mom for how horrible the four years in Arizona was. When I finally vocalized everything that had been bothering me, she put me in my place."

"What do you mean? Was she mad?"

"No, she just made me see a different viewpoint."
He gave me a questioning look, raising one eyebrow dramatically. "It had never occurred to me that Mom was just trying to give us a good life. I was so wrapped up in my unhappiness that it clouded everything else around me. I was so focused on what I didn't think I had I was blind to everything she was trying to provide. Does that make sense?"

"Yeah," he replied thoughtfully. "To be honest, Smiley Riley," he said, using his childhood nickname for me and bumping my shoulder with his, "I can see both your points on this one."

"What do you mean?"

"Well, I was four years younger and I could still tell you were unhappy. And maybe Mom should've done something more to help you. But she was also a single parent and doing her best. For what it's worth though, I think you turned out fine." He said the last part with a shrug, as if he was talking about lasagna, not his sister.

"Thanks," I said, slapping him lightly.

"All I know is that neither one of you is malicious, so if her actions hurt you, it wasn't her intent, and vice versa."

"I know that too," I said quietly. "And thank you." My baby brother had done a lot of growing up since I'd left Arizona. When he moved to Oregon I thought I'd see more of him, but obviously that wasn't the case. "I miss you, you know."

"Aw, shucks, sis," he said goofily. "I miss you too. You and Camden should come visit every once in a while."

"I know. We should. Hopefully things will calm down soon and we can make a trip." I looked over at him.

"Is it possible that you have a new reason to come to Portland more often though?" I asked, batting my eyes at him, my tone teasing.

"Shut up," he said, pushing me again. Although the blush creeping over his face told me I'd hit a nerve.

"Did Rachel stay at her own place last night?" I waggled my eyebrows at him.

"Yes," he insisted, but his cheeks just grew a deeper shade of red.

"Uh-huh. And what time did you end up getting to Camden's condo?"

"I don't kiss and tell, sis."

"So there was kissing?"

"Shut up, Riley." He smiled, but I knew I was pushing my luck.

"Rachel's a friend of mine, okay. And you're my brother. I understand not everything has to be serious, but I don't want either of you hurt. So be careful with her."

Tripp gave me a withering look. "I'm not some playboy dick, you know. I don't just sleep with women and then drop off the face of the planet."

"You slept with her?" I cried, eyes shooting wide open.

"Oh my God," he said, exasperated, and stood up from the couch. "I'm not talking about this with you anymore." He started walking toward the stairs.

"If you're going upstairs, could you take a box with you?"

He didn't answer me, but he did use his hands to make a rude gesture.

I just laughed. "Love you," I called out after he'd disappeared.

It took a moment, but I heard him yell, "Love you too."

Yeah, I missed my baby brother.

Chapter Twelve
Riley

Oh holy hell.

My alarm was blaring and I was too sore to roll over and turn it off.

"I think I'm dying," I groaned into my pillow. The bed shifted and I felt Camden lean over me and grab my phone off my nightstand.

"Time to get up." Camden's voice was raspy from sleep. Super sexy. He rolled back over me but gave my ass a sharp slap before he was completely clear.

I yelped and then moved my hand to the spot, rubbing it but then groaning because moving hurt even more than the stinging on my butt cheek.

"I'm never moving again." I rolled onto my back, whining the whole way.

"That's the idea, babe."

"You be quiet. You don't have to get up for another two hours. I'm not talking to you."

"Don't you need a ride to the airport?"

"I was just going to take an Uber."

He rolled back over and gave me a searing look. "I'll drive you."

Even though my whole body was sore from lifting boxes and walking up and down stairs all weekend, I relaxed a little at his words.

"Okay," I agreed. It was pretty sweet that he wanted to take me to the airport, even though an Uber would do just fine. I wasn't going to argue with him. "I'm going to go take the hottest shower known to man." I stood up slowly, feeling every muscle stretch and strain along the way, and padded into the bathroom. I'd only spent the weekend at the new house, but fuck if I didn't fall in love with my new bathroom. If I wasn't trying to catch a plane that morning, I would've drawn a bath, but instead I turned on the waterfall shower head and made it as hot as I could stand it.

Ten minutes later, I was still standing under the hot water when I heard Camden's voice.

"I'll never again live in a house without a glass shower."

Opening my eyes at his voice, I saw him leaning against the doorjamb, a sexy smirk on his face.

"You perv," I said, even though I really liked the idea of him watching me shower. And even more, I looked forward to the day I could do the same to him.

"Pervy and proud," he said with a laugh. "Here." He walked to the opening of the walk-in shower and held out his hand, showing me two pills. "Advil."

"Ugh," I groaned, taking the pills from him. "You're the best." I popped them in my mouth, then filled my mouth with water and swallowed them down.

"Also," he said, holding out his other hand, which was wrapped around my phone, "it's been going off like crazy for about five minutes."

"Who is it?"

"I don't know. I didn't look."

"Well aren't you the good fiancé who doesn't invade my privacy." I made a loud and exaggerated kissy face at him. "But will you check it for me? It's probably just Hadley with some crazy story from the weekend."

I watched as he swiped across the phone screen and tapped it a few times.

"It's Rose."

"Rose? What did she say?"

"There're, like, ten texts from her." I watch as he scrolls up on my phone and it's obvious he's reading. After a few moments he says while still scrolling, "Looks like she's sick and can't make it to Arizona."

"The trip is canceled?" I asked hopefully, the idea of crawling back into bed for a few hours totally bringing a smile to my face.

"Uh, no, she wants you to go without her."

"What?" I cried out. "By myself?"

"Looks that way."

"What?" I cried again, only that time more hysteria laced my words. "I can't go alone."

"She thinks she ate something bad and has food poisoning. She can't fly." He keeps scrolling and reading. "She already had a car to chauffeur the two of you around, so there should be a driver waiting for you when you land. They'll take you to the hotel and then wherever else you need. She says she'll email you the itinerary."

"Oh my God," I sob dramatically into the water. "This is going to suck so bad."

"Maybe it'll be better by yourself," he supplied, his voice hopeful.

"No, Rose was a really good buffer between Penelope and me. Now I'll have to be the point person and I'm confident it's going to suck."

"Well, at least it's just two days. Tomorrow night you'll be home and it'll be over."

"Uhhhh," I groaned. The day just seemed to be getting worse and worse. Only the thought of a nice alcoholic drink by the pool that evening made the idea of going to Arizona the least bit palatable.

As the morning progressed, I made the conscious decision to just grin and bear it. I gave myself a silent pep talk all the way to the airport, telling myself that if I thought it was going to be a horrible trip, it would become a self-fulfilling prophecy. I had to put positive vibes out into the universe.

Camden pulled my small carry-on bag from the trunk of the Batmobile and set it on the ground next to me.

"Are you going to be all right going by yourself?"

I waved his question away. "I'll be fine. It might be fun even. Everyone loves meeting with caterers. Free samples of yummy food—what's not to love?"

Camden clearly saw right through my positivity ruse but was smart enough not to comment on it. "Call me when you land, okay? I might be in a meeting, but leave a message." His hand came up to cup my face and he leaned in, kissing me softly. "I'll miss you."

"I'll miss you too," I replied with a sigh. Turning and grabbing the handle of my bag, I walked into the airport, repeating under my breath, "It's just two days. It's just two days."

Much to Rose's credit, even though she wasn't there to manage the trip, it went off without a hitch. I was still placed in first class—with free champagne—and there was a driver waiting for me with my name on a sign and everything. This driver, Richard, was friendly and professional and didn't make me feel weird one bit that I was a woman traveling alone. When I climbed into the town car, I turned on my phone and immediately called Camden.

As he'd warned, he didn't pick up, but I left a message telling him I'd landed safely and would call him later. Then my phone pinged with emails and I opened the one from Rose. She'd laid everything out for me with times and addresses; all I had to do was be where she wanted me to be and act on her behalf.

I can totally do this.

I took in a deep breath and tried to keep the positive thoughts rolling through my head.

Richard brought me to the same hotel Rose and I had stayed at previously and waited while I checked in and took my bags to my room. I freshened up a bit and put on a new blouse, then headed back to the car.

"Where to, Miss Smith?" Richard asked as I buckled my seat belt.

I read off the name of the bridal shop and its address to Richard directly from the email Rose sent me.

"Very good," he replied, and then we were off. When we pulled up to a different bridal boutique twenty minutes later, I took a deep and calming breath while Richard opened my door for me. I stepped out and tried to look cool, calm, and collected.

"I'll be waiting for you when you're ready to leave, ma'am."

"Thanks, Richard. You can call me Riley."

He only nodded in reply.

I took one more breath, pushed my shoulders back, tipped my chin up, and walked into that bridal shop like I owned the place.

My eyes instantly found Lily in a sea of white gowns and her eyes lit up when she spotted me.

"Riley," she exclaimed. "Oh, I'm so glad you're here." She welcomed me with a hug. "My mom had a last-minute meeting she had to go to and Rose is sick, and I just didn't think I wanted to do this on my own. I'm so glad you're here." She was obviously flustered. My years of bridal training kicked into gear.

"Don't worry about a thing, Lily. I will help you handle everything," I said as I rubbed a hand down her arm reassuringly. "Have you been assigned a consultant yet?" I asked, my voice soft and gentle.

"Yeah, her name is Buffy," she said, crinkling her nose.

I held back a laugh. "Okay, let's find some dresses."

An hour later, Lily and I were still alone, which I was absolutely okay with. She'd tried on a few dresses, none of which she'd fallen in love with. I went back out to the sales floor and started sifting through the racks again. Unfortunately, I'd already looked through them all and nothing had worked.

I let out a frustrated sigh, pushing heavy weddings dress down the rack when a woman smaller than me pushed a rolling rack full of dresses right next to me.

"Hello," she said with a friendly smile.

"Hi," I responded.

"Don't mind me. We just got a shipment in, so I'll just drop these off and be out of your way."

"These are new?" I asked, hope shimmering around this retail angel like bright lights.

"Yep. Just got them in today." She hung eight glorious dresses in the size eight section where I had been looking for the last twenty minutes. Eight brand new dresses.

I looked around, wondering if any other people had heard the woman and if I was going to have to fight off some bridezillas, but then I zeroed in on the new merchandise.

The first three were clear nos; I didn't even entertain the idea of bringing them back to Lily. The fourth, however, went in the immediate yes pile. It was a stunning pink satin dress with a very low back. It looked elegant and sexy. Dress five went into the no pile, but six and seven were maybes. I decided to bring them back with me just on the chance she'd want to see them on. They were beautiful dresses, but I wasn't sure they fit her vision. However, at that point we were past the point of being too picky. Sometimes, as I'd witnessed many times in the past, you just needed to put dresses on.

The eighth dress, however, took my breath away.

I'd been frantic just moments before, but the dress stopped me in my tracks.

It was a golden champagne color. Not off-white, and not rose, but a dull golden hue. The bodice was lace and it flowed down into a tulle skirt. The intricate and delicate lace pattern of flowers trailed down onto the skirt, mimicking vines of flowers. It had a sweetheart neckline and was only tea length.

It was perfect.

"Hey," Lily said, breaking me from the trance I was in while staring at the dress. "Find something good?"

"Oh, um, yeah," I said, trying to pull my attention away from the dress. "I think you should try these four on," I said, adding the last dress to the pile.

"Okay," she agreed readily with a sweet smile. She was wearing a simple robe the boutique provided to all its brides, and I noticed how even in just a satin robe she looked beautiful.

I followed her back to her dressing room and hung all the dresses on the rack, my hand lingering on the last one.

Lily slowly examined each one and told me what she liked about them. I already knew what she was going to say, as I'd learned her likes and dislikes in dresses over the two days I'd spent shopping with her, but I listened as that was a huge component of my job as wedding planner.

"This one's beautiful," she said breathily as she came to the last dress, and I found myself holding my breath. Her fingers trailed down the delicate lace all the way to the hem of the skirt, pulling it out a little so she could take in the entire dress. "It's such an interesting color, right?"

"It is," I replied, expelling the air I'd been holding in.

"It's nothing like any of the other dresses we've looked at."

"It's very unique."

"But I don't think it would work well for my wedding. Plus," she said, looking over at me, "I really want a floor-length dress. I just have an image in my mind of me on my wedding day and there's lots of material all the way to the floor."

A wave of relief washed over me and I couldn't figure out why, but I tried not to focus on it too much. Instead, I gathered the dresses she didn't want to try on and headed out of the dressing room as she prepared to put on what felt like her twentieth dress of the day.

"You can just put those on the rack outside the door," Buffy, Lily's consultant, said as she entered the room.

"Thanks," I replied. I turned once I was outside the door, found the rack she was referring to, and hung the dresses on it.

"Riley," I heard a voice call from behind me. When I turned, it was very hard not to let my face show the dread I felt when my eyes landed on Penelope. "Oh my word. I have never been this late to anything in my life. Well, except maybe prom senior year." She nudged me with her elbow and then waggled her eyebrows at me. "My date was Anthony Williams. Do you remember him? Well, we were two hours late to prom because once he saw me in my dress, he couldn't keep his hands to himself." She said the words as though they were the wittiest anyone had ever uttered, and I managed an uncomfortable laugh.

"I don't remember him."

"Really? He was the quarterback of the football team? Dark hair? Always wore his letterman jacket?" She looked at me expectantly, but I gave her nothing.

"Nope."

"Hmm. Well, he was hot and he couldn't contain himself around me."

"Penelope? Is that you?" Lily called from inside her dressing room, saving me from having to respond to Penelope's ridiculous assessment of her prom date.

"Hey, Lily. Sorry I'm late."

"No problem. Riley's been a big help." Just as she finished her sentence, she opened the door of her dressing room and came out in one of the new dresses.

"How do you like it?" I asked, smiling at her. She looked phenomenal, like usual.

"I like it," she replied, her voice hesitant. "But I'm not sure it's the one."

"I don't think it's a good look on you," Penelope supplied.

"No?" Lily asked, insecure for the first time that day.

The distinct warmth of rage washed over my body and I knew I had to bite my tongue. I'd definitely dealt with a lot of rude people with my job, but something about knowing how vindictive and rude Penelope was made her harsh words cut even that much deeper.

"Let's go take a look with the big mirrors," I said, trying to distract Lily from Penelope's comments.

Lily lifted the skirt and walked with me to the pedestal she'd stood at on and off all morning. "It's pretty, but I just don't feel like it's *the one*."

"Well, what do you like about it?" I asked as I stood behind her, meeting her gaze in the mirror.

"I like how fitted it is, and I like the length."

"Okay, what about the neckline?"

Lily scrunched her nose a little. "I don't think I like the halter."

"Okay, that's good to know. So, I think back in the dressing room there's another dress that's long, fitted, and satin. It will be a very flattering silhouette, and it has a traditional strap."

"Satin?" Penelope's voice pulled me out of my focus.

"You don't like satin?" Lily asked. It was painfully obvious that Lily cared about Penelope's opinion, which was unfortunate since Penelope was a bitch.

"Satin is very nineties."

"Although satin isn't traditional, it will give you the look you've been saying you wanted. Plus, it's a blush color, which is something you said you wanted." I saw Penelope open her mouth to say something, and I was sure it wasn't a helpful or supportive comment, so I cut her off. "Let's go try it on."

"Okay," Lily replied with her signature sweet smile.

We walked back to the dressing room, and I was a little relieved when I saw the dress Lily had discarded was still hanging on the rack. Penelope followed Lily into the room, so I took another opportunity to drool over the dress.

"It's gorgeous, isn't it? Did Lily want to try it on?" Buffy asked, jolting me out of my dress drooling haze.

"Um, no. She didn't like it."

Buffy tilted her head to the side and narrowed her eyes at me. After a quick moment, her eyes dropped to my engagement ring. "Are you thinking about your own wedding?"

"Oh no," I fumbled. "It's just a beautiful dress. I was just admiring it."

"I could put it in the back for you to try on when you get a moment," she offered, her tone helpful and sweet.

"Are you going to try a dress on, Riley?" Lily's excited voice came through over the door of her dressing room.

"No, no, I was just waiting and looking."

"I think it would look beautiful on you," Buffy added, taking the dress off the rack and holding it out, giving it a thorough look. "You have the perfect coloring to pull off a champagne dress."

"Oh my gosh, Riley," Lily said as she cracked open the door of her dressing room. "This is so exciting! I can't wait to see you in it."

"I can't… I mean, we've got to get to the caterers."

Lily frowned at my refusal. "Can't we reschedule?"

"No, that's not necessary."

"We're open until eight. You could come back later."

"I'm not even sure when I'm getting married. Plus, I don't think you're supposed to try on wedding dresses without your friends and family."

"So call your mom," Penelope added impatiently. "I could call her for you, if you want."

I narrowed my eyes at her. "No, that's not necessary. Let's just focus on Lily, shall we?"

"Tell you what," Buffy said, folding the dress over her arm. "I'll put the dress on hold until tomorrow, and if you feel like coming back to try it on, it'll be here waiting for you."

I opened my mouth to tell her it wasn't necessary, but she cut me off.

"If you don't come back, no harm, no foul." Then she disappeared with my dress.

Well, not *my* dress. I couldn't be trying on wedding dresses—I couldn't even pick a date for my wedding. Thinking about my wedding gave me hives. I didn't have time to think about it, as there were a million other things to accomplish before I could focus on it.

But the dress was absolutely gorgeous.

For the briefest moment, I had a daydream of Camden in a dark tuxedo turning and seeing me for the first time in that dress. His eyes trailed up and down my body from the top of my head all the way to my toes, then back up to my eyes, and I saw tears start to form in his. Then he pulled me to him and whispered, "You look so beautiful."

It was the first time I was able to have an actual visual of anything related to our wedding, and even though I didn't go to that bridal boutique with the intention of trying on a dress, I had a feeling I would regret it if I left without knowing how that dress felt on my body.

"Oh. My. Word."

I heard Lily's voice and knocked gently on her door.

"Everything okay in there?"

"It's perfect," she whispered, and I couldn't help the smile that came over my face.

The next hour was spent telling Lily how beautiful she looked in the dress that was obviously made for her. It was pink, elegant, and sexy—everything she wanted in a wedding gown. After just a few minutes of telling her how perfect it was, her mother showed up and the waterworks began. It was everything the moment was supposed to be, and I'd seen it a million times. But that didn't stop me from getting a little misty too.

"Do you think they have a veil I could try on?" Lily asked me, her cheeks pink from excitement at finding her wedding dress.

"I can definitely check on that for you."

With Buffy's help, we found a few veils that would work and I watched Lily have a special moment with her mother, all the while realizing I wanted that with my mother too.

Chapter Thirteen
Riley

The catering appointment went smoothly and Lily was surprisingly decisive when it came to food, which I could totally relate to. She quickly made decisions about cocktail hors d'oeuvres and main courses. And if I weren't the person helping her plan the wedding, I might have wanted to attend. The menu sounded delicious.

Afterward, Lily's mother invited us all out for drinks. There wasn't a clear company policy on socializing with patrons; it was more of a 'use your best judgment and don't embarrass the company' kind of implied policy. But I knew Rose and Lily were friends and she wasn't just strictly a client. Plus, I was looking at spending the evening alone in my hotel room, so I agreed. I was, however, a little disappointed that Penelope didn't have other pressing plans, since she agreed to go as well.

I was trying to have a good attitude about it though. Besides, Rose and Lily were both friends with her, and I liked both of them very much. And, as if I needed another reason to try and handle being around her, my mother vouched for her too. It seemed as though I was the only one who had a problem with Penelope Price.

And for a while, I was pleasantly surprised.

Lily's mother gave me the address to a super-swanky bar in the nicest part of Paradise Valley and Richard drove me there. In fact, he'd been quietly waiting for me all day. I felt badly for him and offered to take an Uber back to the hotel to give him the rest of the evening off, but he argued that he was contracted for the entire day. I sighed and let him drive me.

Lily's mother was given the royal treatment when we arrived at the bar and we were led directly to a table in the far corner where it was dark and private. The whole bar was elegant, all dark mahogany and candle light.

We all ordered drinks and Lily's mom requested some light appetizers, and then we engaged in what could only be described as a regular old happy hour. Lily waxed poetic about her dress, Lily's mom waxed nostalgic about her daughter, and, much to my surprise, Penelope was perfectly pleasant.

"So," Lily said between sips of her sugary martini drink, "are you going to go back and try the dress on?"

"What dress?" her mother asked, friendly and curious.

"Riley found a dress she was in love with but didn't try it on because she was 'working.' They said they would hold it for her though." Lily's eyes turned back to me. "I think you should go back. You should call your mom and have her meet you there and you can try it on."

I shrugged. "I don't know. I also feel a little bad my best friend isn't here."

"We can totally Skype her. Or video call her. You know you're never going to find a dress like that again. Plus, is your mom planning on going to Portland to go dress shopping any time soon?"

I let out a laugh. "No. I wasn't even planning on looking at dresses any time soon."

"So this is perfect!" Lily exclaimed, practically bouncing in her seat.

"Just call her," Penelope said encouragingly.

"What the hell," I said with a smile and pulled my phone from my purse. I had a text, but I cleared the notification, pulled up my contact list, and hit Send on my mother's number.

"Riley?" she answered with a question in her voice, and I couldn't blame her. It had only been a few weeks since I saw her last and we didn't usually talk terribly often.

"Hey, Mom. Got a minute?"

"Yeah, honey. What's up?"

"Well, I came back to Arizona for some business today and, well…." I realized I was nervous. Nervous to ask my mother to come with me to try on a wedding dress. Sadness crashed over me because I didn't want a strained relationship with my mom. I wanted to feel comfortable talking to her more than every few months, and I wanted to be able to tell her things and call her just because.

"Riley?" she asked again when I didn't finish my thought.

"Sorry," I said, taking a deep breath. I suddenly wished I hadn't made this phone call at a table full of practical strangers. "I'm here in Paradise Valley with a bride, and today at the dress shop I found one I want to try on. So, I was wondering if you wanted to come with me. Tonight. To see it."

At first there were no sounds from the other end of the line, but eventually I heard my mother take in a gasping breath before she asked, "You want me to come with you to try on a wedding dress?" I could tell she was close to tears and, truth be told, so was I.

"I mean, I know it's last-minute and it's getting late on a Monday…."

"Baby?"

"Yeah?"

"When and where?"

I didn't know if it was her calling me baby or just the sound of her voice when she assured me she'd be there to watch me put on my very first wedding dress, but something inside me snapped back into place, something that had been off for a while.

I told my mom which store and asked her to meet me there in an hour, told her I loved her, and then we disconnected.

When I looked back up at the ladies at the table, Lily and her mother were wiping tears from their eyes.

"Can I come too?" Lily asked, her voice wavering.

I shrugged and smiled. "If you want."

"See? It all worked out. I told you your mother would want to come." This came from Penelope. And while she wasn't tearing up like the rest of us, she was giving me a friendly smile.

"Thanks," I said, finding that I meant it. I was, in that moment, thankful for the push to call my mom and make the random, impromptu wedding dress event happen.

"Anytime," she said, then stood from the table. "I've got to run to the ladies' room. Excuse me."

"I can't believe I'm going to try on a wedding dress," I said, finally letting the excitement come over me. I turned my gaze to Lily. "You wouldn't mind holding the phone so my friend Hadley can watch, would you?"

"Of course not! This is so exciting!"

"It has been a rather eventful day," her mother added, lifting her glass and taking a sip of her drink.

"Oh, Mom, I forgot to show you the new floral idea I saw on Pinterest. I think it would look great on the tables." Lily reached for her tiny purse which was resting on the table just above her plate. Her fingers wrapped around it, but as she pulled it toward herself she knocked the dish of cocktail sauce over, spilling the red liquid all over the table and into her lap. "Shit," she whispered. I didn't have time to comment on it being the first unhappy word I'd ever heard her mutter, but I did spring up from my chair.

"I'll go get some club soda from the bar." She didn't respond as she was busy wiping up the sauce from her lap, but I dashed to the bar and grabbed the barkeep's attention. "Can I get a glass of club soda, please?"

"Sure thing," the young woman replied, obviously picking up on the fact that I needed it in a hurry as she moved quickly.

"I just thought you should know what she's been up to in your absence."

I heard Penelope's voice even though it was obvious from the hushed tone she was trying to keep her volume down.

"She spent the whole time with Lily in the dress shop looking for her own dress."

My eyes shot down the bar to where I saw Penelope with her back to me and her phone to her ear.

"Riley is going back to try on a dress this evening. If you don't believe me, text Lily and ask her what she's doing tonight. She's going with her." Penelope paused and I could hear my heart pounding in my ears. "Listen, you're my best friend and I just don't want someone taking advantage of you. You're paying her to be here and assist Lily, not plan her own wedding." Another pause. Rage was flowing through my veins on hot blood. "Well, don't say I didn't warn you." I listened as Penelope said goodbye to Rose, and then I couldn't contain myself anymore.

"What is your problem?" I asked as I came up right behind her.

She turned around with a surprised expression but quickly cooled it to a calmer mask or indignation.

"I was just making sure my friend knew what was going on when she wasn't here to supervise."

"You're full of shit, Penelope. You know what? I knew you were a bitch. From day one I knew you were out to get me, and you haven't changed a bit since high school."

"I wonder if Rose knows how vulgar you are toward clients."

"You're not a client, you're a leech."

"I'll make sure Rose knows exactly what's been happening today. How you used company time to do your own personal business, and how you've spoken to me."

"You go ahead and tell Rose whatever you want. I'm done pretending as though you're not crazy. You always have to be the center of attention." I tilted my head and narrowed my eyes at her. "You wanna know what I think is really going on here? I think you're jealous that Lily is getting married and that Rose is a successful, strong, capable, and powerful businesswoman. I think you find yourself, for once, in a situation where you aren't the focus, so you're finding a way to boost yourself up while bringing other people down. Just like you did all through high school."

"You have no idea what you're talking about." She tried to be firm, but I could see the way her eyes wavered and her lips trembled.

"Don't I?" I couldn't hold back the scoff that escaped me. "You go ahead and tell Rose whatever you want. She knows my work ethic and she trusts me to be here without her. In the end, you'll just end up looking like the pathetic excuse for a friend that you are."

I turned away from her, grabbed the tall glass of club soda the bartender had placed next to me, and returned to the table.

"Here you go," I said, placing the glass on the table with more of a thump than I'd intended.

"Thank you," she said as she dipped her linen napkin in the glass and then went to work on her skirt. She rubbed furiously, then dipped her napkin again and returned to her skirt.

"You should probably get that soaking," her mother offered.

"I hope it isn't ruined. This is one of my favorite skirts."

"Okay," Lily said exasperatedly as she set the napkin on the table. "I think I'm going to run home and change and let this soak. I'll meet you at the dress shop, okay?"

"Sounds good. I hope the stain comes out." I got up and kissed both Lily and her mother on the cheek, then sat once more and let out a deep breath. There had been so many times in my life where I'd thought about what I would say to Penelope Price if I had the chance. If I could let my filter down for just a minute and tell her exactly what I thought about her and the hell she'd put me through. I wanted to tell her how her treatment so many years ago had affected me even still to that day.

"Can I get you another drink?" the waitress asked as she started clearing the table.

"No, thank you. But can I get a glass of water?"

"Sure thing," she said with a smile.

Just as she walked away, Penelope returned to the table. But instead of indignation I saw surprise on her face.

"Where did everyone else go?"

"Lily got cocktail sauce on her skirt, so she and her mom left to go soak it."

"Oh." She looked at me for a moment, as if she wanted to say something but didn't know where to start, but the words didn't come. Instead, she turned and started to leave.

"Penelope," I called out before I could think better of it. "Listen," I started, wondering where all the anger I'd felt five minutes before had gone. Where had the years of pent-up frustration with this woman disappeared to? "Can we start over?"

Penelope's eyebrows darted up, but she didn't say anything in reply.

"Can we talk like grown women? Have a discussion? Face-to-face? Instead of calling bosses behind our backs or taking these feelings with us to the grave? Can we just talk it out?"

Penelope stared at me for a moment but eventually turned back to the table and took a seat.

"I'm listening," she said haughtily.

"Okay," I said, drawing the word out. "I'm sorry." The words stung coming out. I never wanted to apologize to Penelope for telling her to shove it, but apparently I was. "I shouldn't have said those things to you. I was just really upset. It seems that you've been out to get me for a very long time."

Penelope rolled her eyes, but she didn't say anything.

"I guess I've just been harboring some ill feelings toward you since high school. Can I ask why you were always out to get me back then?"

"Out to get you?" she asked, anger clear in her voice. "I wasn't out to get you. You thought you were better than everyone else."

"What in the world are you talking about?" The volume of my voice had skyrocketed, so I tried to rein it in. I continued in a loud, harsh whisper. "I didn't think I was better than *anyone*. I was just trying to survive being targeted every single day by mean girls who picked on me."

"Oh please, Riley. Stop playing the victim. You've been doing it for far too long and it's a tired ploy." She rolled her eyes again and I felt the urge to reach over the table and smack her right in the forehead. I wouldn't do that, obviously. But I could imagine it. And I did. "The minute you moved to Paradise Valley, you decided you were better than everyone and my friends and I were totally beneath you. You never came to parties, you never went to football games, and even when we invited you, you'd ignore us."

"Ignore you? You weren't really inviting me! You were teasing me! You never wanted me to hang out with you." My hands were waving around on their own accord. I had absolutely no control over their gesticulations.

"Maybe toward the end of high school we weren't serious, but that's because you spent so much time ignoring us. When you first moved here, I tried to include you, to bring you into my circle of friends, but you had a cold shoulder from day one."

My mouth was hanging open, but there were no more words coming from it. My mind wandered back to when I was fourteen. I remember Penelope asking me to hang out a few times when I first moved there, but I felt so out of place, so insecure, I turned her down. But I never thought I was too good to hang out with her friends. I honestly couldn't imagine why she and her friends would want to hang out with me to begin with, so I assumed they were just messing with me.

Was it possible that years of insecurity and angst were the result of legitimate miscommunication?

"Let's just put what happened in high school aside for a minute. Why in the world would you call Rose and tell her all those terrible things about me? I wasn't using company time to plan my own wedding. What you saw, me admiring a dress and someone putting it on hold, was the extent of it."

Penelope's eyes fell to her lap where she was fiddling with something. If I didn't know better, I would think she looked ashamed. "It's been hard the past couple years watching so many people around me lead really incredible lives. Rose is running her own business and doing fantastically. Lily has a great job too, but now she's getting married to a really fantastic guy. And I'm happy for them, don't get me wrong, but it's hard being the only person who isn't moving forward." She took a deep breath, her shoulders rising with the inhalation, then let it all out in a whoosh, including her words. "I guess you were right and

I did want to feel better about myself by bringing someone down."

She looked contrite, but then the mask came back down over her eyes.

"You've always had good things in your life and never appreciated them, Riley. Maybe I was trying to give you a little perspective."

"What?" I cried, my face scrunching in confusion.

"Like your mother, for instance."

At the mention of my mom my hackles immediately rose. I had no idea what she was talking about, but I wasn't about to sit there and listen to her trash-talk my mom. "What about my mother?" My eyes narrowed and my jaw clenched tight.

"You were always inconsiderate! She was working her tail off so you and your brother could go to a great school and you were always so rude to her. She worked hard every day and I always watched you mouth off to her. At least your mother cared about you! My mother was too busy going to galas or having lunch dates with her snobby, rich friends to care enough to come see me sing in the choir or watch me cheer. But your mom was there for you all the time. And for me. She was more of a mother to me than my own."

My face pulled back in surprise at her words. Those words were the very last ones I expected to come out of her mouth.

"Wait, you were jealous of me because of my mother?"

Suddenly, Penelope wasn't furious or bitchy—she was just sad.

"Your mom was the closest thing I had to a real mother, even to this day." A tear streaked down her cheek. "Do you know I go to her house every Sunday for brunch? She talks about you all the time. She's so proud of you."

I never liked Penelope, but in that moment, hearing the sadness in her voice, I wouldn't be human if it didn't affect me. We didn't get along, we weren't friends, and I couldn't tell you one thing about her on a deeper level, but I could understand needing someone—especially a mother figure.

"I didn't know." My words were whispered and I fought the urge to reach out and run a hand down Penelope's arm in support. She was obviously fighting back tears.

"Well, all those years she spent in my house, cooking and cleaning, I saw her every day. She was always trying to convince me to befriend you in the beginning, and I tried, but after a while she stopped pressing the issue."

"Even if you and I don't see eye-to-eye, I'm glad my mom was there for you. I know what it feels like when you think your mother doesn't care about you, and I wouldn't wish that on anyone."

Suddenly, it was awkward between us. We weren't friends, but I didn't feel like we were enemies anymore either. We'd obviously just misunderstood each other for the last decade.

Penelope looked at her hands again, a nervous expression coming over her face. "I'll call Rose later and explain what happened. I'll tell her the truth."

"I'd appreciate that." I tried not to let the surprise I was feeling seep into my voice. Penelope had never apologized for anything before, and she'd definitely never tried to make amends. "We don't have to be enemies, you know."

She took in a deep breath and then exhaled in a rush. "I know. And I don't want any more enemies. Maybe one day we can even be friends."

"I can always use more friends." Those were honest words. If Penelope wanted to be friends someday, I wouldn't turn her away. But in that moment, I was satisfied with not having an archnemesis anymore.

"I'm going to go home," she said, stepping away from the bar. "I hope you love that dress. And I hope your wedding is amazing and everything you want it to be."

There had never been a time when I hadn't questioned the sincerity of Penelope's words, but in that moment, I knew she meant what she said. It was refreshing.

"Thanks," I said with a smile I hoped showed her how I genuinely appreciated her words.

Penelope gave me one last sad smile and walked away. I watched her go and then let out a breath. What a strange half hour it had been. I could only hope that Penelope did as she said she would and called Rose to explain. And even if that happened, I still had to hope that there wasn't any blowback on me. It couldn't look good that there was drama happening while Rose was away. The last thing I needed was for my boss to lose confidence in my ability to do my job, regardless of the situation.

I dropped a few bills on the table for a tip, as Lily's mom had already covered the bill, and walked out to meet Richard. Even after all the craziness of the day, I was still secretly excited to try on that dress.

Chapter Fourteen
Riley

"I have something to tell you," I said as I sat in the back of the town car Richard was currently driving to the bridal boutique.

"Oh my God, you're pregnant." Hadley said the words like it would have been the worst news in the world.

"Oh no. Hadley, I'm not pregnant."

"Thank you, tiny baby Jesus." Relief was evident in her voice and also in the loud exhalation that came after the words. "What is it, then?"

"I'm about to try on a wedding dress," I tell her tentatively, knowing it could go one of two ways. She'll either be excited or pissed.

"What? Aren't you in Arizona?" she asked, making me think she was going to lean more toward the pissed side of things.

"Yeah," I replied hesitantly. "But I've got it all worked out and Lily is going to video call you so you can see."

"Really?" she exclaimed.

"Is that all right? I'm so sorry you can't be here. I just saw the dress and I couldn't take my eyes off it—"

"Riley, it's fine," she stated, interrupting my verbal vomit. "Do I wish I could be there? Of course. But I'm just happy I'll get to see it happen. That I'll get to see the look on your face when you see yourself in it. That's all I'm really looking for."

Her words were strangely sentimental. Hadley didn't do sappy normally. Sarcasm was her verbal currency, so to hear her get emotional triggered something inside me and suddenly I was emotional too.

"I just wish you were here."

"Well, I'm there in spirit."

"Okay," I said, taking in a deep breath. "At least this way my mom gets to be there to see me try the dress on."

"Oh, Riley, that's incredible. I'm sure that means a lot to her."

"I think so too." The town car slowed and I saw we were approaching the store. "Okay, I'm gonna go in and get all set up. Do not put your phone down. Lily will call you soon from my number."

"Okay, I can't wait!"

"Oh, and don't tell Camden anything. I want to be the one to tell him."

"Roger that."

We ended the call and Richard opened my door, holding out his hand to help me from the car.

"Thank you," I said as I righted myself, straightening my skirt.

"My pleasure, ma'am."

"I'm going to grab a ride back to the hotel from my mother. I think it would be okay for you to go home now, seeing as how I'm not doing company business anymore."

"If you think that's best," he replied, giving me one more chance to change my mind.

"I do. Thank you for your help today. I'll see you tomorrow?"

"I'll be there at noon to take you to the airport. Call me directly if you need anything before then." He produced a business card like a magic trick with a quick hand movement.

"Thanks," I said with a laugh.

He winked and then walked back around to the driver door. "Hello, ma'am," he said to my mother as she appeared from between two cars. "Lovely evening, isn't it?" I watched as Richard's eyes followed my mother until she met me on the sidewalk.

"It is," she said with a blush.

Richard looked between me and my mother, let his eyes rest on her for moment, then gave us both a nod with a grin, climbed in the town car, and drove away.

"Who was that?" my mother asked.

"That's Richard, my driver for my trip."

"Oh," she said, her voice an entire octave higher than normal. "I'm so glad you called." She wrapped her arms around me.

"I'm glad you could make it. Sorry it's so last-minute. I did not intend on shopping for a wedding dress on this trip. This all came out of left field."

My mother's eyes lit up with anticipation. "Is it gorgeous?"

The corners of my mouth tipped up and my heart fluttered in my chest. "It's the most beautiful dress I've ever seen." There might as well have been big cartoon hearts where my eyes were.

"I can't wait." My mother's voice was raspy now, and I knew she was getting close to tears.

"Come on. Let's go inside and see if they're ready for us."

We didn't make it five feet inside the store before Buffy descended upon us like a moth to a flame.

"I'm so glad you're back," she squealed, clapping excitedly. "I knew you'd come back for that dress."

Lily walked in a few minutes later and everything began to move very quickly.

I was whisked away and pushed gently into a dressing room where Buffy began taking measurements and fitting me for undergarments. I handed my phone to Lily and asked her to video call Hadley for me, smiling when I heard Had's disembodied voice introducing herself to Lily.

I was thrust into a strapless bra and shimmied into a pair of Spanx that were entirely uncomfortable. In all the years I'd been planning weddings, dress shopping wasn't always something the event planner helped with, but even on occasion of being with the bride on the day of the dress, I was never in the dressing room. There was always a consultant from the store for that. I helped more with the theme of the dress, the look. I helped accessorize. I made sure the dress fit the bride's vision. So I'd never seen the moment the bride saw herself in her wedding dress for the first time.

But that's what I saw when I looked in the mirror.

Me. In my wedding dress.

Buffy had slipped it effortlessly over my head and zipped up the back before I'd even been able to blink. And then I blinked a hundred times. I couldn't believe what I was seeing. It was me, but I was a bride.

"This length really makes your legs look incredible," Buffy said, pulling me from my bridal trance. My eyes were drawn down to my legs and sure enough they looked fantastic. Every part of me looked better than it ever had.

"Is this dress magical?"

Buffy laughed.

"I'm serious," I said, turning to look her straight in the eye. "I've never looked like this. Ever. I'm not this beautiful."

"Oh, sweetie. You're definitely a looker, but what you're experiencing right now is the Dress Effect."

"So it *is* magic," I said with a nod, my eyes moving back to my reflection.

"You know what? You're right. It is magic. But it's the same magic every other woman has ever experienced when she found *the* dress and put it on for the first time."

"*The* dress?"

"Her wedding dress."

Holy crap. This is the dress.

"Let's go show everyone. Your mom is a mess." Buffy's words were kind and soft.

"All right." I let Buffy lead me from the room even though I knew the way. As I followed her around the very last corner, I had a mini panic attack, wondering what I would do if everyone hated the dress. In that moment I couldn't even imagine taking the dress off, so hearing they hated it would confuse me and I liked the wonderful happy bubble I'd found myself in. Luckily for me, they didn't hate the dress.

I stepped around the corner and my gaze narrowed in on my mother. Her mouth dropped open and was then covered by her hands, her eyes wide and filled with tears. She was speechless.

"Riley," she rasped from behind her hands, then let out a small sob.

"Holy shit." I heard Hadley's voice and saw my phone in Lily's hand, Hadley's face on the screen, her expression much like my mother's. And Lily's, for that matter. They all looked shocked.

"It's incredible," Lily said, her words a little breathless. "You look amazing."

"You look *fucking fantastic*, Riles. Just gorgeous." I wished Hadley was there in person instead of just a voice on my phone. I missed her.

"It's perfect," my mother said, wiping tears from her eyes. "I can't imagine a better dress."

"Yeah?" I asked. Even though all three of them were losing their minds, I still needed that reassurance. This wasn't any regular dress. This was the dress I'd be vowing my undying and eternal love to Camden in. It was a big fucking deal. Bigger than I ever imagined it to be. I had a newfound respect for all the brides I'd worked with, having rolled my eyes when they tried on a million dresses. If they didn't feel like I felt in that dress, then it wasn't right. I understood that now.

"Yes," Lily said. "It's… I don't even have words." She let out a breath and then asked, "How do you feel about it?"

"I love it," I said as I ran my hands down the skirt, letting my fingers trail over the lace. "I didn't think the dress was a big deal, but this dress is everything."

"It is," my mother agreed. Buffy came up behind her and stealthily handed her a tissue.

"What color is it?" Hadley asked from my phone, squinting.

"It's like a champagne color. Almost gold, but not quite," Buffy supplied.

"Are you okay with not having a white wedding dress?" Lily asked, not unkindly. I was well aware of the fact that choosing a nontraditional dress would raise some eyebrows.

I turned around to face the wall of mirrors behind me, three of them angled so I could see myself from almost every side. A slight twist of my hips and I could see the back of the dress. I looked at how the lace lay against my skin, how the champagne color made everything look more elegant.

"I think so," I said thoughtfully, turning back and forth to examine myself in the dress from every possible vantage point. "Everything about my relationship with Camden so far has been nonconventional, so this isn't too far off the mark."

"Do you want to try a white dress on? I can probably find something similar...."

"No," I say softly, finding her gaze in the mirror. "I don't need to try anything else on."

"You're going to get the dress?" Hadley's voice rang out from the phone.

I turned to face everyone and simply nodded, unable to find words in the moment.

All the women around me let out cries of happiness and excitement, and I'd never in the months since I'd gotten engaged been so excited to get married. I loved Camden, had loved him in some way or another since that very first kiss in the middle of a basketball game. But right then, standing in a bridal boutique with two strangers, my mother, and Hadley on the phone, for the first time, I couldn't wait to marry him.

I stood in front of that mirror for a very long time, just gazing at my reflection. My mother came to stand next to me and fussed over the dress. Eventually Lily had to leave to meet her fiancé, and Hadley had to hang up too, so then it was just my mother and me standing in front of the mirror, admiring my beautiful wedding dress.

"What color shoes are you going to wear?" she asked. "And how will you wear your hair?" She picked my hair up off my nape and rolled it into an impromptu bun, then narrowed her eyes and tilted her head to the side. "Up or down?"

"I'm not sure," I said, lifting the hem of the skirt and letting it float down around my thighs for the millionth time. "Maybe a sparkly pump?"

"That would be gorgeous," my mother said with a gasp.

"Ladies, I hate to break up the dress ogling, but the store will be closing soon," Buffy interrupted, her tone sweet as ever. She'd been more than accommodating, letting me stand there in front of the mirror for who knew how long. "Have you thought about whether you want to order a new custom dress from the designer, or purchase this dress right off the rack?"

"Oh, um, well," I said as I turned and looked at the dress from all the angles again. The only reason to order another dress would be if the one on the rack wasn't the right size, or if it had been tried on so much it wasn't in pristine condition. My dress, however, fit perfectly, and I'd watched it be placed on the rack for the first time. I was the only person to wear it. "I think I want to take it with me."

"Sounds great. Do you want help taking it off?"

"No," I said, smiling. "I think I can manage."

"Sounds good. I can ring you up whenever you're ready."

"Thank you."

Buffy wandered away and I heard her talking to another bride who had also fallen under the Dress Effect when my mother placed her hand on my shoulder.

"Riley, I would love it if you let me cover the cost of the dress."

Her words shocked me and caught me completely off guard.

"What? Mom, no. That's not why I asked you here."

"I know that, sweetie. But I'm your mother and the cost of the wedding is supposed to fall to me."

"Mom, please, I don't want you to worry about paying anything toward the wedding." I turned to her and looked her in the eye. The last thing I wanted was for her to think I expected money from her. Money wasn't even on my radar when I decided to try on the dress. In fact, I hadn't even looked at the price tag.

Her hands came up and rested on my shoulders. "Riley, I won't be able to help much, and I know I won't be able to provide the kind of wedding that's expected of a mayor's son, but I have some money saved up and it would make me so happy to pay for your dress. It will probably be the only thing I can contribute toward."

My heart ached with her words. She wanted to help, but I knew she couldn't afford to give me what she thought I wanted.

"Please," she asked again.

I found the tag and flipped it over to look at the price. There was good news and bad news. The good news was it wasn't the most expensive dress I'd ever seen. In fact, it was pretty reasonable. Probably because it was a nontraditional color and tea length. The bad news was it was still a wedding dress, so there was more than one zero at the end of the number.

"Mom, I know you mean well and want to help, but it really isn't necessary, Camden and I—"

"Just bought a house," she said as she interrupted me. "Trust me, I knew one day you'd be getting married and I knew I'd want to help, even if it's just the dress. Let me buy my baby girl her wedding dress."

I was torn between giving in to something she obviously wanted so badly and making sure she kept that money and used it for something more useful, like retirement. But in the end, I knew it would hurt my mother more to deny her.

"Thank you, Mom." I wrapped my arms around her and felt her shudder with the small sobs of a happy mother.

"You're going to look so beautiful on your wedding day. I can't wait."

Me either.

Chapter Fifteen
Camden

It was only by luck that I saw my phone screen light up on the counter. One thing I couldn't do when Riley was around was play Smashing Pumpkins as loud as my speakers could handle. So, when I found myself with an evening alone and a lot of new furniture to assemble, I turned on my favorite music from high school and got lost in the work. Of course, there was a Guinness within reach.

I'd been on a mission to get a corner of one of the spare bedrooms put together for her while she was away. I had something special planned and I wanted to surprise her when she got home.

I pushed the Mute button on the speaker and answered the phone.

"How's my favorite brunette with a mean Skee-Ball arm?"

"I bought a wedding dress."

Her words were quick and frenzied, as though she was trying to force them out before she lost the nerve to say them at all.

"You what?" I asked for clarification. I'd heard her, but I wanted to make sure I'd heard her correctly.

"Am I crazy?"

"Yes, but not because you bought a wedding dress." I paused, waiting for her to say something, to explain, but she was silent. "You bought a wedding dress."

"Yes! It was totally impulsive and crazy." I could picture her pacing in her suite, biting her thumbnail, worried she'd made a terrible mistake. "But it's so beautiful, Cam." Her voice was suddenly softer, dreamier, and it made me miss her terribly. Riley put on a fierce front for pretty much everyone—me included—so when she went soft and let that side of herself out, it was hard to not want to grab a hold of her.

"Tell me about it," I said, making my voice match her soft tone. I laid back on the carpet and put my hand behind my head, just wanting to listen to her voice and imagine she was in the room with me.

"I can't tell you about the dress! That's bad luck!"

"Okay," I laughed. "Then tell me how you came to impulsively buy a wedding dress."

I spent the next thirty minutes listening to my most favorite person tell me a great story. I only interjected once or twice to ask clarifying questions, but other than that, I just listened. She told me about the run-in with Penelope, but I heard the forgiveness in her voice. She told me about how her mother insisted on buying her dress, but I heard how much it meant to have her mother there and to provide something so important and special for her.

But the best part of the whole story was the end.

"I don't know what it was, Cam," she said, her voice taking on the dreamy quality again. "I don't know if it was the dress, or having my mom there, or feeling for the first time in years that there wasn't something dark hanging over me anymore, but I put that dress on and I wanted nothing more than to marry you. Soon. Like, yesterday."

Her words. *Damn*, her words. They made every part of me sigh with contentment. I knew Riley wanted to marry me. I never doubted, not even for a minute, that she wanted to be with me. But I also wasn't going to push her to plan a wedding. I knew she'd come around and eventually it would happen. I wanted Riley as my wife, but only because it was another way to bind her to me. We didn't need a wedding for commitment, but I wanted that stupid piece of paper more than I cared to admit. Hearing her tell me she wanted to get married, and soon, was like a shot of adrenaline. And lust. When the woman you love more than life itself tells you she wants to marry you *now*, she damn well better be within arm's reach.

"Jesus. I miss you." The words came out with a growl. "What time is your flight tomorrow?"

"Not until the afternoon."

"Damn."

"I know."

"I wish you were here."

"Me too."

We were both quiet for a moment, but then I asked the question burning in my mind.

"What are you wearing?"

"My wedding dress," she said without hesitation.

"Really?"

"No," she replied with a laugh. "I want to be though. There's not much holding me back from putting it on. It's so pretty."

I tried to picture Riley in a wedding dress, and the image my mind conjured up was too sexy for public consumption. Surely Riley wouldn't be wearing a white lace teddy at the altar, but in that moment, that was all I could picture. My mind had officially gotten on the one track that led to Riley and me naked in a bed. Or the floor. A car, even. The only real requirements for the activities flowing through my mind were mine and Riley's bodies. That was all I needed. And maybe just one flat surface.

"I'm sure it's beautiful," I managed, fighting the urge to bring my free hand to the bulge forming in my pants.

"And I meant it about planning the wedding. I want to get started. I want to look at venues and pick out a cake. I want to do all that. But mainly I just want to marry you. Soon."

"Riley," I groaned, rolling to my side. "It's not fair to tell me these things over the phone while you're states away."

"I'm sorry," she replied, sounding contrite. "I just wanted to tell you before I lost this wonderful feeling of just wanting to be your wife. I mean, I'll always want to be your wife, but right now I want it really bad."

"Fuck," I said on a rasp again. "I want you on the next plane home. In fact, I'll charter a flight. Oh, better yet, I'll charter a flight down there so I can get my hands on you faster."

"Where are your hands now?" she asked, her voice coy and shy. Riley rarely took charge in the bedroom; she was more than willing to go wherever I led her and I loved that she trusted me to take care of her.

"I've been trying to keep my hand off my cock since you called."

"Why are you fighting it?"

I let out a sigh.

"Because as turned on as I am right now, and as sexy as it is to think about you touching yourself while you think about me, nothing is as good as being with you in the flesh. And the day you buy your wedding dress, the dress you'll wear when you become my wife, well, that deserves more than mutual masturbation."

She was quiet for a moment, then softly said, "That might be the most romantic thing I've ever heard you say."

I groaned. "That's not true. At least I hope it's not true. I've said lots of romantic things to you, none of which included the phrase 'mutual masturbation.'"

She laughed and the happy sound resonated through me. "I guess that's true. Maybe they're not the most romantic words, but it was pretty high up there as far as romantic intention."

"Aw, shucks."

"I still miss you."

"I still miss you more. Tomorrow I'll make you a nice dinner in our new house and you can tell me all about the dress. And the plans. I can't wait."

"Good, because there's not going to be much of a wait. Think we can fit a wedding in this summer? I don't want to give too much away, but the dress is not made for a winter wedding."

"I think we can get married whenever you want."

"Okay," she whispered. "I can't wait." She was smiling. I could hear it. And it made me smile too.

We talked for another thirty minutes about everything that had happened that day and I listened as she paced around her hotel room, methodically going through her nightly routine. I could tell when she was washing her face, brushing her teeth, then washing her face again with a different product—I swear the girl washed her face with a million different things. I knew that, since I wasn't there, she was putting on her oldest pair of sleep shorts and a T-shirt—probably mine. I took great comfort in the idea that I could imagine everything she was doing, that she was familiar enough to me that I could anticipate her actions.

I also felt extremely lucky to know her in that way. No one else would ever know what her decade-old pajamas looked like.

"Will you be there to pick me up tomorrow? You might want to take my car. I don't think my dress will fit in the trunk of the Batmobile."

"I can do that."

"You sound tired."

"Hmmm." She was right, I was tired. But I would have stayed on the phone and listened to her chatter to herself all night, which was basically what I'd been doing for half an hour.

"Go to bed."

"Okay," I agreed, but only to make her happy. I knew I wouldn't be going to sleep for a while. There was too much to do. "I'll see you tomorrow, babe."

"Love you," she said, a smile still in her voice.

"Love you too." She disconnected and I let out a breath. That woman was going to be the end of me. As well as the beginning. And everything in between.

I sat up, took a pull from my Guinness, and nearly gagged. Nothing was worse than warm beer. I turned the music back to full blast, walked downstairs to grab a fresh beer, and then got back to work on the surprise for my future wife.

The next day I was exhausted. Not only had I gotten up late for work but I'd hardly gotten any sleep at all. All night I was lying in bed, alone, missing Riley and thinking about what she'd said about wanting to get married as soon as possible. The fact of the matter was planning a wedding didn't all of a sudden become less work. Riley was still taking on a lot, and even though she'd suddenly become excited about it, it didn't mean it wasn't going to put a strain on her or cause her stress.

I'd been brainstorming ideas into the early morning. At some point I even took out my cell phone and did some research, all the while fighting the temptation to call Riley and get her input. But I didn't want her to be exhausted while she traveled.

I was on my second espresso when her text came through.

Kinda wishing this banana wasn't so much a banana.

Of course the text was accompanied by a photo of my sexy fiancée with a familiar yellow fruit shoved halfway in her mouth. A sly grin and a wink as well. Her teeth just gently breaching the outside of the fruit.

I had to laugh as I pictured her in the middle of the airport taking a selfie with a banana in her mouth. There weren't many innocent reasons to do that. Fuck, I loved her.

Flight boards in ten minutes. I can't wait to see you. Or your banana.

I laughed again. Couldn't help it. She was so fucking cute.

I can't wait to see you either. Fly safe. Love you.

Love you too.

I managed to finish my day at work and not fuck up any contracts, but my head definitely wasn't in the game. I rushed back to the house to put the finishing touches on

Riley's surprise and then made one stop before heading to the airport.

When I finally spotted her coming from the secure terminal, I couldn't help the huge smile that crept across my face. She looked beautiful walking toward me with a white garment bag, smile plastered across her face as she picked up her pace, closing the distance between us quicker.

When she was finally within arm's reach, my free hand wound around her waist and hers went to my nape and our mouths met in a kiss probably not entirely chaste, but more than likely seen at an airport a time or two before. Lovers reuniting usually didn't care too much if they were being slightly inappropriate. In fact, I couldn't help it much if my hand slipped off her waist and over the roundness of her ass, pulling her into me further.

"Jesus, I missed you," I rumbled against her lips, loving the way I could feel her smiling against me.

"Take me home," she whispered.

"Fuck, yes."

She smiled and kissed me again, then pulled away, making me growl.

"These are for you," I said, holding out the bundle of peonies I'd picked up on the way.

Her mouth opened in a little O that made my dick jump in my pants, and then her eyes met mine as she wrapped her hand around the stems.

"Camden, that's so sweet. You know I love peonies."

"I do," I said triumphantly. Every other fiancé in the Portland Metro area could kiss my ass. No one's girl was as

175

happy as mine was right then. I had a few tricks still up my sleeve.

"Thank you," she said with a blush that crept down her throat. That also made my dick hard.

"Let's go," I said, taking the garment bag from her and then threading our fingers together.

"Careful with my dress," she said, still smiling and happy.

"Is this *the* dress?" I asked, even though I knew the answer.

"Yes, and if you peek at it I'm going to be so mad."

"I'm not going to peek."

"No? You're not curious?"

"I mean, I'm curious, but I've been looking forward to that stereotypical moment where I see you in the dress for the first time and it's a big deal. I want that moment. I don't want to sneak into the closet to look at the dress behind your back. That wouldn't be very groomy of me."

"Aw, you're the best groom ever." She tilted her head up and gave me that dazzling smile of hers. "I can't wait for that moment, babe." She squeezed my hand and I could have sworn I felt it on my heart.

This woman.

She had me.

And I wanted to make it official just as soon as she did.

"Oh," she said, pulling on my hand. "I almost forgot! I had to check my bag since I carried my dress onto the plane. We have to go to baggage claim."

"Okay. Lead the way."

We walked through the airport at a leisurely pace and followed all the signs to the baggage carousel. The belt was already running and people were plucking their suitcases off left and right.

"Oh, that one's mine," she said, pointing. "The one with the flannel scarf tied to the handle."

"Got it," I said and moved to the belt, reaching it just in time to grab the bag and move out of everyone else's way. "This everything?" I asked when I made it back to her.

"Yeah," she said, scrunching her nose in the ridiculously sexy and cute way she did that made me think it wasn't everything at all.

"What is it?" I said with a laugh. "Just tell me."

"I was in a window seat on the plane and didn't want to bother anyone, so I kind of have to find a ladies' room."

I lifted my arms at my sides, complete with dress in one hand and suitcase in the other. "I'll be here."

"Thanks," she said as she rose onto her tiptoes and pressed a kiss against my cheek. She turned and walked away from me, leaving me thinking I'd stand there forever holding anything for her. It was with that thought that I put her suitcase down and pulled out my phone, finally making the decision I'd been mulling over all night and all day.

I pushed Call on a contact and then put the phone to my ear.

"Hey, it's me," I said quietly when they answered. I knew logically Riley would be a few more minutes, but I wanted to get this conversation over with quickly. "I need your help with something."

Chapter Sixteen
Riley

Camden held my hand all the way to the new house, and I was glad for it because I wanted as much contact as possible. We'd only been apart for two days, but they were significant days and things had happened that made me want him close in every way. It was weird seeing him drive my car, but we needed the back seat for my dress.

I'd never felt maternal toward anyone in my whole life, but I was having some serious mother-hen feelings about my dress. I worried throughout the entire flight that something terrible would happen to it and I wouldn't know until I opened the overhead compartment to pull it out. I'd boarded the plane close to last with a plan. I'd found an overhead bin that was pretty full but had enough space above the bags to lay my dress flat across them. The entire flight I worried that someone had smuggled on a bottle of red wine and that it would explode all over my dress from a change in cabin pressure or some other ridiculous nonsense.

Even during the car ride home I must have turned around to check on the dress at least a dozen times. And I might have scolded Camden in my mind for braking too quickly and almost causing my dress to ruffle.

But one gentle squeeze from Camden and I was pulled back into the crazy lust that had been building since I got off that plane and saw him waiting with peonies.

He looked damn good waiting for me too. He was wearing my favorite pair of jeans that hugged his thighs just right and a green polo shirt that showed off his biceps.

He was entirely lickable, which was probably why I jumped him as soon as I saw him.

My eyes darted down to his thighs as he drove. It was so stupid how my body reacted to just looking at his.

He pulled into the driveway of the new house and I took a moment to inwardly gasp at its beauty, still trying to grasp the fact that the house belonged to Camden and me.

He kissed the back of my hand and then released it, climbing out of the car to get my suitcase from the trunk. I stepped out of the car and absently thought about how much cooler it was in Portland than Paradise Valley when Camden came up behind me and handed me my dress.

"Thanks," I said in almost a whisper.

"Come on," he urged, wrapping his arm around my shoulder and leading me inside.

The house looked much the same as it did when I left. There were big pieces of furniture in the space, but boxes were still pushed up against walls and there was nothing out that made it feel like a home yet. We needed to unpack all our things, put our art on the walls, and make it our own for that to happen, and I was kind of glad he hadn't accomplished too much of that while I was away. I wanted to help turn it from a house to a home.

"Where do you want to hang up your dress?" he asked softly.

"Well, honestly, I think I'll worry too much if it's not in our bedroom, but I just need you to promise me you won't look again."

He drew a giant X over his chest above his heart, saying, "Cross my heart and hope to die. Stick a needle in my eye."

I laughed. "Ew."

"Come on."

He led me up the stairs and into our bedroom, which looked pretty much the same as before, though some of Camden's clothes were on the floor. I was happy he hadn't unpacked the downstairs, but I was even more ecstatic he hadn't tackled the bedroom without me.

I headed to the closet and made sure there was enough room for the dress and that nothing was within a two-foot radius of the garment bag. Before I could close the door, I felt Camden behind me and his hands came to rest on my hips.

"God, I missed you," he whispered right against my ear just before he pressed his mouth to my neck, kissing me there and making every single hair on my body stand on end.

I leaned back against him, letting him take my weight, my hands searching for his. The kiss on my neck turned deep, his mouth hungrily searching for something there, and every press of his lips against my thundering pulse sent another wave of lust straight between my legs.

Suddenly, he turned me around, his eyes looking deep into mine.

"You were so stressed before you left and I was trying so hard to think of anything I could do to help you, to make you understand that you could lean on me."

"I know," I said, my voice soft and gentle, emotion taking over. I moved my hands to his face, my belly fluttering when he flipped one of my hands over and kissed the palm. "You're the best thing that ever happened to me."

"The smile on your face as you got off that plane, Riley… I want to see you smile like that all the time."

"You make me so happy. I just had to realize that it wasn't the wedding I needed to worry about, it was the marriage. And I don't have anything to worry about when it comes to being married to you. Our marriage will be the best, easiest, hardest, and most important thing I ever do." His eyes were still searching mine, still looking so deep into mine, but finally he kissed me again.

"I want you happy," he said against my lips. "I'll spend my whole life just making sure you're happy."

"I want that for you too."

He walked me backward until we both fell to the bed, which was just a box spring and mattress on the floor. As soon as we were both horizontal, his hands were all over me and my clothes were disappearing rapidly.

There were no words and no pretenses. I needed him in that moment as much as he needed me. My hands pressed between us, searching for the closure on his jeans, pulling them open and then sliding them down his legs. He pulled back and ripped his shirt over his head, baring his beautiful chest to me, and I made a note somewhere in the back of my mind to admire it better later.

My shirt was soon gone, as were my pants, and everything else along with it. It was just him and me, our naked bodies pulsing with need and lust and love. I craved the warmth his body gave mine as he splayed over me, his hips fitting between my legs and his mouth coming over mine.

He kissed me roughly, groaning as our lips met. I arched into him as his hand snaked down my body and his fingers slid between the folds at my core. He'd find me wet and waiting.

"I promise I'll give you more attention next time," he said, pulling just far enough away from my mouth to utter the words. "But I can't wait."

I knew what he meant. This wasn't about chasing orgasms, although I knew I would find one regardless; it was never a question of 'if' with Camden. But our haste to unite wasn't about pleasure, it was simply about feeling each other, letting each other come home after being apart.

I didn't have words for him, so instead I brought his mouth back to mine and tilted my hips up to meet his length. He slid in, filling me perfectly, and we both gasped at the sensation. He pulled out slowly, then sank back in and stilled, his mouth hovering over mine, both of us breathing each other in.

I was signing up for a lifetime of a lot of things with Camden. Ups and downs. Good times and bad. Births and deaths. Sadness, happiness, stress, joy, disappointment, anger, but most of all I signed up for a lifetime of love. I fucking loved him so much, and there were few times when I realized how much I loved him more than when we were together that way—naked and crazed for each other. Our relationship wasn't all about sex, but that's one way I knew he was the one, because sex with anyone else never made me feel so alive as it did with him. I'd never wanted a lifetime with anyone before, but the way Camden touched me and cherished me in all ways, especially physically, made me realize being with anyone else would be a terrible mistake.

He was mine.

And I was his.

"Riley," he rasped, his forehead dropped to mine, his breaths just grunts and growls. "I can't get deep enough. I can't get close enough."

"You're everywhere," I promised.

"Fuck," he whispered as he pressed his face to my neck, his hands reaching down and pulling my ass up toward him, plunging deeper into me still.

"Yes," I cried, wanting everything he had to give me. I wrapped my legs around his waist, hooking my ankles behind his back, and let him take me wherever he needed.

He was rutting against me and I could've sworn he was trying to crawl inside of me, to eliminate the boundaries where I ended and he began, to meld us into one. With each stroke I was pushed higher, closer to that euphoric cloud of bliss. The white-hot pleasure sparked in my core and grew wildly until the waves of heat were pulsing down my legs and causing my belly to flip and contract, my entire body shuddering under his, shaking with uncontrolled abandon.

"I love watching you come." His voice was a harsh growl, low and gravelly, and it sent me over the edge.

I came hard, my entire body contracting, mouth gaping, cries echoing in the emptiness of the house. I thought perhaps I'd think about it later and be mortified, but in that moment, there was nothing in my mind except Camden and the way he was making me feel. The security he offered, the insatiable depth to which he hungered for me, and the blatant need he had for me. For some strange reason—which I was only starting to somewhat understand—the way he needed me made me feel safe.

I wanted so badly to give that same sense of security back to him too.

"Tell me what you need," I whispered after I'd come down from my mega-orgasm, flutters of electricity still igniting from the rhythmic thrust he was consistently delivering.

"Just tell me you're mine." His words sent me down two paths simultaneously. My heart ached, hating that he needed the reassurance, but it also soared knowing he wanted me forever.

"Always," I breathed against his neck. "I'll always be yours."

My words seemed to be his undoing as his thrusts quickened and his hands became rougher, grabbing me and putting me wherever he wanted, wherever felt best. I would let him use my body until the end of time if he'd let me.

I knew he was close when each time his hips plunged forward his grunts grew louder and longer, until eventually he stilled, seated fully inside me, straining with the exertion of pleasure. He collapsed but rolled to the side so as not to crush me, keeping his arms around me and pulling me toward him. We were both breathing heavily, a sheen of sweat coating our bodies, but I was content to let him hold me. Forever, even, if he'd have me.

I couldn't wait for forever.

"An hour ago I would've said no more business trips because I miss you when you're not around," Camden said, still breathing a little heavy.

I turned to look up at him, wondering what his next words would be.

"But if the welcome home sex is always that good, I might reconsider my stance."

"Hmm," I said, half in agreement and half in jest. "Is the counselor willing to enter into negotiations?" I teased.

"Welcome home sex *and* hot lawyer talk? You're too good to me, babe." His arms wrapped tighter around me, pulling me closer, and he pressed a kiss to my forehead.

We fell quiet again and I began to drift off, completely sated and ready for a nap, when Camden suddenly jerked, his arm tightening around me.

"I totally forgot about your surprise."

"My surprise?" My voice was groggy but I leaned up on one elbow as he jumped out of bed and pulled on his boxer briefs.

"Yeah, here," he said, tossing me his T-shirt. "Put that on and come with me."

I groaned and rolled out of bed, pulling the shirt over my head.

"Babe, I'm tired," I complained as I pulled my panties back on.

"You'll love it, I promise," he said, taking me by the hand and pulling me out of the room.

"Will I love it more than welcome home sex?"

He stopped walking at my words and turned back toward me, his hand coming up to frame my cheek, a sexy smirk on his face.

"Nothing is better than welcome home sex."

I couldn't help but smile back at him.

"Okay, close your eyes."

"Really?" I asked, cocking a hip and resting my hand on it.

"Requirement of receiving the surprise."

I let out a dramatic sigh and rolled my eyes, but then I closed them. He took me by the hand and led me down the hallway, then turned, and I knew we were in the spare bedroom. I heard him position himself behind me and he placed his hands on my shoulders, aiming me in the direction he wanted.

"Okay, open up."

When I opened my eyes, they darted all around at first, trying to land on whatever it was I was looking for, so it took a few moments for my brain to figure out what was going on. The first thing I latched onto was the new chair in the corner. It was oddly shaped, like a circle with a back. It was flat and pretty big. It could easily fit both of us. Then I caught a glimpse of the bookshelves. The next thing I noticed was the books on the shelves. My books. All of them.

"Did you make me a reading nook?" I turned to gasp at him, but then I swept my gaze back to the chair. I walked toward it and then noticed the table next to it with a new lamp that gave off a soft golden light.

"Do you like it?" He sounded shy, as if he was afraid I'd hate what he'd done for me.

"What? Are you kidding? When did you do this?"

He shrugged, and I swear if he'd been wearing pants he would have stuck his hands in the pockets. "While you were gone."

"Babe," I cried, drawing the name out. "Of course I like it. I love it. This is amazing."

"You always used to cram yourself in that tiny chair in your apartment and read by the window. I thought it would be nice if you had a big comfy chair somewhere quiet."

"You're the absolute best," I said as I wrapped my arms around his waist and stared up at him, more than likely with stars dancing in my eyes. I was stupidly in love with the man. He clasped his hands behind my back and rested them right above my ass.

Besides the things he'd put in the room for me, it was bare. "Will you put your desk in here?" I asked, snuggling in closer. "I'm imagining spending nights in here reading while you're working at your desk."

"That can be arranged." He leaned down and kissed my forehead, then pulled back. I noticed the space between his eyebrows crinkled. "You're not upset it won't be a nursery?"

I couldn't help the laugh that erupted from me. "No, I am definitely not upset you didn't surprise me with a nursery." I laughed some more and rested my face against his chest. "Why in the world would you even ask that?"

He shrugged again. "I'm just checking."

"No babies," I said, giving his ass a squeeze with both hands, trying to lighten the mood a little. "Not for a couple years, okay? Let's get the house under our belt, get married, have a fantastic honeymoon where we can drink all we want and not have to worry about who will watch our child, and then we can start talking about kids."

"Counselor is agreeing to revisit the procreation contract at a later date?" he asked and then winked.

"Sure," I replied, feigning exasperation.

"But does the counselor agree to frequent and tedious rehearsal procreation activities?"

"Sure." That time I was giggling as I said the word.

187

Chapter Seventeen
Riley

The next morning, I hadn't even made it to my desk before the phone was ringing.

"Riley Smith's desk," I answered, a little out of breath.

"Good morning, Riley. Can you meet me in my office when you get a moment?"

I hadn't heard from Rose since we'd left the caterer with Lily and her mother. I'd given her a status update, but that was before all the proverbial shit hit the Penelope fan.

"Absolutely, I'll be right there."

"Great." The line went dead and I let out sigh.

I put my things away, grabbed my tablet for notes on the very slim chance I wasn't getting canned, and then headed toward her office.

I caught Rachel's gaze as I walked past the row of desks in the open workspace portion of the office, and she gave me a hesitant smile. Something was up, and if I wasn't unemployed later, I would definitely need to figure out what had her forcing a smile at me. Jasper wasn't at his desk yet, but I was sure if anyone knew what was going on, it would be him. Naturally.

Rose was behind her desk looking just as perfect as she always did. Not one hair out of place, makeup perfectly applied in a way that looked both natural and phenomenal at the same time. She gave me a professional smile as I pulled open the door, and I tried to return it, though I probably looked more like I was going to vomit because that was how I felt.

"Good morning, Riley."

"Morning. Are you feeling better?" I asked as I took the seat across from her like I always did. For some strange reason, I always took the seat on my right, leaving the chair on the left open.

"I am, thank you for asking. I was gone both the days you were, recuperating, but I'm feeling much better now."

"That's good to hear."

"Let's talk about how the trip went."

"Okay," I said slowly, trying to figure out what exactly she wanted to know. Rose had always been a straight shooter, very no-nonsense, so it was a little alarming that she would ask such a broad question. I needed her to be the old Rose in that moment. I just wanted her to rip the bad-news Band-Aid right off. "Well, Lily found a dress and it's perfect for her theme and colors, and she looked stunning in it. Did she send you a photo? I have one on my phone if you want to see."

"She did send me a photo, and I agree—it's perfect."

"Right." I nodded, feeling like I was completely floundering. "Well, after the dress appointment, we moved on to catering, which was also a success. The chef had everything prepared and it was all incredible. Lily made some great choices and, again, stayed true to her vision for the reception. I'm confident we're in line for a successful event."

Rose didn't respond for a moment, then said, "That's great. Thank you again for covering for me. I wish I'd been well enough to go."

"I totally understand. I thought it was a productive trip."

"And I hear you found yourself a dress even?" she asked, her tone unreadable. She didn't sound angry, but she didn't sound like a girlfriend asking for details either.

My heart rate spiked and I immediately went into panic mode thinking about how difficult it would be to make a mortgage payment without an income. I had images flashing through my mind of myself with a headset on taking orders at a drive-thru, covered in grease every day and coming home smelling like fried food.

"Oh, um, well…." I couldn't find any words. I was torn between apologizing and acting as though everything was fine. I truly didn't feel as though I'd done anything wrong, but damn, I wanted to keep my job.

"Listen," Rose started as she stood from her desk.

This is it. This is the moment I lose my job.

I'd never been fired before in my life. I didn't want to do the walk of shame through the building with a box full of my personal belongings, escorted out by security. We didn't actually have security, but that wasn't the point.

"Penelope and I have been friends a long time," Rose said as she walked around her desk and took the chair I'd left vacant, sitting right next to me. "No one understands better than I that she can be a little dramatic at times."

Say nothing. It's a trap!

"I also understand that you and Penelope have your own past, which complicates the situation further."

I still remained silent.

"I think it's best we just lay everything out in the open and get this over with."

Shit. Shit. Shit.

"Between you and me, Penelope is still trying to find herself. I love her and she's so brave and smart, but she hasn't found her niche yet. When Lily asked me to help her plan her wedding instead of leaning fully on Penny, well, I think that hurt her feelings. She was feeling a little useless and a lot sorry for herself, so she fabricated some drama. I'm sorry you found yourself in the middle of it."

My moral fiber wouldn't let me stay quiet any longer.

"She didn't fabricate it though, Rose. I did find a wedding dress. But I want you to know that I was *not* using company time for personal business. I happened to see a dress, Lily noticed that I liked it, and the consultant put it on hold for me. I didn't even try it on until after all my business with Lily was complete. I would never do something as unprofessional as try on a dress while assisting a client. *Never.*"

Rose smiled, and that time, it looked genuine and inviting.

"Riley," she said with a laugh. "Of course you wouldn't, and you have to know I already knew that about you." She reached out and rested her hand on my forearm for a short moment, but I couldn't deny that it helped ease the tension that had been building. "I knew without a doubt that Penny was having a moment and she needed somewhere to place her frustration. She's my best friend, but that doesn't mean I can't see her faults. I knew you weren't doing anything inappropriate."

"Oh my gosh." My breath rushed out of me, my hand coming to my chest. "I'm so glad to hear you say that. I thought for sure you had called me in here to fire me."

"Fire you? What? No, you're my best coordinator."

Her praise was so welcome in that moment; it almost shocked me how badly I needed to hear her say those words.

"I just heard what she was telling you and it sounded terrible."

"Yes, but it also sounded like someone who needed an ear. I wasn't your boss when she called me, I was her best friend. And you should know that Penny called me back an hour later and apologized and told me the truth about everything that had happened."

"I'm sorry. I should have been the one to tell you."

"Don't apologize, Riley. That's my job today. You found yourself in a difficult situation and I think you handled it wonderfully. You were alone, on a job location, and dealing with personal issues that weren't your own. I put you in that position by asking you to step in for me with my friends. This is one of the issues that arises when you mix friends and business. So if anyone's at fault, it's me. I hope you won't hold it against me going forward."

I had to keep my mouth from dropping open in shock at her words. "I have to admit, this is not the way I pictured this conversation going."

"I'm sorry you were worried."

"Okay, now you don't have to apologize. I didn't think I'd done anything wrong, aside from maybe having words with Penelope, but I definitely didn't think you had any blame. So let's just agree it was a tricky situation and move past it."

Rose sagged with what looked like relief and then smiled again. "I'm happy you feel that way. Now," she said as she reached for my forearm again, "can I see your dress? Lily said it was beautiful."

Rose and I both knew from extensive personal experience that no bride who'd chosen a wedding dress walked around without a photo ready.

"Yes," I said with excitement. I'd show that picture to a stranger on the street if I thought they might want to see it. I pulled up the photo gallery on my phone, found the one of the dress on the hanger, and turned the screen toward her.

"Oh, Riley," she breathed. "It's beautiful."

"I know, right? I saw it and couldn't look away."

"I totally understand. And with your legs, it probably looks fantastic on."

I swiped the screen to the left and a photo of me in the dress appeared.

"Yep, legs look great," she said with a laugh. "Looks like you'll be planning a summer wedding with that length."

I shrugged. "Or we'll get married somewhere warm."

"Are you thinking of a destination wedding?" she asked excitedly.

It occurred to me that Rose and I had never just had a regular conversation like the one we were having then. Rose's guard had dropped around me in the past couple of weeks, and I couldn't help but notice that I *liked* Rose. A lot. She was a considerate and warm person when she dropped the icy glass walls she usually had around herself at all times.

Perhaps it was because I'd traveled with her and spent time with her and her friends, but she didn't feel just like my boss anymore. She also felt like a friend.

"I was having a hard time planning the wedding, or even choosing a date, but once I put the dress on, all of a sudden the wedding can't happen fast enough. So if we can't make it happen this summer, we might just have to go somewhere warm."

"Well, I hope it goes without saying, but if you need any help, don't hesitate to ask or use Rachel or Jasper." She reached out and that time her hand rested on my arm and she gave me her warmest smile yet. "You deserve the best wedding, Riley. I mean that. Anything I can do to help, it would be an honor."

"Thank you," I managed to squeak out, overwhelmed by her sudden, yet genuine, offer and support.

"Any time." She took a breath and then stood, walking back to her desk. "I took a look at your schedule this week and you're packed. Let me know if you need anything in terms of support or backup." And just like that, Rose fell back into her boss role beautifully. Honestly, I was almost more comfortable with Boss Rose—she was more familiar to me.

"Ah, yes, busy days. Rachel is working with me on most of it though, so I should be okay."

Rose nodded and then sat in her high-back chair. "She does great work."

"Indeed. Thank you for everything, Rose."

"Like I said, any time."

I nodded and then made my way out the door, taking the hint that I was indeed being dismissed. I'd spent a good amount of time between Arizona and that morning worrying about what Rose would have to say regarding Penelope, and even in my most rational and reasonable imaginings, none of them ended with me walking out with praise from Rose, let alone an apology.

I headed to my office, sat down, and let out a high sigh, dropping my head into my hands. I spent a few moments just breathing, thanking my lucky stars that I still had the job I loved.

I was pulled from my breathing exercises when I heard a light knock on the door. I snapped my head up and saw Rachel in the doorway, hand paused from rapping on the doorjamb.

"Hey, welcome back," she said hesitantly.

"Hi, come in," I said, waving her in the room. "Do you have time to status right now?"

"I'm all yours."

"Promises, promises," I teased. "Hey," I said a little louder than I meant, caught off guard by the thought that popped into my mind. "What happened between you and my brother over the weekend?"

I watched with interest as a blush crept over her cheeks.

"Not much at all," she answered.

"That is clearly not enough information." I leaned back in my chair and crossed my arms over my chest. "Spill, woman."

"We talked a little at your party, had a drink, and then he drove me home."

"Did you exchange phone numbers?"

Her blush deepened to a dark red and her eyes widened, obviously not expecting me to ask her such specific and prying questions. I didn't feel bad about it though; he was my baby brother, and I held rights to ask anything I wanted. And even though it took her a few moments to spit the words out, I knew the answer before she gave it to me.

"Yes." She drew the word out, sounding like she was worried about what I was going to ask next.

"I love you, Rachel. And I love my brother. Just make sure he doesn't jerk you around."

"We just exchanged phone numbers, Riley. I haven't even heard from him. It's nothing."

"Oh, it's something. I saw the way he looked at you."

"Well, it doesn't matter how he looked at me if he never contacts me."

The burn in her voice made me think she really wanted to hear from him and might have been a little hurt that she hadn't. It almost made me think there was more to the story than just a ride home.

"He will," I promised. I sort of also hoped he would. Even though I was protective of both my brother and Rachel, there was a big part of me that thought they'd make a great couple. "Okay, let's talk about work. We've got the Gellerman event next weekend, so we're focusing on tying up the loose ends and nailing down the final details. What's on your schedule?"

Like I expected, Rachel switched into work mode effortlessly. "I'm meeting with the site coordinator today, actually, to do a final walk-through. Then early next week I planned a status with Mr. and Mrs. Gellerman to make sure we've got everything they need under control. I was hoping you'd join me for that meeting, but if not, I can definitely handle it on my own." Rachel delivered her spiel all while staring down at her tablet, and I knew she was looking at her calendar.

We spent the next twenty minutes going over schedules and making notes about ideas that came to us or things we needed to check into.

"I feel good about where we are. Lots of work to do, but I think we've got it all covered."

"Busy is good," Rachel replied, then set her tablet on my desk. "How was Arizona?"

"It went all right. It was a little stressful going without Rose, but I managed."

"I think it's really cool that even though she couldn't go, she still sent you. That speaks a lot about how much she trusts you."

"Aw, geez, Rach, stop."

She shrugged. "Just saying."

"Okay, well, thank you, but believe me, having Rose trust me is both wonderful and stressful."

Rachel laughed. "Oh, I believe that."

"I'm going to catch up on some emails and get to work on this proposal that's due tomorrow."

"Okay, I'll keep you posted on anything interesting that pops up."

"Great."

I smiled as she left, thankful to have her on my team and grateful to have a job still at all.

Hours later, I'd only left my desk twice—once for coffee and once for the restroom. Lunch had come and gone, but my butt had not left the chair for food and my stomach was angry at me for it. I opened the bottom drawer of my desk, sifting through the random items I'd accumulated since moving into the office months before: tampons, hair clips, ChapStick, vitamins I never remembered to take, a random cardigan sweater, a phone charger, a travel-sized deodorant, a small hairbrush, a travel coffee mug, a few takeout menus, and what I was looking for—a small box of granola bars. I peeled off the wrapper and took a bite, my stomach growling the entire time I chewed.

Murphy's Law dictated that the first moment I put food in my mouth that day, the phone would ring. I chewed quickly and then swallowed way before I would've liked, then picked up the phone.

"Riley Smith's office, Riley speaking."

"Hey, bitch."

I relaxed at Hadley's preferred greeting.

"Hey, whore."

"Oh, I love it when you talk dirty to me."

"I know. What's up?"

"Calling to see if you want to go shopping with me after work. I need new jeans and I need my official butt judge with me to take in the view from the back."

I couldn't help but laugh. "What kind of best friend would I be if I didn't tell you how good your ass looked in denim?"

"The worst kind."

Again, I laughed.

"I'm swamped today, but I could probably get out of here by six." My stomach rumbled again. "But can we eat first?"

"Dinner and shopping? Sounds like the perfect date."

At her comment, I thought about probing about Justin, but the other line started ringing so I made a mental note to ask her about it over dinner. Or jeans. One or the other.

"Gotta go, Had. Phone's a-ringing."

"Okay, text me where you want to meet. See ya later."

I hung up with a smile, excited to see my best friend after a crazy couple of days.

"What about these?" Hadley turned and bent at the waist, showing me her ass.

"Hmmm," I said while formulating my answer. "Those look like a little too much junk in the trunk."

"In a bad way?" she asked, genuinely perplexed.

"Yeah. Less junk, please." I laughed.

"I didn't realize too much junk was possible," she said as she stood straight. She turned and then considered her own backside in the mirror. "Do you think it's the pockets?"

"I think it's your ass."

"Hey," she whined.

"It's not a bad thing. You just need a pair of jeans that properly cover all that glorious booty. Maybe something with a higher waist."

"Oh, good idea. I have a pair of those in here somewhere."

Of course she did. Hadley was a serious and experienced shopper. I knew my role when she invited me along for this journey—I was expected to offer my opinion, but only really when asked. I knew from experience that if I tried to pick anything out for her, it would be denied. Not because Hadley was some sort of fashion snob, but because I could never quite nail down her ever-changing style. And even though I wasn't quite capable of picking pieces for her, apparently I was qualified to give feedback, which she always considered even if she didn't always agree. And it was a job I was happy to do.

The funny part was, on the flipside, Hadley was always great at picking pieces out for me. But that could be because my style hadn't really evolved much since I met her. I went a little more business professional after we graduated from high school, but my casual wear had always been comfortable and flirty. I wasn't hard to nail down, apparently.

"Did you show Camden the dress?" she asked from behind her closed dressing room door.

"No. That's bad luck. Everyone knows that."

"I just figured you weren't going the traditional route."

"Just because we met in a strange circumstance and then fell hard and fast into a very serious relationship doesn't mean we're untraditional, and it also doesn't mean I'm going to tempt fate by breaking all the rules."

"Well, he's going to love it when he sees it."

My pulse picked up speed at the thought.

"I cannot wait to see his face," I said with a dreamy smile.

"How about these?" she said as she opened the door with flair, then strutted past me in a new pair of jeans.

I watched as her ass sailed by, part of me jealous of all the gifts bestowed upon her back end. Then the other, more rational part of me chimed in and I was reminded that shopping for jeans was never this difficult for me.

"I think those look much better. Your trunk is now full of sexy things, not junk."

"These do look better," she said contemplatively.

"What does Justin think about your ass?" Sometimes it was better to try to catch Hadley off guard.

"He likes it just as much as any other man I've let fondle it."

Even though it wasn't close to what I thought to be the full story of what happened between them, I was shocked she admitted even that much.

"So you let him fondle your ass? Did he get to fondle anything else?"

Hadley and I both turned our heads when we heard a *harrumph* come from another dressing room. The door flew open and an older woman who looked to be about my grandmother's age did her best to stomp toward the exit. The scathing looks she sent both Hadley and me clued us in to the fact that she wasn't impressed with our choice of conversation topic.

The door banged closed with a loud thump, and when my gaze met with Hadley's we both lost our composure to a fit of laughter.

"Oh my God," Hadley said with tears streaming down her face as she bent at the waist. "That granny definitely needs to have her junk fondled."

I laughed so hard I fell over and had to lie down on the bench, my arms wrapped around my belly that ached from laughing too much.

Neither of us was concerned about whether there was anyone else in the dressing room, letting the laughter take us away.

"Oh my word," Hadley finally said, wiping the tears from her face. "That was, by far, the best part of my whole week."

"The granny or the laughter?" I couldn't say it without initiating another small gigglefest.

"All of it." She collapsed on the bench next to me, both of us trying to calm our breathing. "I miss us. We used to laugh like this all the time."

"I know." It was always strange when the really happy moments in your life also made you sad. The emotional roller coaster was real and Hadley and I were in the first car, just about to go over the first drop.

"Why'd you have to go and fall in love with that fantastic man who treats you so well and worships the ground you walk on?" Even though Hadley was trying to make her words sound like a joke, I knew she was serious.

"I'm sorry," I said, leaning my head over against her shoulder.

"No, you're not."

"Well, I'm not sorry I met Camden, but I am sorry you're feeling neglected."

"It's not even neglect. I don't expect you to be single with me forever. It's just kind of alarming watching your best friend fall madly in love. Kind of makes you realize how far apart you are in terms of life goals."

"Hey, just because you're single and I'm getting married doesn't mean you aren't still my very best friend. Nothing changes for me when Camden's around. You know that. If anything, now we have a manservant to bring us drinks and paint our toes."

Hadley laughed again, which was exactly what I was going for.

"He would too."

"I know." I shrugged, trying to look nonchalant. "He loves me."

"I love you too, ya know. He might get to be your husband, but I get to be your oldest and best friend for life."

"Aw, Hads. I love you too." I wrapped my arms around her and tried not to laugh when she let out an incredibly undignified sniffle. She may have even wiped her nose on my shirt, but I didn't bring it up. "You'll find it too, one day. You know that, right?"

Hadley stiffened in my arms.

"One day someone's going to come along and just blow every other man you've ever been with out of the water. He's going to love you for the smartass I know you to be, and he's going to go to the ends of the Earth to make you fall in love with him."

"Well, let's not hold our breath, shall we?"

I laughed. "Okay."

Hadley pulled away, wiping away more tears, then squared her shoulders and pushed her chin up.

"So, these jeans are good, yeah?" She stood and examined herself in the mirror.

"Yeah. Exactly the right amount of junk."

Hadley's gaze met mine in the mirror and she gave me the smile I knew so well.

I knew she'd be okay.

And so would we, because I wasn't willing to allow any other outcome.

Hadley purchased her ass-complimenting jeans and we proceeded to walk through the department store, browsing and stopping to look at anything that caught our eye.

We passed the lingerie section and Hadley's eyes lit up, making me laugh.

"Have you gotten anything to wear under your wedding dress yet?" she asked, eyes wide.

"No. I haven't really had a chance. There's no rush though."

"Oh come on. Let's look. I didn't get to be there when you tried the dress on, so this is the next best thing. Oh, and shoes! Come on, please?"

"Sure," I conceded. I would need lingerie and shoes.

After I told her my size, she dragged me farther into the section, fingering lacy bras and silky panties.

"So, what kind of lingerie do you imagine yourself in?" she asked, paying very close attention to the black leather bralette in her hand.

"Uh, nothing like that." I laughed.

"Obviously. This is for me."

"Of course."

"So, what do you want? Soft and flirty? Super-hot and sexy? Functional?" She stuck a finger in her mouth and made a gagging noise after the last suggestion.

"I think maybe a combination of all three would be best, right? I don't want to be dressed like a sex kitten under my dress, but I definitely want it to be sexy. And it has to hold the girls up or else what's the point?"

She considered my words for a moment, then said, "So let's find a sexy corset top with matching panties. Maybe crotchless."

I had to laugh.

"I don't think they sell crotchless panties at the department store, Had. I think you have to go to a specialty store for that."

"You're probably right. We'll find something that works here, and then I'll see if I can't locate some crotchless panties for you before the big day."

"Aw, what a good maid of honor you are."

Hadley, who had been thumbing through racks of merchandise, halted and turned back to look at me.

"I'm your maid of honor?" Her eyes were wide, her voice so soft.

"Of course you're my maid of honor. Aren't you? I mean, you will be, right?"

And then the tears started again and Hadley and I were crying in the middle of the lingerie section of the department store.

"Are you premenstrual?" she asked as she hugged me, both of us sniffling.

"No, are you?" I said through a little laugh.

"Maybe," she admitted.

We pulled away and were, again, wiping our eyes. "So, is that a yes?"

"Absolutely."

My only response was a smile.

Chapter Eighteen
Camden

I heard Riley's car pull into the driveway, the sound of the engine reminding me that we needed to look into getting her a new car. Her old college clunker was not nearly safe or reliable enough to get her to and from work anymore. I smiled at the idea of trying to convince her to get a newer vehicle, knowing she'd argue with me and I'd be able to persuade her using my favorite negotiation techniques—the kind that involved her naked on the bed and giving me everything I want from her.

When the front door closed, it snapped me out of my daydream and I schooled my features, trying to look calm, cool, and collected.

"Hey, babe," she called out.

"Hey, in the family room."

I heard her heels clicking against the hardwood floor. I couldn't tell you why, exactly, but that sound totally turned me on. It was like she was announcing her entrance, giving me and my body a warning.

She walked right to me, toed off her shoes, sat in my lap, wrapped her arms around my neck, and kissed me hello.

My hands instinctively came to her ass—only to make sure she didn't fall off my lap, of course.

Her kiss was short but effective, her tongue just barely brushing over my bottom lip, teasing me. But when she pulled away, she looked tired.

"Everything okay?" I asked, smoothing my hand up her back.

"Yeah, I think I'm just overly tired. All the traveling and today I was absolutely swamped, and then I went right from work to hang out with Hadley. I think I just need to go to bed."

"Did you have fun with Had?" I reached up and pushed a lock of hair behind her ear, waiting for her response.

"I always have fun with Hadley. She's my favorite."

"Good. What did you end up doing?"

"Dinner and shopping. Oh, I'm sorry I ditched you for dinner. Did you manage all right?"

"Yep, called Justin and we met at a bar." I didn't tell her that Jasper had come with us and that I'd instructed Hadley to keep Riley out for a few hours. "Did you get anything while you were shopping?"

I was prying, but I wanted her to confess to what she'd bought. Kind of wanted to see it too.

"Wedding stuff. Nothing for you to see."

"I thought I couldn't see the dress?"

"Well, I can't show you what I'm going to wear *under* the dress either. That's a surprise too."

Mission accomplished.

"Riley Smith, did you bring sexy things back into this house? And are you keeping them from me?" I asked, running my hand back up her back, trying to coax her closer.

"Oh no," she said, standing. "You are not going to see what I bought. It's for the wedding." She crossed her arms over her chest and I could've sworn she was one second from tapping her foot on the ground.

I held up my hands as if to surrender.

"Okay. I won't see it until the wedding, but it better be worth the wait."

Her shoulders relaxed and her hands dropped to her sides.

"You know it will be."

"Yeah," I agreed. "You ready for bed? I'll rub your back until you fall asleep."

"Hmm," she moaned, making it difficult to not revert to the images of all the sexy things she might have in her bags. "You're the best."

I stood and took her hand, leading her up the stairs to the bedroom where I listened to her tell me all about her day. She told me how Rose didn't fire her, and how Hadley opened up about being sad that Riley was moving on with her life and seemed to be pulling away from their friendship. Women were strange creatures. Justin and I never busted each other's balls for being absent. If I hadn't seen him in a while and I thought about him, I called him up and we went out for a beer. But Riley loved Hadley, so I knew she'd be upset if her best friend told her something like that. The fact of the matter was both Riley and Hadley were prime. I was lucky enough to lure Riley into my snare and keep her, but someday someone was going to snatch up Hadley too. It was inevitable.

She was a little wild and a lot crazy, but that was part of her charm.

Plus, she was hilarious.

Riley told me a story about an old woman in the dressing room, but I couldn't really understand her through all the laughter, so I just watched her while smiling, nodding when I thought it was appropriate.

Riley fell asleep approximately three minutes after I started rubbing her back, which was pretty typical, but I waited a few extra minutes just to make sure she'd stay asleep. When I was confident she was out for the night, I rolled toward my nightstand and picked up my phone, tapping out a text.

Nice work, tonight. She didn't suspect a thing.

I waited for a reply, but it didn't take long.

Don't thank me yet. Wait until your wedding night. I set you up so good, Camden. Don't you forget who shouted her last name to you when she was blowing you off. None of this would be happening if it weren't for me.

I realize this. And I am grateful.

Just remember: my birthday's in September and I like diamonds.

Haha, noted.

She loves you, Cam, and that makes you damn lucky.

I know that too. See you Saturday?

Wouldn't miss it for the world.

The next two days were a strange juxtaposition of passing slowly yet still not filled with enough time. There was so much to do, so many loose ends to tie up. I was afraid we wouldn't get everything done, but somehow we managed. Thursday and Friday, Riley left for work like normal and I got up and readied myself for work just like I always did, but after she kissed me goodbye and drove away, I took off my suit, changed into jeans, and went to work on the plan that had a very short window of opportunity.

Truth be told, Friday night I probably didn't get much sleep at all. I was too wired. Too nervous, too anxious, too excited, too scared out of my mind. But I was also so fucking happy.

When the sun rose on Saturday, part of me wanted to shake her as soon as the light filtered in through the window. I wanted to wake her up and shout my news to the rooftops with her, but I reined myself in—barely.

We'd worked everything out, planned every detail practically down to the minute, and I knew I needed to let her sleep as long as possible. The minutes ticked by slowly, but I cherished every one as I watched Riley sleep.

Finally she roused, eyes fluttering open, back arching, arms stretching over her head.

She finally met my gaze and smiled back at me with the warmth of so much love in her eyes.

"Hey," she said, her voice still scratchy from sleep. "How long have you been awake?"

"A while," I answered, opening my arms and watching as she scooted toward me, wrapping one arm around my middle and resting her head in the crook of my shoulder, just like I knew she would.

"Feeling okay?"

"Yeah, just thinking."

"About?" she prodded.

"Us, the wedding, life."

"So nothing too heavy for a Saturday morning," she said with a laugh.

Her laugh. It was the best sound in the world. I never thought myself to be excessively sentimental, but I loved the way she looked when she laughed and how it made me feel. If Riley was happy, then everything was right in my world.

"Marry me," I asked her quietly.

The side of her mouth tipped up into a small smile. "I've already agreed to that. Are you sure you're feeling okay?"

"Marry me. Today."

"Today?" Her head pulled back and she examined me closer, her brow furrowing in the middle.

"Go with me to Vegas. Marry me. Today."

"We can't get married today."

I expected the resistance at first. Riley was a planner and needed control over all aspects of her life, so I was prepared for a small fight.

"Why not? You've got a dress, and some sexy things to wear under it. I've got a suit. Why wait?"

"What about our parents?"

I gave a shrug. "We'll have a reception sometime this summer."

"You don't think your parents will be mad you got married without them?"

"They'll get over it. Besides, the only person I really want at my wedding is you." I leaned forward and kissed her gently. She kissed me back, but I could tell her mind was reeling.

"We can't elope."

I brought my hand to her face and rubbed my thumb over her bottom lip.

"We can. I want you to be my wife. Let's be wild and crazy, throw caution to the wind, just like we did during halftime on the Jumbotron. Trust me."

"You really want to just get on a plane and get married?"

My heart began thundering as she started to actually consider it. I wanted her to say yes, to agree to focus on us and do something for just the two of us.

"I really want to be your husband."

"Today?"

"Today."

Her eyes darted wildly between mine, back and forth, as she considered my words. I knew she was weighing everything in her mind, trying to justify leaving all our friends and family in the dust and doing something so incredibly huge without them. But finally she gave me the answer I was looking for.

"Yes," she whispered.

"Yes?"

"Yes," she said excitedly, nodding and smiling, eyes filling with tears.

I rolled over her, kissing her, hoping to show her what it meant to me, the relinquishment of control, the fact that she'd give up everything for me, even if I knew shortly she'd realize she wasn't giving up anything.

She kissed me back, her knees bending and pulling up to capture my waist, allowing my hips to sink between her thighs. *Fuck*, how I wanted to peel her clothes off and sink into her, to take that moment and brand it with more than just a kiss, but we had to get moving.

I kissed down her throat and chest, then grabbed her hands and pulled her to a sitting position.

"We've got to get a move on. I'm going to start packing while you get in the shower."

"Is this really happening?" she giggled.

"Yes, get up," I said, tossing a pillow at her.

"Shouldn't we check flights?"

"Babe, it's Vegas. They've got flights all the time to Vegas. We'll book one when we get to the airport."

"Oh my God," she cried, covering her face with her hands. "Hadley's going to kill me."

"She'll be fine. *Get. Up.*"

She threw the covers off her body and went to the bathroom, mumbling to herself about her whole family hating her. But she was smiling, so I knew it was all right.

I heard the water turn on and could tell Riley had gotten in a minute later, so I grabbed my phone and sent off a text.

Operation Vegas Shenanigans is go for green. I repeat, Operation Vegas Shenanigans is go for green.

Read you loud and clear. Bridal squadron is on the move and our ETA is eleven hundred. All soldiers present and accounted for. Over and out, old buddy.

You totally ruined the military theme of this whole operation by calling me old buddy.

Beggars can't be choosers, Camden. I am far from a military man.

Right, but your sign off sounded more like a trucker than a navy seal. I'm just saying.

Shut up and get your bride to Vegas.

I had to laugh. It was going to be a great day.

I helped Riley pack, which turned out to be more of a production than I'd anticipated. Packing for a quick trip was not the same as packing for your wedding. That was obviously an oversight on my part. She was putting things in her bag I'd never even seen her use before. Who knew eyelash curlers were even a thing? And more contraptions to straighten, curl, or dry her hair went into the bag than I even knew she owned. Needless to say, by the time we got out the door, we were pressed for time. I couldn't let it show though. No, there was still one more surprise in store for Riley, and I desperately wanted to watch her enjoy it.

Chapter Nineteen
Riley

The Batmobile sped down the freeway toward the airport and I still couldn't believe what was happening. So many thoughts were filtering through my mind, and I couldn't land on just one. I was worried about my mom, about hurting her feelings by getting married without her. I was also worried about hurting Hadley's feelings. I'd just asked her the night before to be my maid of honor and now I was completely ditching her.

I felt terrible.

But I also felt wonderful.

I wanted nothing more than to end the day as Camden's wife. I wanted to fly to Vegas and find a chapel, get married, and just be with my husband. Sure, I wanted my family and friends around, but I wanted Camden more. I wanted this experience with him, to wake up one sunny morning and just *get married*. It was crazy and perfect.

In the back of my mind I suspected that everyone I cared about would be understanding in the end. They might be shocked or surprised, but they'd know it was perfect for Camden and me.

And of course Camden would do something like that. He'd listen to me, hear my worries and frustrations, and he'd take matters into his own hands to ease whatever was a burden to me. So there we were, getting ready to fly to Vegas and become husband and wife.

"Do you think I should text Hadley? Just tell her what's going on? I don't want her to be hurt."

He shrugged and said, "If it'll make you feel better."

Camden took the airport exit off the freeway as I pulled out my phone and tapped out a text to my best friend.

Don't be mad. Camden and I are eloping. It was a last-minute decision and I'm so happy, but I don't want you to be hurt.

I waited for a reply, but after a few moments of nothing, I knew I'd just stress until I heard from her.

"I should've called. Now I'm just worried that she's read the text and is really mad."

Camden's hand came to rest on my knee.

"It'll be okay, babe. Promise."

He parked the car in long-term parking and we loaded onto a shuttle, all the while my nerves starting to get the better of me. Was this really the best decision? Were we being irrational? Impulsive? Just when I hit my anxiety threshold, the point where I felt like I might start hyperventilating, Camden took my hand and brought the back of it to his lips, kissing me gently, absentmindedly. He didn't even look like he'd done it on purpose or with any thought or consciousness. It was within his nature to comfort me, to smooth my rough edges.

And I decided to simply let it go. At that moment, I was at peace with the decision we'd made. In fact, I was downright excited about it.

"I love you," I said, leaning my head against his shoulder as we drove toward the main departure terminal.

"More than anything, I love you," he replied, kissing the top of my head.

Yeah. We were going to be all right.

The shuttle stopped and everyone unloaded. I immediately realized I had no idea what we were going to do. We still needed tickets. We had no plan whatsoever besides being unprepared.

"Should we go check the departure board and see if there are any flights coming up? Or should we just start at one carrier and try our luck?" I pulled my phone from my purse. "We could probably find out online."

Suddenly my phone was snatched from my hand and Camden put it in his back pocket.

"No phones."

"No phones? We're going to Vegas, not back in time. Give me my phone back."

"Just trust me."

He arranged the luggage, stacking it in some magical way so he could take my hand, and led me through the airport. My free hand was holding the garment bag with my wedding dress. I could think of no reason to not do as he said, so I followed.

He walked until he came to the beginning of the line to a major airline, then took me with him as he wove his way through the serpentine line.

"So we're just going to see when their first flight is?" I asked anxiously.

"Babe, relax," he said and kissed me on the nose condescendingly. Well, he more than likely didn't mean it that way, but I didn't like being shushed.

"I can't relax. We're at an airport with no real plan. This is, quite literally, my worst nightmare." Panic was edging every word I spoke.

Camden bent his knees so our eyes were even and said, "Trust me." He held my gaze for a moment and then stood up straight. All I could do in response was let out a breath I'd been holding for too long. He squeezed my hand and it almost helped. Almost.

It took a few minutes to get to the front of the line, but finally we were called to a customer service agent and she greeted us with a smile.

"Hello, there. Where are we headed today?"

"Las Vegas," Camden said coolly, placing his driver's license on the counter. "Babe, give her your license." He nudged me with his elbow.

"What?" I asked, confused.

"I'll just need your license to check you into your flight," the woman on the other side of the counter said with a smile.

"What flight?" I'd never been more confused than at that moment.

"The flight I booked us a few days ago," Camden said, as though he'd just told me about loading the dishwasher.

"What? You booked a flight a few days ago?" I practically screamed.

"We can talk about this while we're waiting in line for security. Our flight leaves in an hour, so get a move on, yeah?" he said, a smile twinkling in his eye.

I gaped at him for a moment but then finally pulled myself together enough to get out my license.

"Any exciting plans for Las Vegas?" the woman asked as she typed on her keyboard and checked our IDs.

"We're getting married," Camden said proudly.

"If I don't kill him before then," I added, only half joking.

"I'm sure you'll work it out." She winked at Camden and gave us our boarding passes. He handed over our luggage and then took my hand again. "Enjoy your trip," she said sweetly as we walked away, heading toward security.

"Camden Joshua Rogers, you better tell me what the hell is going on. Right now."

"You came home from Arizona and were talking so much about getting married sooner than later, so I decided to just make it happen. I didn't want you to stress about it, so I booked the tickets ahead of time. I wanted to surprise you." He looked over at me. "Did it work?"

That sexy, playful, mischievous gleam was back in his eye, and it was difficult to stay mad at him when I knew he did all this because he thought it would make me happy.

"I'm definitely surprised."

"Mission accomplished, then." He leaned down and kissed me quickly, then pulled me to the line that would lead us through security.

I tried to ask him questions, to figure out how he got all this past me, but he seemed preoccupied with getting through the security line.

I gave the TSA agents a very thorough lecture about how my dress was very delicate and instructed them to be very careful as they ran it through their machine. Lucky for them they heeded my advice and used gentle hands.

"What gate are we at?" I asked Camden as he pulled his shoes back on his feet after being scanned.

"E-14."

"Are we late?"

He looked at his watch. "No, we're good."

I held out my hand to him. "Let's go, then."

We walked silently through the airport, both of us familiar enough with it to know which direction to go in.

I saw the E gates starting at number one, and my stomach slipped a little thinking that we were getting close to boarding a plane to get married.

"This is crazy," I said quietly, almost to myself, but he heard me.

"It is crazy, but it's also awesome."

I laughed. "That too."

"Anything in particular you want to do in Vegas aside from marry me?" He tugged me closer and I went willingly.

"Anything, really. I've never been there."

"I'll have to show you a good time, then." He waggled his eyebrows at me, making me laugh.

The numbers on the gate were getting higher, and when fourteen finally came into view I could hardly contain myself.

"This is probably the best surprise in the history of surprises," I said wistfully. I looked up at him, hoping he could see how happy I was.

"Well, hold off on that award for just a minute."

"What? Why?"

"Surprise!"

I heard a chorus of voices yell and startled at the noise, my head snapping toward the gate. It was then that I realized what was really happening.

Standing in front of me was everyone I was sad would be missing our wedding. My mom, Hadley, Camden's parents, Justin, Tripp, Jasper, and Rachel.

"What the fuck?" I gasped, my hand covering my mouth. Everyone swarmed me, laughing and hugging.

When Rachel wrapped me in a hug, she took my dress from me, giving me a wink. "What in the world is going on?" I asked, still overwhelmed at the sight of all the people closest to me waiting at the gate for our flight. "What are you all doing here?"

"You didn't think I'd let you go to Vegas without me, did you?" Hadley asked.

"But how?" I asked, my hand still covering my face.

"Your husband-to-be put us all to work planning this whole thing," Jasper added with a smile. "You came back from Arizona all dreamy-eyed and armed with a dress, so Camden made a plan and we executed."

I turned to look at Camden, who had stepped back and was now just observing the situation.

"You did all this? You planned this?"

He shrugged, always trying to let my praise roll right off him. "I knew you wanted to get married, I knew you'd want your friends and family around you, and I knew if you tried to plan it you'd lose your mind. Vegas seemed like a fun way to combine a wedding and a family vacation."

I walked straight to him and threw my arms around his neck.

"I love you so much, Camden Rogers."

His strong arms wrapped around me, holding me so close I could feel his heartbeat through his thin shirt. I loved the way his body felt pressed against mine, and I wanted to feel the way we lined up perfectly for the rest of my life. "I know, Riley. There's nothing I love more than what just happened. Watching you smile and light up with happiness, the last few days was worth all the stress just for that moment." He pulled back and smiled widely. "You should have seen your face. You had no idea."

"I really didn't," I said through laughter and a few tears. "And you." I turned, pointing at Hadley. "You knew about all this and didn't tell me? I sent you that text a half hour ago so worried you'd be mad at me for eloping and you didn't even respond."

"Listen, if you eloped without me, I *would* be mad at you."

"Wait, did you know about this when we went shopping?"

"Of course I did," she said, pointing at her jeans. "I needed these for the trip. And you needed some stuff too, if I'm not mistaken." She winked at me and all I could do was shake my head.

I was baffled.

I'd never been so surprised.

My mom hugged me and told me how she'd flown up the day before and stayed with my brother. It was when her arms were around me that I nearly broke down, realizing what Camden had really given me. He was responsible for so much goodness in my life, I didn't know how I would ever repay him for making it so easy to love him, and to let him love me.

"Don't cry," my mother whispered as she took in the tears welling in my eyes. She framed my face with her hands and kept whispering. "This is the happiest day of your life, sweetheart. That man would walk through fire for you. You're going to spend the rest of your life with him and it's going to be so wonderful."

It was a whirlwind. Every emotion imaginable was swirling around me while my closest friends and family stood by, caught in the storm. I was so incredibly happy but still wiping a tear away every few minutes, completely overwhelmed. We boarded the plane and I was sure the flight crew was going to kick us off. We were happy and loud and rowdy. Luckily, I think the crew and the other passengers saw us as excited, not disruptive. Everyone was on their way to Las Vegas, and they all seemed down to party too.

We took our seats, Camden on one side of me, Hadley on the other—very reminiscent of the first time we met. I let my gaze trail over him, from head to thighs, and had a flutter in my belly.

"So," Hadley said, pulling me out of my Camden haze. "Once we land, we'll go to the hotel and drop off all our stuff, but then it's go time. You've got a hair appointment, followed by a makeup appointment, and then a wedding to get to." She smiled widely and clapped her hands excitedly. "This is going to be so fun."

"Wow, maybe you missed your calling as a wedding planner," I teased.

"Hey, I don't want to do this for a living, but you know I'd do anything for you."

"I know. And you don't know how much I appreciate all this. I still can't even believe it."

"Well, Rachel and Jasper helped a lot. I can't take all the credit."

"You're still going to stand up with me, right? Be my maid of honor?"

"Of course. I even have a killer dress."

"You're going to kill Justin, aren't you?" Camden added, interjecting himself into the conversation.

Hadley just shrugged. "I look amazing in my dress, and he's going to have to deal with it."

"Is Justin your best man?" I asked Camden, realizing we'd never spoken about it.

"Actually, no. Greg is on a flight to Vegas as we speak."

I'd heard a lot about Greg, even talked on the phone with him a time or two when Camden had put him on speakerphone. They'd been best friends since childhood, but Greg moved to the East Coast for college and never returned. His wife had their second baby around the time Camden and I met, and Greg, now a father of two, wasn't traveling much.

"Are you serious?" I asked, shocked and excited that Camden would get to have his best friend by his side for his wedding.

"I am. I called him, told him what was happening, and he made it happen. His brother, Ben, is coming too. It's going to be good to see them."

"We owe his wife a fruit basket or something. What a saint, letting her husband go to Vegas while she stays home with two kids. Too bad she couldn't come." I was looking forward to the day I could meet Greg and his wife.

"She wanted to but wasn't ready to leave the baby."

"Understandable," I replied. "Maybe soon we can go visit them."

"That sounds like a great idea."

"Is this Ben guy single?" Hadley asked, and I shot her a withering look. "What? I'm just curious."

"You can't seriously be thinking about hooking up with someone with Justin around."

She shrugged. "He doesn't have a say in anything I do."

I kept my mouth shut and fought the urge to roll my eyes. I had a feeling Justin had a very strong hold on her, and she was fighting it tooth and nail.

"So, what color is your dress?" I asked, attempting to change the subject. Luckily, she took the bait. The next two hours was spent ironing out all the last-minute details of a last-minute wedding.

It was the best two hours ever.

Chapter Twenty
Camden

The last few days had been ridiculously stressful. Keeping secrets from Riley wasn't my favorite thing, even if I knew she'd love them. I loved surprising her, and I was fairly certain she'd enjoy what I'd planned, but it was always risky to plan a woman's wedding without her input. Luckily for me, in so many ways, Riley only cared about marrying me, not about when or how. The fact that she'd agreed to elope before she knew her whole family and all her friends would be there meant more to me than she'd probably ever realize.

The flight went smoothly and it was the most relaxed I'd been in days. I looked out the window, Riley's hand in mine the whole time, and listened to the woman I loved chattering happily with her best friend about our wedding.

My parents were a few rows ahead of us, sitting with Riley's mom. Justin was next to Jasper, and Rachel and Tripp managed to snag two seats next to each other as well. I didn't think Riley had noticed, and I wasn't going to be the one to point it out to her either.

"Oh no," I heard Riley say, her tone suddenly worried. "You didn't get a bachelor party." She rested her hand lightly on my thigh. Fuck, I loved her hands on me. Any spot would do, but I knew how much she liked my thighs, always caught her sneaking peeks at them, so to feel her hand there was a huge turn-on.

I had to laugh at her concern.

"Babe, I don't need a bachelor party."

Her eyebrows drew together in confusion.

"You don't think a week or month from now you'll regret not having one last crazy night with your man friends? You don't want to watch a woman take her clothes off while she spins around a pole? Stick dollar bills in her G-string?"

"Is the woman on the pole you?"

Hadley snorted in her seat.

"You don't want to see me on a pole," Riley scoffed. "I tried one of those pole dancing classes before and I was a hot mess."

"She really was," Hadley added with yet another snort.

"Okay, first of all, we're going to talk about this you getting on a pole thing again. I can't believe I didn't know this about you. In fact, I think I might have one waiting for us when we get home." Truly, the image of Riley seductively swinging around a stripper pole with only thin scraps of lace covering her body went straight to my dick. I was beginning to regret inviting everyone to come with us. Surely they'd never let us live it down if I dragged Riley into the bathroom of the airplane. "And secondly, no, I don't need to watch some random woman take her clothes off. I've been there and done that, and I refuse to treat our marriage like the death of a time in my life that I can't wait to be rid of. Marrying you isn't the end of something, it's the beginning."

Her eyes went soft like they did whenever she thought I was being sweet. The truth of the matter was it was easy to be sweet with Riley. I loved her, and that love was evident in the way I treated her, revered her, cherished her. I didn't understand how a man in love *didn't* treat his woman with utter respect and kindness. It seemed like second nature to me.

I used my forefinger and thumb to gently tilt her chin up so I could look her in the eye.

"Do you need a bachelorette party?"

"No," she whispered.

"Sure?"

She nodded slightly, as much as she could anyway with her chin between my fingers.

"Okay," I replied and then kissed her gently.

"Don't worry, guys. When I get married we can have huge bachelor and bachelorette parties. I'll make up for it," Hadley said, then took a sip of her Coke.

I rolled my eyes and Riley laughed.

The thing was I believed her. Hadley would definitely mourn the end of her single life. I couldn't even imagine her ever settling down anyway.

"Good afternoon, everyone. This is your pilot speaking. We are about to make our final descent into Las Vegas. The temperature is a cool ninety-two degrees, and the skies are sunny as far as the eye can see. We hope you enjoyed flying with us. Flight crew, prepare for landing."

"I'm so excited," Riley said, practically bouncing in her seat.

I gave her leg a squeeze and then took her hand.

The plane touched down and Jasper and Rachel went immediately into event planning mode, which I couldn't have been more grateful for. Everything was planned, every last detail taken care of. We made our way to baggage claim and that's where I saw Greg and Ben waiting.

"Hey, man," I said, shaking Greg's hand and pulling him into a hug, patting his back. It had been too long since I'd seen him, and I couldn't fully express how much it meant that he was there. "It's good to see you."

"I wouldn't have missed it for the world, Cam." We pulled back, but I held onto him for a moment more. "Ally is sad she couldn't make it. She sends her best."

"We totally get it," I replied honestly. Ally was a wonderful mother and I couldn't hold it against her for staying home. "I guess I'm just lucky she let you come at all," I added with a laugh.

"Ha-ha," he said, also laughing. His eyes slid to my side where I knew Riley was standing. "This must be the woman crazy enough to take you on."

With more pride than I could verbalize, I put my arm around Riley and introduced her to my best friend. "Greg, this is Riley, my fiancée and soon-to-be wife. Riley, this is Greg, my best friend since forever."

"It's nice to meet you," she said, holding her hand out to him.

"None of that," he said as he playfully took her hand and pulled her into a hug.

"Ben," I said, looking to Greg's brother. "I'm so glad you guys could make it." We hugged and I introduced him to Riley as soon as Greg let her go.

"I've heard so much about both of you," Riley said sweetly, wrapping her arm around my waist and leaning into my side, fitting herself against me, exactly where she belonged.

"Same goes," Greg replied with a warm smile. I knew I wanted Greg at my wedding, but it hadn't occurred to me how much his presence would make everything feel even more perfect—if that was even a thing. I would have married Riley under any circumstance. Seriously. But having my best friend to stand by my side made everything better.

"Okay, folks, I don't want to rush a reunion, but we only have a limited amount of time to get to the chapel, so let's get the show on the road." Jasper's voice pulled us all out of our bubble and I had to laugh.

"Is he always like this?" I asked Riley.

"Yes. That's why he's so awesome at his job."

"Thanks, babe," Jasper replied, winking at my girl. "But your praise isn't going to save you today. Get your sweet ass moving."

Everyone laughed, but we all did exactly what he said.

Just like Jasper had promised, there was a large SUV limo waiting for us after we'd all retrieved our bags. My parents had graciously offered to pay for everyone's hotel, the limo, and the wedding site. It was a pretty big bill, but nothing compared to what a huge wedding would end up costing if we'd planned to stay in Portland. My mom was so excited and insisted on covering most of the expenses.

The ride to the Bellagio was invigorating. Everyone was riding a wave of excitement, people were laughing and smiling, and I couldn't help but notice a few had opened a bottle of champagne. It was, by all means, a celebration.

When we arrived at the hotel, my parents checked everyone in and handed each person their room keys, and people started to disappear.

"I'll be up to get you in thirty minutes," Hadley said to Riley. "Thirty minutes, Camden. Do not get her all flushed or sweaty. There's no time to shower before the hair and makeup appointments. So no funny business."

Riley blushed at Hadley's words, but I promised her we'd be on our best behavior.

My mom handed us a key card and, with an enormous smile, said, "They had a suite available, so we upgraded you."

"Mom," I said, shaking my head. "You don't have to do that. We don't need all this. You've done so much already."

"No, no," she said, pushing the key card toward me. "This is what we want to do. We're so happy to be here and we're so happy for both of you. It's the least we can do."

I pulled my mother into a hug, knowing she was close to tears and I didn't want any crying. Not yet, anyway.

"Okay," I whispered. "Thank you."

"We'll see you at the chapel." She pulled back, then turned and walked away. I knew she was trying not to lose her composure.

"She'll be all right," my stepfather said, reaching out to shake my hand. "She's just happy."

"Thank you, for everything," Riley said sincerely.

"For you, Riley, we'd give anything."

"Okay, enough," I said, pulling Riley close to me before she lost it too. She and my stepfather had a tumultuous history, even for such a short relationship, but things were good between them and I knew that meant a lot to Riley.

"Go," he said with a smile. "Get ready for a wedding."

I smiled at him and aimed Riley toward the bay of elevators to take us up to our suite.

A bellhop helped us by wheeling all our bags and Riley's dress up to the room, leaving her and me to take in the opulence of the hotel.

"This is a little crazy," she said right before we entered the elevator.

"It's nice," I agreed. "I can't believe you've never been to Vegas."

She shrugged. "Never had the money to go when I turned twenty-one, and then after that it seemed kind of silly."

"It can be a fun town. Lots to do. You can see concerts, shows, sit and gamble, drink—there's a lot of ways to spend time."

"Well, I'm glad my first time will be with you."

I smirked at her.

"I might not be your first, but I'm gonna be your last," I whispered right before I pressed a kiss against her mouth. I kissed her until the elevator pinged, knowing the bellhop had probably seen way worse than two adults sharing a kiss. It was Vegas, after all.

We followed him down the hallway and it was clear to both of us that our floor was the nicest.

"I think this might have cost your parents a fortune," Riley whispered as the bellhop opened the door.

"Don't think about it. They wanted to give this to us, so let's enjoy it."

The bellhop placed our luggage in the bedroom, showed us the impressive features of the room, and left twenty dollars richer for it. I closed the door behind him and locked it, then walked back to the bedroom, stopping at the threshold and leaning against the doorjamb.

Riley had opened her suitcase on top of the bed and was sorting through everything she'd brought, appearing to make a pile of things she needed to take with her. Suddenly it hit me that in just a few hours she was going to be my wife. I was going to be someone's husband. No, not someone's—Riley's.

I didn't know how I got so lucky to find her and convince her to stick around, but I'd spend forever making sure she never regretted it.

I placed my hand over hers, which was moving around at lightning speed. I'd brought her here to avoid stress, but I could tell her eyes were about to pop right out of her head.

"Babe, calm down. Come here," I said, pulling her away from her things. "Just be with me for a minute."

I sat on the bed and spread my legs, bringing her to stand between my knees. Her hands came to rest naturally on my shoulders, and my hands went to her ass… naturally.

"I can't believe this is happening."

"Don't blink. It'll be over before you know it."

A smile crept across her face. "Good."

"Are you okay with the only sex you have for the rest of your life being married sex?" I used my thumbs to push up the back of her shirt, letting my hands roam against her skin, and watched as she shivered at my touch.

"Is married sex different than what we've been doing for the last couple months?" she asked, breathily.

I shrugged, pulling her closer, lifting her shirt so I could place kisses around her navel. "I don't know," I said between kisses. "I've never had married sex."

"Oh," she panted as I pulled her even closer, forcing her to straddle me. I'd been trying to distract her, to get her mind off the million things surely running through it, but now I was invested. Now I wanted to feel her writhing beneath me. Or on top of me. I wasn't picky.

She came willingly, putting her knees on either side of my hips, settling her core right against my dick, making me groan and wish I could do all sorts of things to her.

I pushed her shirt up over her breasts and took the top swells in my mouth, thumbing her nipples over the lace of her bra.

"Hadley said no funny business."

"I don't want to talk about Hadley right now," I said as I moved my mouth from one breast to the other.

"Okay," she breathed.

I smiled against her skin, then put my mouth over the lace covering the rosy peak and pulled it into my mouth, eliciting a moan from her.

"Cam," she whispered, rocking her core against me, letting out small whimpers at the friction.

"Yeah, babe?"

"We can't have sex right now," she said, even as she ground against me.

"Oh really?" I laughed, pulling down gently on her hips, causing her head to fall back on a sigh.

"No, we shouldn't," she said, even if her body was saying something completely contradictory. She brought her head forward and rested it against my shoulder, wrapping her arms tightly around my neck, pressing the front of her body against mine so that every part of her fit against me. "I don't want to put my wedding dress on all sweaty and sticky."

I wouldn't admit the idea of marrying Riley with part of me still between her legs made me even harder. No. I was going to let that one go. Instead, I simply kissed her. Then we were both startled by a knock at the door.

"See? We didn't even have time." She kissed me quickly and then climbed off my lap.

I let out a frustrated groan and fell back on the bed, thinking about all the awesome husband and wife sex coming my way. I listened as the door opened and then Hadley's voice rang out.

"I told you two no sex," she scolded.

"We didn't have sex!"

"Then why do you look like a cheerleader climbing out of the back seat of the quarterback's car?"

Then I heard Riley's sheepish response. "It was just a little over-the-clothing stuff."

My hands came to cover my mouth to muffle my laughter.

"No time for hanky-panky, Riley. Time to get a move on." I heard Hadley push her way into the room. The next ten minutes were filled with me watching the two of them run around like crazy people, making sure they had everything they needed. They were halfway out the door when I called Riley back.

"Babe?"

"Yeah?" she asked, quite nearly out of breath.

"Aren't you forgetting something?" I asked with a smile.

Her eyes widened a little and she came running back to me, pressing up on her toes to plant a kiss on my lips. "See you at the altar," she said, then laid one more peck on me.

I watched as she ran back toward the door and I called out again. "Babe."

"What?" she said as she turned, that time a little exasperated.

"Dress?"

"Oh shit," she exclaimed and then ran back into the bedroom, only to reappear a few seconds later with the garment bag draped over her arm.

"Thank you," she said as she ran past me. "I love you!"

"Love you too." I was left in the suite alone, laughing.

Chapter Twenty-One
Riley

There'd been so much happening in the last five hours that I couldn't wrap my mind around it all, but the last hour had been the worst. I was never good with hurry up and wait.

Hadley and I had practically run from the hotel back to the limo. My mom, Camden's mom, Rachel, and Jasper were already waiting for us. I was told that the boys would follow after us.

"Where are we going?"

"To the chapel, silly," Jasper had replied.

In my mind, I'd been picturing something really tacky: strobe lights, plastic flowers, and Elvis. But when we pulled up to the chapel I was pleasantly surprised. There were no flashing signs, no one-hour-wedding advertisements. It looked like a perfectly normal and even cute chapel.

"This looks nice," I said, unable to hide the surprise from my voice.

"Trust me," Rachel said with a smile, "Jasper and I were not going to let you get married in some dive. This is the nicest chapel in Vegas, even if it does have a drive-thru window."

"You can get married in your car?" I asked, disbelieving.

"Honey, this is Vegas. Almost anything goes," Jasper said just before exiting the limo.

I'd been sitting in the same chair for an hour, and it wasn't terribly comfortable.

"Are you about ready?" the woman doing my makeup asked.

"I am," I replied, trying not to sound impatient.

"Okay, here you go." She spun the chair around and I faced the large mirror that covered most of the wall.

I almost didn't even believe it was me I was looking at.

I looked like me, just… beautiful. Different, but the same. Bridal. It was strange.

My brown hair had been pulled up into a French twist with curled tendrils framing my face. I knew immediately Camden would appreciate the unobstructed view of my neck. My makeup was light and perfect, dewy pinks and rose colors. I looked like a bride, and it made me realize how close I was to the biggest moment of my life thus far.

"Oh my word," I said, then started fanning my face with my hands.

"Don't cry," the makeup woman said sweetly, swiftly pulling out tissues from her case and dabbing under my eyes. "You'll ruin all my hard work."

"I'm sorry," I replied, still trying to hold back the tears. "I just didn't expect to look so… beautiful."

"Oh, baby," my mother said, coming up behind me and placing her hands on my shoulders. "You look just gorgeous." She was tearing up as well. In fact, everyone in the room had tears in their eyes.

"Stop it, everyone," I said with a laugh. "No more crying. Only laughter."

Everyone followed directions and laughter rang throughout the room. The makeup artist dabbed something on my face again, apparently fixing anything I'd ruined by my few tears.

"Dress time," Hadley singsonged.

"That's my cue to leave," Jasper said, making me laugh. He came to where I was sitting and kissed the air right next to my cheek, avoiding actual contact. "You look amazing, Riley. You're gonna knock his socks off."

"Thank you, Jasper, for everything."

"Are you kidding? This is the most fun I've had since the last time I was in Vegas." He winked and then headed toward the door.

"I'll see you out there, Riley. You do look gorgeous," Rachel gushed.

"Thank you," I said softly. She gave me a small wave as she followed Jasper.

I watched as Hadley started unzipping the garment bag that held my dress. My stomach went absolutely silly with butterflies. I wasn't nervous—I was excited. I was also in shock that any of this was even happening. It was still a little unreal.

"Riley? Before you get into your dress, can I talk to you for a minute?" Meg asked.

"Sure. Of course." Her tone was strange, off a little. She had a smile on her face, but it was forced and looked as though it could fall away any moment and reveal sadness that was just below the surface. "Is everything okay?"

"Oh, sweetheart, everything is wonderful." She sat in the chair next to me, seeming nervous. She took a deep breath and then met my eyes. "I don't want to overstep my boundaries, and you can absolutely say no if you don't feel like this is right, but I wanted to offer it to you anyway." She held out her hand and opened her palm to reveal a men's platinum wedding band. I couldn't help but notice her hand was shaking slightly. "This was Camden's father's ring from our wedding. I couldn't bear to bury it with him, and I've been saving it for Camden ever since."

"Meg," I said, my voice a whisper, new tears forming in my eyes. Her cheeks were wet with them, tears streaming down her face. "Oh, Meg," I said again, rising from my chair and wrapping my arms around her. She cried softly for a short moment, allowing me to comfort her, but then she pulled away and seemed to steel herself.

"I understand if you don't want to use it. I would've offered it to Camden himself, but I didn't want him to feel pressured, and I also thought it might be a nice surprise."

It would be a surprise. Camden had picked out his own wedding band when he'd purchased my engagement ring, but I knew having his father's ring would mean a lot to him, maybe even more than he knew.

"Does Camden know you have this?" I asked, gingerly taking the ring from her hand.

She shook her head. "No. I wanted to save it for him as a surprise."

"I think he'll love it," I said quietly, looking back up at her. "Thank you."

"Are you sure? I don't want to force you into anything. He doesn't even have to know I have it."

"Meg, don't be silly. I think it will mean a lot to him." Camden and I had spoken about his father a few times since we started dating. He told me everything he remembered about his death and had insightful things to say about how losing his father at such a young age impacted him, but it wasn't something we spoke about often. Camden was a very well-adjusted man, and the death of his father didn't seem to affect his everyday life, but I knew he missed him and the relationship he might have had with him. I also knew that Meg had been desperately in love with her late husband. That wasn't taking anything away from Camden's stepfather, as he was a wonderful husband and stepfather. I just knew losing her husband was traumatic.

The idea of Camden dying tragically before we had enough years together, well, I was crying again at the thought.

"I think he'll love it," I said, holding back tears and wrapping Meg in my arms again. "Thank you," I whispered to her.

"No," she said, pulling away. "Thank you. You're the best thing that ever happened to him, and if I have to give him up to anyone, I'm so glad it's you, Riley."

"Stop it," Hadley said from the other side of the room, tears in her eyes. "Right now."

Luckily, everyone laughed.

"Okay, I'm going to go check on Camden and then I'll see you out there," Meg said, giving me one last hug before making her way out of the room.

"Meg?" I called out to her just before she left.

"Yes?"

"Tell him I love him, okay?"

Her face softened at my request and she said, "Of course, dear."

"I gotta tell ya," the makeup artist said right when the door closed, "I have never seen anything as sweet as what just happened, and I've seen *a lot*." I smiled at her as she closed her case. "Here is your lip color, yours to keep reapplying as needed. You look beautiful. Happy wedding

241

day." She gave us all a big smile and then left the room, leaving me alone with just Hadley and my mom.

"Holy shit," I said, eyes wide. "I'm getting married."

We all laughed again.

"Let's get the dress on, Riley," Hadley said with a smile.

I took in a deep breath and then pushed it out. "Okay, let's do it." I jumped around from foot to foot, trying to amp myself up, attempting to fight off the nerves that were swarming in my belly. They weren't butterflies anymore—I was harboring the scaly dragon cast of *Game of Thrones* in my stomach.

When we'd arrived at the venue, Hadley had given me all the lingerie I'd bought with her just days before, along with a white satin robe with the word 'Bride' embroidered on the back in blue, and that's what I'd been wearing since we'd arrived. It was perfect for getting my hair and makeup done.

Hadley pulled my dress from the bag carefully and walked toward me with the biggest smile.

"You're going to look so fucking beautiful, Riles," she said, eyes shining.

I slipped the robe off my shoulders and laid it on the chair, trying to ignore the fact that my mother and my best friend were seeing me in some pretty sexy lingerie.

"He's going to fucking lose his mind when he takes this dress off you later," Hadley added, making my cheeks burn with embarrassment.

I tried to give Hadley a look that read 'Shut the fuck up, my mother is right next to you,' but apparently I wasn't covert enough because my mother started laughing.

"Oh, Riley, don't be embarrassed. I'm no virgin. I know what happens on a wedding night. And Hadley's right—Camden will lose his mind."

"Okay," I said quickly, "Let's stop talking about all the sex I'm having later and put the dress on."

The next half hour was a blur. The dress went on, more tears came, Hadley and my mom both changed into their dresses, the venue photographer came to take pictures, and then suddenly I found myself standing outside the doors to the chapel, seconds away from walking down the aisle to my husband.

And I was about to hyperventilate.

"Riley," Hadley said, gripping my shoulders and looking right into my eyes. "Breathe."

"I can't," I replied breathlessly, panicking a little.

"It's going to be okay. You're going to walk down that aisle and you're going to marry the sexy man who is practically bursting at the seams waiting for you."

"You've seen him?" I asked, suddenly distracted by the idea of Camden waiting.

"I have. Just for a moment. He looks so incredibly handsome, Riley. And happy. He looks happy."

I tried to take a deep breath. It kind of worked. And then I exhaled.

"I'm not nervous about marrying him," I said, trying to make sure no one was worried about me running. "I can't wait to be his wife. I'm just nervous about the whole thing. I don't like being the center of attention."

"We know," my mother said from beside Hadley. "Think of how much worse it would be if there were a hundred people in there."

"Good point," I said.

The side door to the chapel opened and the coordinator came out. "Ready?" she asked, polite smile in place.

"Sure," I said with a maniacal laugh. "Why not?"

She cocked her head at me and her smile turned a little worried, but Hadley came to the rescue.

"She's just losing her mind a little. She'll be fine once the whole thing starts."

"Well, it starts now." The coordinator blinked at me.

"I'm ready," I said unconvincingly as the coordinator raised an eyebrow at me. "I swear. Let's go."

"All right," she said, still not looking too convinced. "The doors will open and you and your mother will be standing over here," she said, motioning to the area to the side. "Maid of honor walks first, doors close behind her, and you and your mom take your place once they do." She turned to Hadley and said, "Take a left at the end of the aisle."

"Got it," Hadley said with a smile.

"Next, doors open and the mother walks the bride down. Any questions?"

I gave her a blank look. "Nope. Can't think of anything."

"Okay, the music will start and the doors will open. Congratulations."

She disappeared with a smile, and then I was in Hadley's arms. "I love you, Riley. I'm so happy to be here with you today."

My best friend had always been supportive and present, but emotional, sensitive Hadley wasn't someone I

244

was terribly familiar with. I knew the sarcastic, loving, and brash Hadley. This girl, the one who held me close, whispered to me, and sounded incredibly sincere, she was sort of new, but I loved her nonetheless.

"I love you too, Hadley. Thank you so much for being here for me and doing all this."

"Anytime," she whispered. She pulled away and wiped the tears from just below her eyes, then turned toward the door and readied herself.

My mom and I took our spots out of sight and I heard the music start.

It was the typical "Canon in D" that I associated with weddings, and I was instantly on edge. I was going to walk down the aisle in just a moment. To get married. To Camden.

When I'd woken up that morning, I thought maybe we'd go for a walk downtown by the river, or get some coffee and unpack some boxes. Maybe if we were crazy we'd go to Ikea.

I never could have imagined I'd be at a chapel in Las Vegas getting married.

I was so lucky.

Hadley disappeared through the doors and my nerves took off, knowing I was next.

My mom led me over to the door to wait for our turn and took my hand, saying, "I am not the best source of marriage wisdom, but I want to offer you one piece of advice."

I looked over at her, not sure if I was going to cry, laugh, or puke.

"Everything will always be all right as long as you communicate. Tell him how you're feeling, both in here," she said, pointing to my forehead, "and in here," she finished, pointing to my heart. "Don't hide your feelings from him, and don't keep him at arm's length."

"I won't," I promised, knowing I'd done exactly that to my mother for so long. "Promise."

"Good," she replied, eyes shining. "I love you."

"I love you too."

Suddenly the doors were opening and I was getting married.

Chapter Twenty-Two
Camden

To say I was anxious was an understatement, so when the doors finally opened and revealed my Riley, it was a relief. A breath pushed out of me and it was almost as if my body was relieved to even lay eyes on her.

My wife.

She walked toward me, arm linked through her mother's elbow, and even though the room contained many other people, it may as well have just been us. Our gazes locked and nothing in the world could have pried my eyes off her.

There'd never been a woman more beautiful than my Riley as she walked down the aisle to me.

I'm sure her dress was stunning, and all the added attention to her makeup and hair was probably good too, but it wasn't how she looked that made her beautiful, it was how she made me feel. I felt so fucking lucky to be the one who got to spend forever with her. I could hardly contain my emotions and was caught off guard as a tear slipped down my cheek.

I wasn't usually an overly emotional man, but seeing her and knowing she was mine, that we got to spend our entire lives together making each other happy… well, it was all hitting me hard.

Riley and her mother made it all the way down the aisle, both of them smiling widely. When she was within reach, I held out my hand. She came willingly and I leaned over to kiss her mother on the cheek, trying to convey with one gesture how thankful I was for the opportunity to love her daughter, then led Riley back to the officiant.

The music stopped and everyone took a seat, but I couldn't take my eyes off Riley.

"Hi," she said softly, tears brimming in her eyes.

"Hi," I replied, watching as one of the tears broke free and streaked down her face. I brushed it away with my thumb and then mouthed, "I love you." That made more tears fall, but she smiled and mouthed, "I love you too."

"Good evening," the officiant said to everyone. I'd been introduced to the man just a few minutes before, but I couldn't remember his name for the life of me. And that was fine. Ten, twenty, thirty years from now, I wouldn't want to remember his name or even what he looked like. I did, however, want to remember the way Riley looked as she walked toward me, how we felt standing in front of each other, her hands in mine, ready to get married.

"People don't usually come to Las Vegas to get married in a lengthy service, so I'll make this short and sweet."

His quip made everyone laugh, Riley and me included.

"Marriage is not just a piece of paper, it is a commitment to be a partner every single day of the rest of your life. Marriage isn't about a dress or a ring, it's about two people promising to put the other person above anyone else until death. You kids look plenty happy, and I'm sure you love each other a lot, but I'm here to tell you there will be days in the years ahead where you'll question that love, where you'll wonder if you have what it takes to stick it out until the end. Remember, love is a feeling, but marriage is a choice. You must choose, every day, to be true to the one you love, to give your marriage as much attention as it needs, and even when you think it's fine, put the effort in anyway."

Riley smiled at me and I squeezed her hand. Even though this man was a Las Vegas marriage officiant and he probably married hundreds of couples every year, I took his advice to heart. I never wanted to be complacent with Riley. I never wanted to take our relationship for granted or fall away from the closeness I felt with her in that moment. I vowed to work every day at making her happy.

"Did you want the traditional vows, or have you prepared your own?" he asked us with a smile.

Before I could answer, Riley spoke. "Is it okay if we just wing it?"

"You want to *wing* your marriage vows?"

She shrugged. "Yeah?"

He laughed but then said, "Be my guest."

Riley turned and handed her bouquet of peonies to Hadley, then took both my hands in hers and looked up at me with the most brilliant smile.

"Camden," she started, then stopped to cry a little. Hadley handed her a tissue and she started again after a few moments. "Camden, I think often about how so many things had to line up just perfectly for us to meet the way we did. To think that someone else could have sat down next to you, or that the Kiss Cam could have landed on two other people, or if I didn't have a loudmouthed best friend who gave you my personal information, we wouldn't be standing here right now and I wouldn't be the luckiest woman in the world to be marrying you. But I want you to know that I am well aware of the part I'll play in our forever. I know life won't always hand us happiness, so I promise that even in the bad times I'll hold your hand. I'll live in the beautiful house you bought us, but I promise I'd be happy with you in a crappy apartment in the bad part of town. When you're sick, I'll make you soup, and when you're sad, I'll hold you. When you're angry, I'll help you plot your revenge, and when you're happy, I promise I'll be happy with you. I promise I'll always keep Guinness in the house, even if it's the grossest beer ever made, and I'll always let you win at Skee-Ball. I promise I'll always put the life we've built together first, and I will make you a priority every single day."

Not a damn dry eye in the house. *Jesus.*

I rubbed my thumbs over the back of Riley's hands and tried to put two thoughts together.

"I don't know why I'm surprised to find myself standing in front of you, speechless. You've had that effect on me a lot since that first night we met. But rest assured, Riley, no matter how we would have ended up meeting, the two of us were destined. Nothing as perfect as you and me together could be anything but fate. I'm not sure how I'll ever top this," I said, waving my hand around for emphasis, "but I promise I'll never stop surprising you. I live for the look on your face when I give you something you didn't even realize you needed. Your smile can make the worst day better, the saddest day happy, and I intend to see you smile every day for the rest of my life. I'm also going to bust my ass to provide for you, not because you can't provide for yourself but because I want to give you everything I can. It's the least I can do since you've given me everything I've ever dreamed of."

I heard the females in the chapel sighing, but I continued.

"I'll try my best to make sure you have everything you want, but I'll always be there to give you what you need. I'll get you out of your head, because I know sometimes you get lost in there. I'll make you laugh because I know you love it, but also because the sound of you laughing is the best sound in the whole world. I'll hold you close when you feel like you're floating away, and I'll rub the tension from your shoulders every night since you seem to want to carry the world on them all on your own. No one would have loved you like I'm going to love you."

Because I couldn't stop myself or hold back any longer, I pulled Riley toward me and pressed a kiss against her lips, then smiled against her mouth when I felt her arms wrap around my neck.

The officiant cleared his throat and then laughed. "You, uh, skipped ahead a few steps."

"Sorry, not sorry," Riley replied spritely, making everyone laugh.

"Do you have rings?"

Riley and I both turned to our best people to retrieve the bands.

"Camden," he said once I'd turned back to face Riley. "Place the ring on her left ring finger and repeat after me."

I held the ring at the tip of her finger as he spoke the words and I repeated them, knowing I'd never say them to another woman.

"I give you this ring as a pledge of my love and commitment. With this ring, I thee wed."

I slid the platinum eternity band down her finger and then grasped her hand in mine, watching as she sniffled and smiled all the while.

"Repeat after me, Riley," the officiant said.

I watched as she placed the ring on my finger and looked into my eyes, saying, "I give you this ring as a pledge of my love and commitment. With this ring, I thee wed." I looked down as the ring slid into place, but something was off. The ring I'd chosen was titanium, but the ring on my finger was platinum. I looked up to Riley and even more tears were shining in her eyes.

"I hope you don't mind," she said through a cry, "but I switched your ring out with another."

"What?" I asked, looking back and forth between the ring and Riley. Behind me I heard my mother crying, and I glanced over to see my stepdad consoling her. "You switched my ring?"

"That's your father's ring. Your mom thought you might like to have it."

"What?" I said again. "My father's ring?"

"Yeah," she replied, nodding as more tears fell. "I hope that's okay?"

I looked back at my mom again, then to Riley.

"His wedding ring?" I looked down at the ring on my finger. Suddenly it all clicked into place, and along with understanding came emotion. My fist clenched and I brought it to my mouth, pressing the closed fingers against my lips, trying to keep in the sobs that had caught me off guard. Riley was immediately as close to me as she could get, one arm around my waist as the other hand came to my cheek.

"I'm sorry, Camden. I'm sorry. We thought it would be a nice surprise. I should have asked you first."

On instinct, I opened my arms and wrapped them around her, pulling her chest against mine and burying my face in her neck. I cried silently against her for a minute, trying to pull myself together but failing. I'd never experienced emotion so raw before. All the while, Riley was running her hands up and down my back, apologizing over and over.

Once I'd gained some composure, I pulled back and took her face in my hands, bringing her gaze level with mine.

"I'm sorry," she said again. "I can get your new ring. I think Hadley might still have it."

I silenced her by kissing her again, softly that time.

"Thank you," I said against her lips. "I didn't even know this existed."

"You're all right with it?"

"Yes." I smiled, our noses still touching, her body pressed against mine. "Yes. I was surprised, but a good surprised. Thank you."

"You're welcome."

I kissed her again, which prompted the officiant to clear his throat one more time.

"I'm going to assume neither of you has done this before, so I'll give you a hint: You're supposed to wait to kiss until the end."

"Sorry, not sorry," Riley said again, and that time even the officiant laughed.

It was with tears in my eyes and Riley in my arms when he finally said, "By the powers vested in me by the state of Nevada, I now pronounce you husband and wife. You may kiss the bride… again."

So I did.

Chapter Twenty-Three
Riley

"Would you like another drink, Mrs. Rogers?"

Shivers raced down my spine at Camden's words. Not only from the way his breath hit my neck as he spoke, but also hearing him call me Mrs. Rogers. I never thought taking someone's last name would be such a turn-on, but apparently it was. Something else that became apparent to me as he wrapped his arms around me from behind was that my husband was also turned on by my new last name, the evidence pressed against my ass.

"I'm good," I said, grinding my hips into his erection. Nothing too obvious—we were out in public still.

"Oh no, Mrs. Rogers, I think you're a little bit naughty."

I giggled as his mouth found my neck and he peppered kisses along the sensitive skin.

"Seriously though," he said, spinning me around so I was facing him, "can I get you something?"

My hands slid up his chest, admiring the navy suit jacket he still wore and how well his awesome fucking muscles filled it out.

My husband was hot.

My *husband* was hot.

"Babe?" he asked, a smirk on his face. "Drink?"

I bit my lip and shook my head.

His hands slid down from my waist and back to cup my ass through my dress.

"Have I told you how beautiful you look?"

I nodded. "Too many times."

"Not enough times," he argued. His gaze smoothed over me, from my face down my chest and over the rest of my dress. "*Fuck*. This dress, Riley. It's the sexiest fucking thing you've ever worn."

I rose onto my toes, which wasn't easy in my stilettos, and whispered in his ear, "You should see what's *under* my dress."

"So, we're done here, then?" he asked, pulling away and hauling me toward the exit.

"Camden," I giggled. "We can't just leave. This is our reception."

He stopped, but only to pull me back into his arms.

I didn't complain.

We'd had a hard time keeping our hands to ourselves, but everyone seemed to understand. Even strangers. Turns out, when a woman in a fancy, even-close-to-white dress and a man in a snazzy suit walk down the Vegas Strip, everyone knows you got married. It was almost as if the entire city was attending our reception.

We'd gone from the chapel to a fancy dinner where all our friends and family raised their glasses and toasted to our marriage. We ate amazing food and drank our weight in champagne. Everyone was laughing and smiling most of the time. Camden's mother did sit next to him for a minute, and I covertly eavesdropped as they discussed Camden's wedding ring. Hearing Cam tell his mother that he was glad to have the ring and honored to wear it made me feel much better about bombarding him. I knew eventually we'd talk about it, have a deeper conversation about what it meant to him to have that ring on his finger, but for that night I was content to let it be. He was happy. I was happy. We had our whole lives to talk about sad things.

After dinner our parents politely declined to come out and party with all of us, even though we tried our best to convince them. After dropping them back off at the hotel, I commandeered the wedding party and gave Camden my own surprise, taking him someplace I knew he'd love.

When we'd pulled up to the arcade, Camden laughed for a good three minutes.

"Come on, Skee-Ball shark, go in there and show everyone how it's done."

And he did.

We'd played Skee-Ball and air hockey and Pac-Man for hours, and it was the best night ever.

And it wasn't over yet.

"The bride and groom are always the first to leave the reception. It's tradition," Camden said, his lips finding my neck again. But he suddenly pulled away and gave me a serious face. "In fact, it's our weddingly duty to walk out of this establishment right now. Our marriage may be cursed if we don't."

"Well," I replied, trying to keep a straight face and failing miserably, "we can't let that happen."

He kissed me again, his mouth lingering on mine for longer than necessary, but I didn't mind. When he finally pulled back, it was with a smile and a wink.

God, I love this man.

He took my hand and we made the rounds, saying thank you and good night to everyone. I wasn't sure when our flight back home left, but I figured someone would fill me in and I would see everyone the next day to go back to our normal lives.

Well, they'd be going back to their normal lives. I'd be going back married.

I squeezed Hadley harder than the rest.

"Thank you for everything, Had. There's no one else I would have wanted with me today."

"Shut up, bitch," she said, trying to sound tough, but I heard the crack in her voice.

I pulled back and looked over her shoulder where Justin was standing, staring at her. As soon as he caught me looking at him, he turned away.

"Everything okay with Justin?"

"Hmm?" she asked, pretending as if she hadn't heard me.

"Are you going to be all right here with Justin?" I knew he would never intentionally hurt Hadley, but that didn't mean he couldn't upset her. I wanted everyone to have a good night. "Do you want to ride back to the hotel with us?"

She scoffed. "Right. And sit next to you guys while you grope each other in the limo? No, thanks. I'll take my chances with Justin."

I gave her a careful look, then decided that Hadley was a big girl and could make her own decisions. I just wanted her all right at the end of the evening.

"Okay, but use the buddy system. Don't go back to the hotel alone, all right?"

"Yes, Mom." She rolled her eyes at me.

"Love you," I told her.

"Love you too."

As soon as we were in the limo, Hadley's prediction became reality—Camden was, indeed, all over me. I was okay with it though, because ever since I saw him standing at the end of that aisle in the crisp blue suit, I'd wanted to get my hands on him. On his thighs, specifically. All night the blue fabric clung to his thighs, and it was all I could do not to lean over and bite them.

Yes, bite them.

Did I mention I'd had a lot of champagne?

We were too drunk and too in love for seat belts, and I was too turned on to remain in my seat, so I climbed over him, straddling one of his legs, and smirked at his eyes lit up with lust.

"You're in for it now, husband."

"Is that right?" he asked as his hands started at the backs of my knees and slid slowly up my thighs until he met the edge of my lacy thong.

"Yep," I said, popping the P. "You're my husband, and it is your legal obligation to let me use your body for all my pleasure." Even as I said the words I rocked back and forth on his leg. I wasn't going to ride his thigh to orgasm in the limo, but there was nothing wrong with getting a little riled up on the way to the hotel. I could always finish what I'd started once we got there.

"Well, by all means," he said, squeezing my ass.

I kissed him then, my mouth crashing over his, my hands threading through his hair, and everything about it felt more right than it ever had before. It was different, kissing my husband. As soon as Camden and I were officially together, it hadn't occurred to me that we'd ever be apart, but kissing him as his wife was a strange and wonderful kind of different. I'd always wanted to kiss him forever, but now it seemed as though that would happen. He was mine. Forever.

Thinking about the wedding and our commitment, it was strangely arousing.

I wanted to fuck my husband. Bad.

In some part of my mind I'd always thought wedding nights were supposed to be loving and sensual. There was supposed to be candlelight and romance.

Nope.

I just wanted to be filled with him, to be connected, to feel him inside me knowing it was him and me forever.

"I can't wait to get you out of this dress, babe," he growled just before moving his mouth down my jaw to my throat. I craned my neck, offering him more to taste, all the while my hips moving back and forth as he palmed my ass, his fingers dipping scandalously close to my opening.

The limo came to a stop and we heard the driver door open, so I climbed off Camden and headed for the door I knew the driver would be opening soon. I wasn't even planning on trying to pretend I wasn't dry humping my husband in the back of the limo—it was Las fucking Vegas and I was sure shit like that happened all the time.

So it was with a big smile that I hopped down from the big limo and held out my hand for Cam. He tipped the driver but said nothing, and we made our way into the hotel.

It took a few minutes to wind our way through the casino and get to the elevators, but his hand was in mine the whole time. Fortune smiled upon us when the elevator doors closed and we found ourselves alone. His arms were immediately around me and his mouth was instantly covering mine. He kissed me hard and it was exactly what I needed, especially when he thrust his hips against me and I could feel every ridge and outline of his erection.

The elevator dinged and the doors opened on our floor. We practically ran to our door, but before Camden inserted the key, he lifted me at the waist and my legs instinctively went around his hips, my hands in his hair, my lips on his neck.

Once the door was open, there was absolutely nothing stopping us.

His mouth found mine again as he growled down my throat, and I used every muscle I could isolate to grind my core against his cock, still very hard and still very much inside his pants.

I heard the door slam closed and then my back was against the nearest wall, Camden pinning me with his hips.

There were no words exchanged, no loving or tender caresses.

We were both riding a wild high created by lust and I just needed him. My husband. Inside me.

I unfastened his belt and then the closure on his pants, all the while kissing him senseless. I managed to push his pants down far enough to free his cock, and within seconds my thong was pulled aside and Camden pushed into me.

"Fuck, yes," he grunted as he seated himself fully inside of me, pushing in far enough that I felt him bottom out against me.

I gasped and clutched him tighter, holding him to me, just wanting to feel full of him for a moment.

There'd been no foreplay once we'd reached the room. We'd had hours of it beforehand. Just marrying him was foreplay enough. The image of his smiling face as he said his vows was the biggest turn-on. It was with that picture in my mind that I pressed my lips to his. He kissed me back hungrily, and after a few moments he finally pulled out and pushed back in, both of us groaning with the movement.

"More," I rasped between kisses. "Please."

I didn't have to ask him twice. His hands moved to my ass, holding me up as he pistoned his hips at a punishing speed. It was blissful.

"Fuck," he growled again. Just his voice pushed me closer to the edge I'd been dancing around since we left the arcade. "Touch yourself, Riley. I want to feel you come around me."

My hand snaked between us, slipped under my lacy thong, and I found my clit and circled it, matching his pace.

"Get there, babe," he ordered, and I knew he wasn't going to last much longer. It was so hot, the idea of how keyed up we both were, that just a few strokes would set us both off. We were like fireworks, dynamite, our fuses so short.

"Yes," I moaned as he picked up speed.

"I want my wife to come."

And that was it. That was all I needed. Camden Rogers called me his wife as he thrust his cock so damn deep inside me I could barely see straight. I convulsed around him, shuddering, crying out, and holding on to him for dear, dear life.

"That's it," he grunted, then picked up even more speed until he finally stilled and shuddered himself.

Our breaths both panted out heavily, my forehead resting against his shoulder, his hands still holding me under my ass. It wasn't sweet, and it wasn't candles and rose petals, but it was fucking fantastic.

"Hey," he said quietly after a moment, causing me to lift my head and look at him. "I love you."

That was all the romance I really needed. Just him, loving me.

"I love you too."

He kissed me then, slowly, and I could feel his love for me down to my bones.

He pulled away and gave me a smirk.

"I still want to see what you've got on under this dress."

"Okay," I whispered, finding myself strangely close to tears.

"You all right?"

I nodded. "I'm just really happy."

He smiled. "Me too, babe." He kissed me once more, short and sweet. "Let's take this dress off and let me get a good look at you. Then we'll get in that huge tub and clean up."

"Okay," I replied.

"Then I'll get you dirty again," he said with that sexy fucking smirk.

"Sounds perfect."

Chapter Twenty-Four
Riley

One would think a 3:00 p.m. flight would be late enough in the day to not feel crappy when boarding. But one would be wrong about that if they had a Vegas wedding hangover.

Granted, I wasn't the worst of the bunch.

Hadley looked like she wanted to die.

Honestly, everyone except the parental units agreed that one night in Vegas was not the best plan they ever made.

Camden checked us into our flight as I chatted with Rachel and Hadley. Well, Rachel and I chatted while Hadley stood there looking as though she was about to vomit everywhere. My brother had caught an earlier flight, but by the blush on Rachel's cheeks when I mentioned him, I assumed she gave him a thorough goodbye. She was pretty tight-lipped about it, but I knew with time I could get some details out of her.

We'd made it through security and approached a gate with the flashing sign above the door saying 'Portland.' I saw it and let out a sigh. Portland was home, but I didn't really want our little trip to end. So much had happened in just twenty-four hours and I hadn't grasped it all yet. I wanted more time to adjust, to take everything in.

"Okay," Camden said as everyone took their seat to wait for boarding. "Say goodbye to everyone, Riley."

"Goodbye? Why? Where are they going?"

"It's not where they're going, it's where *you're* going."

"Where am I going?"

Camden smiled as he produced our boarding passes, handing me the one that had my name on it. I looked at him with a furrowed brow, still confused. But then I looked closer at the boarding pass and realized it didn't say Portland.

"Camden…," I said slowly.

"Yes, wife?"

"Why does my boarding pass say Maui on it?" My heartbeat raced and my hands started shaking.

"I couldn't plan a surprise wedding without also planning a surprise honeymoon, now could I?"

All our friends and family started laughing and clapping, and I stood there like an idiot with my mouth hanging open.

"Are you serious?"

"Babe, I'm good, but I can't get the FAA to print me fake boarding passes to pull one over on you. We're going to Maui."

My hands flew up to cover my mouth and Camden took a step closer, running his hands down my arms.

"Are you surprised?" he asked softly.

All I could do was nod in response.

"You told me once that you had never been to Hawaii. I couldn't really make an international trip happen on such short notice, so I hope Hawaii is okay."

"Are you serious? Are you even real?" My words were choked with tears and laughter as I let him pull me into a hug.

"Say goodbye, babe. Our plane boards soon."

"Wait," I said, pulling away, panicked. "I have to work tomorrow."

"You've got two weeks off, courtesy of Rose," Jasper said from behind me, where he was standing with Rachel.

"Your room will have fresh flowers, fruit, and champagne waiting, also courtesy of Rose," Rachel added.

"What? Rose knew about this?"

"Jasper and Rachel helped me get you the time off. I'm surprised you really thought our entire wedding celebration would be only twenty-four hours." He *tsked* at me.

"I can't believe you," I whispered to him, shaking my head in disbelief.

His arms came around me again, holding me close, and his mouth found the shell of my ear.

"Like I said, I'm going to spend forever finding ways to surprise you. Don't ever get used to it. I like watching you light up too much."

I leaned back so I could see his face. "I don't have anything packed for Hawaii."

His smirk appeared again. "Babe, all you need is a bikini, and we can buy one there."

I smiled in response.

"You ready for a lifetime of adventures?" he said quietly enough so that I was the only one who could hear him.

"Yeah," I whispered.

A lifetime with Camden seemed like the best idea I ever had.

Books by Anie Michaels

The Never Series

Never Close Enough

Never Far Away

Never Giving Up

Never Standing Still

Never Tied Down

Never With You – *pre-order available – releasing August 15th*

The Private Serials

The Love and Loss Series

The Absence of Olivia

The Presence of Grace

The With A Kiss Series

Kiss Cam

<u>Riled Up</u>

Stand Alone Novels

The Space Between Us

Instead of You

Acknowledgements

First, I really have to thank Hot Tree Editing and Pink Ink Designs for working on an unexpected quick turnaround. Both of these professional companies did everything they could to help me with a very tight deadline and I couldn't appreciate it more. Not only did they fit me in at the last minute, they did phenomenal work. Thanks also to Edeline Wrigh for proofreading with a very narrow window.

As always, thanks for my teamsters for giving me great advice when asked upon and also for just listening to me vent most of the time. It might not seem really important, but having a safe place to bounce ideas of readers and to let out frustration, happiness, and sadness, is something I don't take for granted. You all know what I went through the first half of this year and it was that special group of readers that really kept me pushing forward. Thank you from the bottom of my heart.

Thanks to my husband for always being supportive and understanding when I have to chain myself to my computer and for listening when I tell you exciting things about my job, even when you don't know what I'm talking about.

Thanks to all the early readers who helped find those pesky last-minute errors. I appreciate the help!